I Will, Through the Veil

What gay man hasn't fantasized about hot sex with those repressed Mormon missionaries in their white shirts and conservative ties? But there's more to Mormon fantasy sex than curious young "elders." What about temple workers going at it in the baptismal font after hours? Group sex during a Court of Love?

How about an ex-Mormon who throws a "pity party" (or "pity orgy") for men whose physical flaws prevent them from getting laid regularly? The ex-mo trapped by a snowstorm in an adult video store overnight?

And what collection of gay Mormon porn would be complete without an adventure involving the sexual practices the Three Nephites have perfected over two thousand years?

Got cum, anyone?

Praise for Johnny Townsend

In *Zombies for Jesus*, "Townsend isn't writing satire, but deeply emotional and revealing portraits of people who are, with a few exceptions, quite lovable."

Kel Munger, *Sacramento News and Review*

In *Sex among the Saints,* "Townsend writes with a deadpan wit and a supple, realistic prose that's full of psychological empathy….he takes his protagonists' moral struggles seriously and invests them with real emotional resonance."

Kirkus Reviews

Inferno in the French Quarter: The UpStairs Lounge Fire is "a gripping account of all the horrors that transpired that night, as well as a respectful remembrance of the victims."

Terry Firma, Patheos

"Johnny Townsend's 'Partying with St. Roch' [in the anthology *Latter-Gay Saints*] tells a beautiful, haunting tale."

Kent Brintnall, Out in Print: Queer Book Reviews

Selling the City of Enoch is "sharply intelligent...pleasingly complex...The stories are full of...doubters, but there's no vindictiveness in these pages; the characters continuously poke holes in Mormonism's more extravagant absurdities, but they take very little pleasure in doing so....Many of Townsend's stories...have a provocative edge to them, but this [book] displays a great deal of insight as well...a playful, biting and surprisingly warm collection."

Kirkus Reviews

Gayrabian Nights is "an allegorical tour de force...a hard-core emotional punch."

Gay. Guy. Reading and Friends

The Washing of Brains has "A lovely writing style, and each story [is] full of unique, engaging characters....immensely entertaining."

Rainbow Awards

In *Dead Mankind Walking*, "Townsend writes in an energetic prose that balances crankiness and humor....A rambunctious volume of short, well-crafted essays..."

Kirkus Reviews

I Will, Through the Veil

Gay Mormon Porn

Johnny Townsend

Contents

Sweet Cheeks

The first time it happened was on the ferry from the mainland of Italy to the island of Sardinia. It was early 1981, and I'd arrived in Rome the day before to begin my Mormon missionary service. My first assignment would be in Quartu, just outside Cagliari. Rather than fly me there, the mission president bought me a train ticket to Civitavecchia, where I then caught the ferry.

Since the trip took thirteen hours, the vessel offered tiny rooms where passengers could sleep. My room, barely the size of the upstairs bathroom back in my family's home in Salt Lake, contained a bunk bed and not much else. No one else seemed interested in sharing the space with a religious fanatic, so I had the place to myself.

For a while.

I'd taken the lower bunk and was surprised to discover I wasn't seasick, given the stormy weather. I lay in bed with the lights out, smiling gently as the ferry rocked slowly back and forth. I almost didn't hear the door open.

The room had a tiny nightlight somewhere, so it wasn't pitch black, even though we were many miles from land and light pollution. I opened my eyes ever so slightly, just a slit, knowing it wouldn't be detectable in the dimness. I'd practiced the technique back in the Missionary Training

Center in Provo so I could watch my companion change clothes in the morning.

The man sharing my room stood beside the bed for a moment and then slowly began pulling off his clothes. Shirt first, then shoes and socks. A bit surprising, given how cool it was in mid-February.

I was even more surprised when I saw the man lift the socks and heard him sniff deeply. His face was just out of range, blocked from view by the bunk above me. But he must have pressed the socks to his nose.

That's when I could feel my erection starting.

It's not that I was "into" anything kinky. I was still a virgin, after all, at the age of nineteen. Sure, I beat off back home before my mission, but usually just thinking about cute guys and their dicks and asses. Nothing weird like this guy was doing.

But as I listened to the man drop one sock at a time to the floor, I could feel my dick growing even harder. I watched through my slitted eyes as he unbuckled his belt and unzipped, pushing his pants to the floor and stepping out of them. In the dim light, I could see he still wore underwear. Not boxers, not tighty whities, but something else hard to make out.

The man rubbed his crotch a moment. By this point, I was hard as a rock. Was he going to masturbate right in front of me? This promised to be the best night of my life!

I watched as the man pulled off his underwear, his cock springing upward once freed of the fabric.

So, so difficult to keep my eyes almost closed. The man was only a couple of feet away in the tiny room. Even in the dim light, I could see he had a much larger girth than I did, his dick straight, unlike my slightly curved one. I'd never looked at porn and didn't have much to compare my own against, but the cock before me also looked at least an inch or two longer than mine.

I suppose I should have seen this as a trial of my faith. Instead, I saw it as a blessing. It would have been a sin for me to fantasize, a sin to be a creepy voyeur, a sin to seek out a naked man anywhere. But if Heavenly Father was providing, there was really nothing to do but lie there and enjoy the view.

The man lifted his underwear somewhere out of view, and I heard another deep sniff.

I could feel a tiny bit of dampness in my garments. I'd always issued lots of precum and could feel it starting down there. I'd only been wearing my garments, the one-piece Mormon underwear every adult wore after their first trip to the temple, just three months. An old man had pulled them on me during the initiatory while I wore nothing else but a white sheet. They were basically a T-shirt attached to long underwear that reached down to my knees, with embroidered markings at specific spots to remind wearers to keep their covenants.

I continued looking at the man standing beside the bed. He wasn't climbing up into the top bunk. He stood there slowly stroking his cock. My heart was beating so hard I was afraid he'd hear and know I was faking. Would he stop if he knew I could see?

Or…

The man continued stroking himself, slowly, quietly. My companion in the MTC had beat off once during the night and couldn't keep himself from moaning just a little, even knowing I was in the room with him. This guy didn't make a sound.

I suddenly wondered if my companion had *wanted* me to know what he was doing.

I rustled ever so slightly in my "sleep" now. The man paused, but once I stopped moving a couple of seconds later, he continued. His hand never lost contact with his cock, pulling the skin up and down his shaft, the friction underneath the surface rather than on top.

I'd tried it that way at home and found it satisfactory, but I preferred the chafing from moving my hand back and forth across the surface.

The man's hand began moving faster. And then a little faster. Finally, I watched as he pulled his other hand in front of him.

Please, don't block the view! I cried out in my head.

I saw a thick white glob burst forth and land in the man's palm.

This was the best night of my life!

But it was what happened next that changed me forever.

The man stood there in the dim light for another long moment, lifting his hand out of range, where I heard him sniff deeply. My own dick was so hard now it downright hurt.

The man crouched down and I saw his face for the first time. Swarthy, even by Italian standards, with a thick, bushy moustache and eyebrows almost as thick. His hair was thick and wavy though not curly. He couldn't have been much over thirty.

He began to reach into the space above me in the bottom bunk, and I wondered if he was going to touch me. I'd resisted physical contact with another guy, even that day in gym class when Danny and I had been alone and he asked. I was going to be a good boy.

But I was a man now, and my body was producing so many hormones every few milliseconds I wasn't sure even Joseph Smith could resist the temptation I was facing. I wouldn't "wake up," I told myself. I'd let the guy do whatever he wanted and pretend to sleep through the whole thing. Whether he believed I was truly asleep or not didn't matter. I simply couldn't let him know I knew what he was doing.

The man didn't touch me. Instead, he held his hand over my face and tilted it sideways. It wasn't until I felt something wet hit my cheek that I realized *which* hand was above me.

I didn't flinch, didn't jerk, but even in my sex-addled mind, I knew I had to demonstrate some kind of reaction to pass convincingly as still asleep, so I murmured slightly and adjusted my face on the pillow.

The man didn't move. I felt some of his cum sliding slowly down my check, a single drop slipping along the crack between my lips.

This must be what the Celestial Kingdom was like!

Finally, the man withdrew his hand and lifted it out of range again. I didn't hear any sniffing this time. Instead, I heard him licking his hand.

Dear sweet Jesus.

I continued lying in bed motionless as the man climbed into the bunk above me. I wanted more than anything to pull some of his cum off my cheek into my mouth but didn't dare move, though I did lick my lips as quietly as I could. Then I somehow managed not to fondle myself, concentrating on feeling his cum drying on my cheek. Smelling him on me for the next twenty minutes.

When I heard his deep breathing above me, I finally fell asleep, too.

If that were the entirety of the experience, it would have been enough, but in the morning, despite a desperate urge to pee, I waited in bed until the man above me slipped quietly to the floor. There was no porthole in the tiny cabin, so the lighting was the same now as it had been the evening before.

Would he, I wondered? Would he do it again?

It would be a sin to pray for such a thing.

I prayed for such a thing.

I lay on my stomach, my cum-covered cheek still facing the man. What I wouldn't give for a fresh coating. But the ferry would be pulling into Cagliari soon. I'd have to wash up before the other elders saw me.

That thought alone made me go flaccid.

But the man still stood beside my bed, and *he* wasn't flaccid.

This was the best morning of my life!

I watched again as the olive-skinned man beat off, a sight I knew would never get old. But he did something different this time, something even I, with all the fantasies I'd played out in my head the past several years, had never considered.

After he shot into his hand, this time he held his palm over my ass. I'd deliberately pulled the covers down as soon as I woke up, hoping that despite my funky Mormon underwear, the sight of my ass might still inspire him to masturbate a second time this morning. Whether my ass had been the catalyst or not, he seemed smitten by it now.

The man bent over me. I could smell the scent coming from his armpits, his breath, earthy but not unpleasant. I could feel the heat emanating from his body.

With his empty hand, he reached gently for my garments and pulled the slit over my ass toward him. I murmured slightly, just to pretend I was still asleep. He paused, but when I grew silent again, he tilted his hand.

A glob of wetness landed in my crack.

At every missionary homecoming, the missionary announced to the congregation, "That was the best two years of my life."

I understood now I'd be saying the same thing.

And yet this wonderful morning *still* wasn't over. The man continued leaning over me in the bottom bunk. What else could he be thinking? What else could he want? Once I came, I was usually ready to clean up and get on with my day.

But this guy wanted something more.

He still held onto my garments, keeping the slit open, and he leaned down toward my ass. He sniffed deeply, smelling his own cum on me. Then he withdrew just slightly, and with his hand still slick with cum, pushed down gently with a single finger.

He was pushing his cum deeper into my crack. I could feel him now against my asshole.

No one could sleep through such a thing. The fact that I wasn't making any sound at all now had to be complete giveaway. But it didn't seem to fazed him. He scraped more of the cum downward toward my asshole and fingered my hole for a moment.

Then he pushed his finger ever so gently inside.

I still made no sound.

I was lucky, I suppose, he didn't laugh at my fakery. But he was a gentleman, standing there a few more moments, pushing his cum inside me again and again with his finger.

When he was finally done, he pulled back, and our eyes locked. He didn't look nervous. Why should he? It was clear I'd enjoyed every second of what he'd done. I could have protested long before if I'd wanted to.

We stared at each other a long moment. And then he smiled.

That was even more beautiful than his cock.

He motioned for me to turn over and I did, my dick straining against my garments. The man knelt beside me and pulled me out through the slit in front. He stared at the glistening precum on the tip and leaned forward to lick it off.

And then he took me completely into his mouth.

After I came, he pulled back and smiled again. Then he leaned forward and kissed me on the lips. I'd never kissed anyone before, not even my high school girlfriend. I wasn't quite sure how it was done, despite people kissing in practically every movie I'd ever seen. The real thing required practice and technique.

I tried to follow the man's lead, and when he thrust out his tongue to pry open my lips, I let him. I wasn't expecting the rush of cum from his mouth into mine, but when I tasted it, I reached around him and pulled the man on top of me.

Fifteen minutes later, while he was fucking me, we heard the announcement over the loudspeaker that we were about to dock. After he finished, we didn't have time to clean up but dressed quickly.

We still hadn't said a word to one another. My Italian was so weak at the time I probably wouldn't have understood much in any event.

But I understood the hand offered to me as we left the cabin together.

I never did meet the other elders in Cagliari. I went home with Gino, who lived in Sassari up north. We've had some rough patches, and I struggled at first learning how to be a responsible adult both as part of a couple and simply in the world of work. But we've been together now over forty years, and even at the age of seventy, that man continues to come up with new things for us to try in bed.

He can still put a smile on my lips, whether we have sex or not. We have an awful lot of "not" these days, and Gino's good at that, too.

But we do manage to get it up at least some of the time.

There's nothing better for an old man like me than taking an afternoon nap smelling my husband's cum drying on my beard and feeling his weight on top of me.

Whether there's a heaven after this life, I don't know, but I do know I've had a lifetime of it right here in Italy.

Master of the Mormon Dungeon

I struggled my entire life to suppress my gay feelings, but after a lifetime of service to the Church, and years of large financial donations, Heavenly Father blessed me with the Second Anointing. The first thing I did was arrange to pass that pre-emptive amnesty on to my fellow temple workers who I also suspected were gay.

We were all in our upper fifties, a bit late for a mid-life crisis, but I could sense a rising level of frustration among my endowment friends. Friday night was often Date Night at the temple, at least for those Mormon couples who wanted to save Saturday night for the real thing. It was always a bit disconcerting doing initiatories on a man who'd be sharing his body more fully with his wife later that evening.

Shaking a man's hand through the veil and pulling him into the Celestial Room was far more intimate than a Sunday handshake in the chapel. But performing sealings all evening for couples who'd died without temple marriage was the most challenging task any of us faced.

"I don't think I can make it tonight, Trent." Mitchell shook his head wearily. "I want to see that movie about Tolkien, and a late showing is the only time I have to do it."

"I set up a new dungeon," I whispered in his ear. "I promise you'll have a good time." I put my hand on his shoulder. He looked about to see if any of the other temple workers had noticed. Most of the others, of course, were straight. And if Dungeons and Dragons had taught us anything, it was that supposed allies couldn't always be trusted.

"I—I might need to talk to the bishop about playing with you in the temple." He continued looking about nervously. "It's so blasphemous."

"I promise I'll take care of that, too."

Mitchell frowned for a moment but then nodded. "See you in the basement after we close."

I'd prepared carefully for tonight, smuggling in necessary supplies little by little on my last several assigned days. Temple suitcases were so tiny I couldn't fit in much extra on any one trip. I started setting up next to the oxen tonight as soon as the Date Nighters and other temple staff left the building, standing next to the font as Mitchell and the others arrived. I'd already set the table with a map, our dice, a sealed Rubbermaid container filled with cookies, five tall, plastic Tupperware glasses Karen had bought decades ago, and a two-liter bottle of orange-flavored seltzer water.

"What's with the bucket?" Warner asked, pointing.

"Sit down and take off your slippers," I said. They all did so. "Socks, too." The guys complied, exchanging some confused looks. I kneeled down and took Mitchell's right foot in my hand.

"What the—"

I cleared my throat. "A couple of weeks ago, I was given the Second Anointing." I'd kind of hoped for a gasp or two at this revelation, feeling a little disappointed not to hear one, but everyone's jaw still dropped, and that was satisfying enough.

"I'm not *supposed* to perform the ordinance on anyone without approval," I went on. "Or without assistance. But given that my calling and election are already made sure, what are they gonna do?"

I grinned and began washing Mitchell's feet. Within ten minutes, my pals were all immune to divine punishment as well. I stood up and poured the bucket of sinful foot water into the baptismal font.

"I'm not sure I feel any different," Mitchell said.

"Oh, you will," I promised. I clapped my hands together lightly. "All right, everyone, strip down to your garments."

"What?" Warner folded his arms across his chest.

I handed a pair of one-piece garments to each of them. Most of us had started out with the one-piece decades ago but had adapted to the two-piece underwear at some point over the years. "You'll need to wear these tonight."

Mitchell tentatively grabbed one, looking about at the others nervously. I held the rest up until the others all took one. We'd changed together in the dressing room many times before. I'd noted early on that these guys were not particularly self-conscious, and I'd quickly been able to tell that their "casual" glances while we changed clothes lasted longer than those of straight guys. There'd been a few verbal hints as well during the time we'd served together in the temple, almost two years now. I'd soon find out if I was following the lead of the Holy Ghost in my assessment or not.

I pulled off my white shirt and pants and nodded for them to do the same. Then I pulled off my T-shirt and my knee-length underwear. Boxer briefs didn't even come close to what Mormon men wore every day. I stroked myself just once before stepping into my one-piece garments through the neck, deliberately letting the rim catch the edge of my penis so that I had to "struggle" a moment to slip it underneath the fabric.

Dean undressed quickly and stood naked, watching the others slowly disrobe. No one seemed to want to put on their new garments, staring at the fresh garments in their hands and then at each other as if unsure what to do. Mitchell kept turning his garments to look at the front and then at the back, as if he couldn't quite remember which was which. I caught him glancing at Daniel's dick, the vision of which seemed to make his own bob upward briefly before returning to its flaccid state.

Once the guys were standing before me in just their one-piece garments, I gave them all a nod. I'd purposefully bought them garments a size too small so that their nipples pointed forcefully through the fabric. Their asses strained against the back flaps and, most importantly, every millimeter of their balls and dicks stood out in sharp relief. Smiling in as friendly a manner as I could, I pulled out some special seat cushions I'd made for tonight. I set them on the chairs I'd arranged next to the font and pointed. This time I did hear a gasp.

"What the frack?" Warner's eyes moved from the cushions to me to the other guys and back to the cushions. He'd divorced Catherine four months ago but never told us why. It was none of our business, of course, but I couldn't help suspecting the reason had something to do with the fact that he spent Date Nights working in the temple rather than with his wife.

"You can't possibly…" Mitchell seemed unable to go on.

Daniel's hands moved to cover his crotch, which could only mean one thing. More than a brief bob was taking place. I handed green temple aprons to everyone, and the guys quickly tied them on. Daniel's apron tented outward. Neither Adam nor Eve nor God would have been fooled by those fig leaves.

"Here's a small bottle of lubricant for each of you," I said, passing them out. "Just pull apart the slit in the seat of your garments and sit down."

I reached behind me and applied some lube to my asshole. I hovered over my seat, aimed my ass over the five-inch dildo I'd affixed to the cushion, and slowly sat down. "Ahhh," I said. I'd practiced at home several times in the past week, but my sphincter was still taken unawares.

"Oh my god." Mitchell clapped a hand over his mouth.

"Taking the Lord's name in vain is no longer a problem," I pointed out. "You've all had the Second

Anointing." The men stared at the dildos pointing upward from their seats. Dean moved his head about as if trying to get a better glimpse through crowded bleachers of his favorite baseball player.

"Come on, guys," I said. "You know you want to." I paused just a second. Mitchell's right hand reached out gingerly as if he were debating strategy in a Jenga game. "And nothing you do now can ever be held against you." I motioned again to the seats. "Sit down so we can get on with our D&D."

Daniel squeezed some lube onto his fingers, rubbed some on his ass and on his dildo, and sat down quickly. And I mean quickly.

"Arlene used to strap on one of these things," he said, his voice trembling. "She said in the Celestial Kingdom, women and men would be equal, and that would mean…" He wiggled about on his cushion, his eyes closed, a little smile on his face.

"Oh my god," Mitchell said again.

Arlene had died of breast cancer nine months ago. Daniel confided to me at the time his worry that the illness might be his fault because he'd never fully appreciated his wife's breasts. It wasn't that he believed the Lord was teaching him a lesson. He simply wondered if Arlene's subconscious had felt spurned over her tiny breasts and reacted physically. Such a confession had added to my suspicions, but lots of straight men didn't like small breasts on a woman, so I still couldn't be sure.

I was sure now.

Mitchell's eyes focused on Daniel's face, giving him an expression of intense longing. He hesitantly reached behind himself and applied some lube. His tube was the only one containing lubricant boasting a "warming sensation," to go with the dark red cinnamon dildo I'd chosen for him.

Still staring intently at Daniel, Mitchell slid down onto his cushion. He grimaced the entire way down, a strained smile on his face as he settled into his seat as far as he could. "It's—it's okay, guys," he said, stifling a grunt. The mixture of relief, pain, and guilt on his face reminded me of his expression when he informed me ten months ago that his wife Brenda had been killed in a car accident. She'd been traveling at ninety miles an hour when she hit a bridge support.

Mitchell's eyes were closed now as he mouthed, "Oh my god. Oh my god. Oh my god," over and over and over.

Dean was next, and it took him almost half a minute to allow the full five inches inside him. I'd specifically planned that his dildo offered a larger girth than the others. He'd confided in me once that after Tammy bore their first child, he'd switched to anal so they could continue to have sex without condoms and not have to worry about another pregnancy.

"Whew!" he said, shaking his head to help him adjust to the slightly curved dildo. Tammy had put up with Dean's commitment to inconceivable sex for years until she couldn't take it anymore. "Ooh, boy!" Dean said, wiping his brow. He and Tammy hadn't had sex in almost ten years.

Tammy had died of a sudden stroke six months ago. Dean told me the week before that he was going to confess a serious transgression to her that he'd committed "just the one time" a couple of years after she'd shut down her rear entrance. I suspected, naturally, that he was referring to some kind of homosexual activity, but he'd never told me specifically what the issue was. When Tammy died a few days later, I couldn't help but wonder if the news had so shocked her it triggered the stroke.

After all, Karen had cried for three days when I told her a year ago I was gay. I promised I'd remain faithful but explained I didn't want to have sex with her again until we were in the Celestial Kingdom and Heavenly Father fixed my inability to find women attractive. Karen had awakened on the fourth day still crying and died of a heart attack while saying her morning prayers.

I looked back at Dean. He often regaled us with stories of the priesthood in action. I wondered if Tammy had threatened to go to the bishop, and Dean had raised his arm to the square in self-defense.

As unhappy as we'd all been trying to abide by gospel principles, it was clear we'd made the lives of the women we loved far more miserable. We all desperately needed the Second Anointing if there was to be any chance at happiness in the next world.

Was this how Heavenly Father got away with forcing us all into marriages that could cause nothing *but* grief? I'd often wondered why so many things God was recorded doing in the scriptures seemed so nasty. He'd clearly had the Second Anointing himself before even becoming a god. So he could do whatever he wanted, nice or not, and it was okay.

How else could the unjustifiable be justified?

We all turned our attention to Warner, who still had his arms folded across his chest. After another moment, he threw up his arms. "What the hell?" He squirted out some lube and soon joined us, chanting, "Hell, hell, hell, hell" as he slid down onto his dildo. I'd chosen a dark brown one for him with an extra-large head. He'd never come out and said anything blatantly racist, but he'd come close a couple of times.

I waited thirty seconds before pulling out some reusable plastic straws and placing one in each glass. Nude men cavorting in different positions were attached to the ends, the straws themselves extremely long penises. I opened the Rubbermaid container, revealing penis-shaped cookies.

I was perhaps overdoing it, but D&D guys liked to immerse themselves in the experience. I grabbed a penis cookie and bit off the tip. I poured everyone some seltzer water, and we got down to playing the game.

"Laban has refused to give you the brass plates you need," I said. "When you come back to steal them, you find him sitting on the ground drunk." I paused. "Dean, you're first. What do you do?"

"I cast a spell to make sure he stays asleep."

I rolled the dice and looked up. "He doesn't stay asleep. Mitchell, what do you do?"

He looked about nervously at the others. "I jump out boldly and knock him on the head with the blunt end of my Goliath battle axe."

We rolled the dice, I referred to my story plans, and I told him, "You've broken his spinal cord. He's paralyzed from the neck down but can still breathe. And shout. Daniel, what do you do?"

The game continued for another hour as I dragged the others away from Jerusalem, through a desert filled with sand orcs and biting brass flies, down to the ocean, where they battled acid-spitting sea turtles before setting sail for America.

On the open sea, my men fought salt-water dragons and violent half-brothers who'd caught STDs from sexual encounters with demon seals. As they were tied up by Laman and Lemuel, I passed around leather jesses and had everyone reach over to wrap the bindings gently around each other's penises.

When I saw Daniel wipe a drop of pre-cum off Mitchell's dick and then lick his finger, I felt a little thrill and asked what he thought of it. So far, I'd only tasted my own pre-cum.

"It is delicious to the taste," he said, "and very desirable."

Mitchell's jaw dropped at the words, and Daniel took the opportunity to pick up a clear drop from the end of his own penis and put it on Mitchell's tongue.

The best thing about role-playing was the unembarrassed enthusiasm of the participants. So many of the regular visitors to the temple seemed only to want to finish their sessions and go home. Most of the temple workers weren't much better.

But Dean and Warner and Mitchell and Daniel had caught my attention my first day on the job. They *enjoyed* being here. Gay men liking theater was a stereotype, and my endowment friends didn't necessarily have flair, but they had *something* the other workers didn't have.

"Has it a name?" I asked. I stuck out my tongue and wiggled it a little.

Mitchell stared at me in horror, blinked several times, and then laughed. Warner discovered that his lube was cherry flavored and let Dean and Daniel lick his fingertip. I recalled a time Karen had dripped chocolate syrup onto my penis, not for use as a lubricant but simply for fun.

If only we'd both been straight.

I led my friends through Lehi's dream, in which they had to enter the great and spacious building to rescue Lehi, who'd been seduced by a succubus in the form of Sariah. I presented them with the challenge of convincing Laman and Lemuel that their anger stemmed from suppressing their love for each other. Warner, with the help of the dice, convinced them to become lovers, and the biggest threat to the safety of the group was dismantled.

By the time we reached the Promised Land, the guys looked like they'd been sitting on dildos and sipping seltzer water through penises their whole lives. Being middle-aged, we all had to urinate at some point during the game, but rather than pulling ourselves off the dildos, we nudged the bucket to each other across the floor with our feet, lifted our fig leaves, and took turns pissing as we continued to play. Finally, though, it was time to wrap up.

I reached into a bag and handed everyone a small towel. "Okay, guys, we have one last activity before we call it a night." I motioned for the guys to stand up.

The noises that followed reminded me of summers on my grandparents' dairy farm. A cow pulling its foot out of the mud made a very specific sound one didn't forget.

After we wiped ourselves off, I motioned for Daniel and Warner to climb down into the baptismal font. We were all still dressed in our garments and green aprons. I sat just outside the font and handed them more lube. I explained what we were going to do, and not one of them offered the slightest protest.

The Second Anointing was a powerful thing.

Warner applied some lube to his penis, pulled apart the slit in the back of Daniel's garments, and placed the tip of his penis on Daniel's asshole. He raised his arm to the square.

"I fuck you for and on behalf of Arlene, who is dead." He paused. "Will you accept my penis?"

"I will, through the veil."

Warner pushed inside Daniel, and we watched for the next few minutes as they fucked in the baptismal font. We all leaned forward to study every movement, listen to every squeak and squish, smell the earthiness of man-on-man love. The whimpering, the grunts, the panting, and the final "Ahhh!" were sweeter than any hymn I'd ever heard.

The sound of ministering angels?

Over the next twenty minutes or so, we all took our turns. Daniel fucked Mitchell. Mitchell fucked Dean. Dean fucked me. And I fucked Warner. "For and on behalf of the man you will someday marry in the temple."

We cleaned up, changed back into our two-piece garments, and headed upstairs to the dressing room where we could put on our street clothes before leaving the building.

"I'll need to work tomorrow morning on my Sunday School lesson," Daniel stated matter-of-factly, zipping his pants.

"This is my Saturday to clean the chapel," Warner informed us, fastening his belt buckle.

"I promised to help one of the families in my ward move," Dean reminded himself.

"I was supposed to work on a talk for stake conference," Mitchell said, "but I've decided I'm going to see that movie about Tolkien instead."

I put my hand on his shoulder and gave it a squeeze. "I'll see you all again next Friday," I said. I noticed for the first time how cute Mitchell's ear was and quickly thrust my tongue into it, making him giggle. He slapped my butt playfully in rebuke.

"Bring your own lube, though," I told everyone. "That stuff's expensive." I was already trying to think up a new scenario for our next adventure. Perhaps we could use the Old Testament this time, eat each other's "manna" in the Celestial Room.

"Good night, Trent."

"Good night, Daniel."

"Good night, Warner."

We all hugged, locked the door of the temple behind us, and walked back to our cars. I watched them all pull off before I started my ignition. On top of the spire, Moroni held his horn for all the world to see.

From now on, sinning after Date Night at the temple was going to be redemptive.

I turned on The Piano Guys and stepped on the gas.

Gandolfo's Staff

"Run!" Elder Pratt pointed to the train about to leave from Corridoio 18. "We can still make it!" He took off, elbowing aside a middle-aged commuter. The man's dark arm hair and firm buttocks testified of continued virility despite his cane. I thought about Barnabas Collins.

"Eeeeiii!" the man said, lifting the cane in protest.

"Andiamo!" Elder Pratt urged me onward again.

"I'm coming." I remembered a scene from *Jaws* a couple of years earlier. On my first official date—a double date, of course—all I could think about was Richard Dreyfuss, not the bishop's daughter my parents had encouraged me to ask out. "Don't wait for me!" I called back to my companion.

I put my hand on the middle-aged man's arm as I caught up to him. "You okay?" I asked.

"Your friend isn't very friendly," he said.

"Mi dispiace," I told him, for what it was worth. "I gotta go." I squeezed his arm slightly in parting and hurried after Elder Pratt. He was my third companion since I'd arrived in Italy as a Mormon missionary four and a half months ago.

I watched him jump up the steps of the orange and yellow commuter train just as the doors closed, clamping him firmly at the entrance. I could see the conductor through the glass, an expression of horror and exasperation on his face. He pulled on Elder Pratt's arms as forcefully as he could, and after a few moments, Elder Pratt finished squeezing through, the doors slamming shut behind him.

I watched my companion talking to the conductor while pointing back to me, with no sound, like a silent movie. The conductor shook his head, pointing his finger in Elder Pratt's face. The commuter train jolted and started moving away from the station.

"Stronzo," the man with the cane muttered, stopping beside me.

I had to admit the guy was right, though I'd never have allowed myself to use such vulgar language. The whole reason we were late getting back to our apartment for lunch with our housemates was Elder Pratt's insistence we call a gypsy beggar near Piazza della Repubblica to repentance. Some battles, I'd learned, were not worth fighting. I'd already pretty much concluded that attempting to convert Roman Catholics in Rome to Mormonism was one of them. Gypsies didn't strike me as any better a target.

"What's your stop?" the man asked, pointing to the empty tracks.

"Ciampino."

He nodded. "The next local leaves in eight minutes." He looked at his watch. "It's over on Corridoio 23. *I* get to *my* trains on time." He continued on, limping only slightly. I couldn't help but notice how his gait forced his butt cheeks to contract in an especially attractive manner. I felt an incredible longing to feel the friction the two cheeks created by twisting against each other. The man paused a second, looked over his shoulder, and waved me to follow.

Caspita. I hoped he hadn't seen the angle of my gaze. "I'm Anziano Andrews," I said, offering my hand.

"Anziano?" He chuckled. "You look twenty."

"I'm nineteen."

"Dio mio." The man shook his head. "I'm Stefano."

There weren't many empty seats on the train, which gave me a good excuse to sit next to him. I should use this opportunity, I knew, to ask him the Golden Questions. Baptism or not, this would make a good faith-promoting story for my family back home. Get the other elders here off my back.

"And where do you get off?" I asked.

"Castel Gandolfo."

The little town where the Pope had a summer home. The four of us from Ciampino had spent a few hours there one Preparation Day after finishing our grocery shopping. The town's best feature was a brilliant blue crater lake. And a jukebox that played "Sará perche ti amo" on the shore.

"Bello," I said.

"Want to stop by for lunch?" Stefano glanced at his watch again. "You don't have to catch up with Signor Stronzone right away, do you?"

"That's *Elder* Stronzone," I corrected sternly. Stefano looked at me blankly for a second and then chuckled.

"Ottimo," he said with a faint smile. "I don't get much company these days." He wiggled his cane as corroborating evidence.

I remembered trying to use the blunt end of a wooden backscratcher a few years ago but couldn't get it more than half an inch past my sphincter without searing pain.

"What happened?" My companions insisted we be discreet and delicate when talking to prospective investigators. Even with each other, for that matter, and our mission leaders. We had to pretend we liked the new rule banning any other music besides the Mormon Tabernacle Choir. We had to pretend we enjoyed wearing our suits while sightseeing on P-Day. We had to pretend we liked being missionaries, when it was clear almost all of us felt trapped.

"I was attacked by a couple of thugs coming out of a bar."

I frowned. That meant Stefano drank. And probably a bit too much, if he was tipsy enough to become a target.

"How awful." Stefano looked strong even now, after what must have been a convalescent period with limited opportunities to exercise. A period long enough that he was feeling the lack of social interaction.

Stefano took my hand and placed it on his upper thigh. "You can feel one of the scars through my pants."

I felt a surge of adrenaline flood my bloodstream. It wasn't unlike the sensation I'd experienced once after having iodine injected for an imaging test. My doctor had been concerned about blood flow in my feet. He'd held them in his lap and examined every square centimeter carefully over fifteen or twenty minutes before ordering the test.

"Go on," Stefano said. "Feel my leg."

I stared at my motionless hand, breathed in deeply, and moved my fingers back and forth a few centimeters. I could in fact detect a small ridge under the fabric.

"Were there any other injuries?" I wasn't sure why I asked. Was I hoping he'd ask me to rub some other scars? It was unlikely, after all, there'd be a scar running the length of his penis, even if I succumbed to the temptation to touch it. The entire surface of his body was not going to be covered in scars. His lips weren't going to be covered, his tongue, his nipples.

Stefano shrugged. "I also had two cracked ribs. A black eye and a busted lip. A few other things. And then, of course, the worst injury of all."

"The leg?"

"They kicked me in the groin over and over."

I stared at him.

"The doctors had to remove one of my testicles."

"Oh my heck!" I said in English. "Cioé…mannaggia!"

"My other ball works just fine," Stefano assured me. "But I can't deny it's a psychological blow." He lifted his cane a few inches. "And I can't wear tight pants anymore." He paused before whispering conspiratorially, "My box makes rather less of a statement these days."

I didn't recognize some of the words, but I understood the gist. The man really must be lonely, I thought, to reveal so much personal information to a complete stranger on public transportation.

We were taught that Heavenly Father made people emotionally vulnerable so they'd be more receptive to the gospel.

No one else in the seats around us seemed to even notice we were there. I looked past Stefano to the aqueduct running alongside this portion of the rail line.

"It feels good to be touched again."

I jerked my hand away as if the Pharaoh's magicians had just turned Stefano's cane into a serpent.

"Please," Stefano said softly.

Aaron's staff had devoured the staffs of the magicians.

The train slowed down as it reached Ciampino.

I put my hand back on Stefano's thigh a few moments later as the doors closed and we continued on our way.

He talked about Juventus for the next several minutes while I stared at the dark hair on his arm.

I wondered if he was uncircumcised.

"Eccoci." The train slowed to a stop again, and Stefano urged me out the door. "We can walk from here." He took a few steps, his limp more pronounced after sitting for twenty minutes. Then he paused and held out his free hand.

I hesitated, remembering when the Italian elder in my first district used to hold his companion's hand. The gesture didn't mean the same thing in this culture.

I took Stefano's hand.

There were noises—birds chirping, traffic moving past, the occasional voices of passersby—but the weight of Rome had lifted. I could feel the tranquility of small-town life. Even walking up a slight incline, I felt relaxed.

"Eccoci," Stefano said again a few minutes later.

I followed him into a small apartment building. The lack of an elevator had probably never been a problem before his injury, but he slowed as we climbed the last flight of stairs. The view from behind brought back the thoughts I used to have about one of my Italian instructors in Provo.

Interesting how the name of the city where Brigham Young University and the Missionary Training Center were located meant "I'm trying." I watched Stefano's ass twist attractively until he paused to rest.

Would an offer of assistance be welcome or upsetting?

I placed my hands on the seat of his pants and gave a gentle push.

"Grazie."

A moment later, Stefano unlocked his door, and I followed him into his apartment. When he shut the door behind us, I saw that the inside portion resembled the door to a bank vault, covered with huge, thick bolts going in four directions.

Stefano was safe here from hoodlums.

I wasn't going to be able to leave without his permission.

"Bibita?" he asked. He poured us both some aranciata.

"Do you mind if I make myself more comfortable?" He kicked off his shoes.

"É casa tua."

"But I want my guest to feel comfortable, too." He pulled off a sock. "Or you might not come back."

Would he be more receptive to hearing the story of Joseph Smith's first vision if he was relaxed? Or did he still need emotional distress to be open to the truth? Letting him think I was going along with his plans and then stopping might cause the requisite amount.

But that sounded distressful to me, too. And what if my suspicions were all in my mind? While I'd only been on five real dates, I'd had sex in my brain hundreds and hundreds of times. It meant I carried sex around with me everywhere I went. Perhaps actual sex might leave less of a mark on my soul.

Maybe all we were going to do was eat lunch. He'd never said he was gay.

"Take off your tie, Signor Andrews."

"Anziano."

"Giovanotto." Stefano reached for my neck. "Let me help you." He began fumbling with the knot.

I remembered a scene from *Strangers on a Train*.

"That's better. You can take off your shoes, too."

I pulled off my black dress shoes, watching as Stefano unbuckled his belt, and feeling another infusion of contrast dye flowing through my veins. "In tutta la storia dell'umanitá…" I started reciting the first missionary lesson in my mind.

"I need my legs to feel free," Stefano explained.

So why was he taking off his shirt, too?

My eyes traveled to the various scars across his body but didn't linger on them long. If the bulge in his underwear had looked more impressive before his attack, it had looked mighty impressive indeed.

Stefano took my hand and placed it on his chest. "Feel this scar," he said. I fingered a short scar on his left side, wondering why a beating would have left such a mark. Would doctors have performed surgery on a broken rib? And why was there a scar on his shoulder? Did the men kicking him wear sharp boots?

I rubbed my fingers gently over each of the scars. Stefano moved half a step closer.

I remembered watching *The Graduate* one evening when my parents weren't home.

"Will you feel the last scar?" Stefano whispered.

I should raise my arm to the square, I told myself. I should call him to repentance. What would Ammon do?

I thought about Elder Pratt's gypsy as I reached past the elastic of Stefano's underwear.

I wondered if he'd even been beaten in the first place. Maybe he'd been in a car accident driving drunk and was just trying to manipulate me. Gay men were always recruiting.

Stefano unbuttoned my shirt as I continued fondling his sack and penis. He unbuckled my belt and unzipped my pants, letting them fall to the floor. He didn't say a word about my own underwear, the one-piece union jack certainly as unsettling as any scar he carried.

"The bedroom's this way." He tilted his head and moved off to the left. I stepped out of my pants, pulled off my shirt, and followed. Stefano had already removed his underwear before I could join him. He reached forward to help me remove mine but paused, clearly unsure how to approach the task.

"I'm not allowed to take them off," I said. If I kept them on, the Lord might protect me. Keep me from committing a terrible sin.

I could still testify, talk about the importance of holding onto the iron rod, of enduring to the end. I could tell him how baptism would make him pure as the driven snow.

I thought about his dark pubic hair showing through his wet white pants in the font.

Stefano turned me around and slid his hand through my back slit, his fingers tentatively exploring my asshole. I remembered my first prostate exam during my final physical before sending my papers to Salt Lake. I'd been seeing my doctor since before I was ordained a deacon. He'd been first counselor in the bishopric at the time, eventually moving up to bishop when I dated his daughter, and was now first counselor in the stake presidency. He'd explained that since I might be sent anywhere in the world, it was important to make absolutely sure my prostate was okay before I left.

As the exam continued into its third minute, then its fourth, I stared at the wall and begged Heavenly Father to keep the doctor from noticing my erection, shouting when he pressed hard with no warning and a stream of fluid shot out of my penis. He caught it with his ungloved hand. "Sorry," he said. "I thought I felt something that needed checking out, and I didn't want to drag this out any longer than necessary, so I made a split-second decision to get a sample for testing. I'll be right back. Hang tight."

He returned a few minutes later. I was still leaning over the examining table with my pants around my knees. I knew I'd be naked at some point my first time through the temple, so I kept pretending this was all a part of taking out my endowments. "Turns out your seminal fluid is fine. You don't have to worry about a thing. Let me just check back here one more second to make sure I didn't hurt you." He pulled on another glove and rubbed my anus for another few moments. Then he took a towel and wiped me carefully for several more seconds after that. "Okay," he said, "you can get dressed now. You should be all set for your mission."

I felt something wet on my anus. Stefano must've been using some kind of lubricant. I remembered hearing one of the Laurels in Seminary gossiping about another girl who always carried Kentucky jelly with her.

A finger pushed past my sphincter. I thought about camels passing through the eye of a needle.

I stared out the bedroom window. Stefano had a partial view of the papal palace. I could just make out the observatory where the telescope was housed, hardly used anymore, I'd heard, because of the light pollution this close to Rome.

I was supposed to be a light set on a hill. I needed to bring light into Stefano's life. The Lord had called me on a mission.

"I work up there," Stefano said, apparently aware I was staring. "Used to, anyway." He sighed. "It was two of the priests there who followed me to the bar in Rome and…"

I felt something larger than a fingertip pushing against my anus. Then it slid in without any further warning, my sphincter reluctantly protesting the welcome intrusion. Stefano's penis seemed to slide in six inches, eight, twelve, fifteen. I remembered a TV movie I'd seen, *A Short Walk to Daylight*, about a subway in New York.

I gasped as Stefano's abdomen slapped up against my ass, the tip of his penis seeming to collide with the bottom wall of my stomach.

What kind of spiritual scars was this going to leave on me? And on him? I was causing more damage than anything those priests could have done.

"Do you and Elder Stronzone do this?" Stefano asked, pulling out ten or eleven or twelve inches and then pushing back in.

"No." I groaned.

"Do you *wish* you and Elder Stronzone did this?" He pulled out eleven or twelve or thirteen inches until the tip of his penis popped all the way out. I was about to answer when Stefano lunged forward, his penis gliding deep inside again.

"Unh." I thought about the two kilo salami I'd bought the last time it was my turn to cook for the week.

"Are you going to ask Elder Stronzone to do this to you tonight?"

Stefano started pumping slowly.

"N-no."

"Are *you* going to do this to *him*?"

"No."

Stefano squeezed his arms about my chest like a vise and nuzzled the back of my neck. He held on tightly as he continued to pump slowly. Then he squeezed more and more tightly as he began to pump faster. Even when he slowed down briefly, his crushing embrace continued forcing me to take shallow breaths. "Are you going to let me do this to you again?"

"In tutta la storia dell'umanitá…"

Stefano stopped moving, and the stillness was like an itch. I pulled forward a few inches and then pushed my ass against him as hard as I could.

"I'm glad," Stefano whispered. "I want to see you again, too."

He didn't know anything about me, I thought. How could he tell if he liked me?

Neither of us spoke for the next several minutes. I concentrated on the pressure of his penis against the walls of my rectum, on his arms constricting my chest, on his sweat dripping onto the back of my garments. I concentrated on the observatory in the distance.

"It's lovely, isn't it?" Stefano asked.

Catholics definitely had Mormons beat when it came to beautiful buildings. I nodded.

"I didn't mind so much the aspergillum being shoved up my ass," he said, sliding slowly in and slowly out, "but being beaten with that sharp crucifix…" He pushed himself in so hard I was sure he was going to tear through the lining of my stomach. I had no time to think about some of the unfamiliar terms.

"No one gave a damn."

I began to understand why his social life had declined. "I'm sorry," I said.

"Your hot ass feels so good." He squeezed me more tightly. "I wasn't sure I'd ever…"

Could the priests in the summer house watch us through the window with their telescope?

I wondered what excuse I'd give Elder Pratt for being late. I wondered what I was going to tell the mission president. How would I pay for my plane ticket if I was sent home in disgrace?

"Do you want me to cum inside you?" Stefano whispered in my ear. I felt a drop of his sweat hit the back of my neck, and then I felt him lick it up.

"Sí."

"I *want* to cum inside you. I *want* to…"

"But?"

"I won't unless you promise to fuck me, too."

Such language. This was all wrong. If I didn't have an orgasm myself, maybe letting him inside my ass wouldn't count as sex. Maybe…

Stefano started to pull out.

"Cum inside me," I ordered. He kissed the back of my neck, squeezed me even more tightly, and started pumping away with more determination than before. The friction made me wiggle my ass like a bear trying to scratch its back against a tree.

Was this what women felt when men were inside them? It didn't seem possible. Wouldn't they want to feel this all the time? I always thought women didn't like sex, that they only did it because they had to. But this…this was…this was enjoyable.

I reached behind me, placing my right hand on Stefano's right ass cheek and pulling him toward me. I remembered how difficult it had been to wash in the community showers of the Missionary Training Center. To have permission now to touch a man's ass erased any sensation of confinement the vault door or Stefano's muscular arms created. To be able to give another man permission to spread apart my cheeks seemed a greater blessing than anything I'd ever conferred with my consecrated oil and Melchizedek priesthood.

Why did I need permission from God to be kind to someone?

Why would the Lord disapprove of Stefano's kindness toward me?

Stefano seemed to push deeper and deeper with each thrust, fifteen inches, sixteen, seventeen inches, as if his penis—no, his cock—grew longer with each transgressive act.

Was that why finocchio was the Italian word for gay?

"Aaagghh!!"

Stefano sounded like he'd just been beaten with a club. But he sounded happy about it.

"My physical therapist," he panted, "said this was good for my recovery."

For the first time since being set apart, I felt like a missionary.

Stefano pulled out and handed me a bottle of lubricant. As I extracted my dick through the slit in the front of my garments and dabbed some of the lubricant on it, I was shocked to see that his cock appeared to be a mere eight inches long. What had I been feeling in there? The Spirit?

With Stefano's arms no longer around my chest, I felt light and free as I pried apart his cheeks and probed for his opening with my lubed fingers. His sphincter already felt a little dilated in anticipation.

Or was that particular muscle just heavily used?

"Put in your two index fingers," Stefano guided me, "and pull my hole open wide."

He was soft and warm and wet inside, and I wanted to be a part of Stefano's heat. I aimed my dick at the beckoning hole in front of me, feeling like the brother of Jared entering a barge headed for the Promised Land, and slid all the way inside him with no resistance.

I remembered a crude joke the son of the first counselor had told before Seminary class one morning. "If God had meant for a man to be fucked, he'd have given him an asshole."

I slid in and out as slowly as I could, afraid of overstimulating myself. Every skin cell in my shaft tingled. My asshole still burned, too, like the time my doctor's son had handed me the wrong leaves to wipe myself during a ward scouting trip.

I used to listen to the Osmonds singing, "He Ain't Heavy, He's My Brother," before the music ban.

The road was long.

I pushed all seven inches of my dick inside Stefano.

I needed to stay on the strait and narrow path.

If I had an orgasm, there'd be no going back. I'd be damned. I'd be sent home. I'd be excommunicated.

I pulled out.

And then pushed myself in again.

It might still be possible to salvage my soul, and his, too.

When I shot inside this man who was no longer a stranger, I started trying to figure out how we'd be able to do this again when I came back with Elder Stronzone to teach him.

I was just about to finally ask those Golden Questions when Stefano spoke up first. "Caro mio, what do you know about being gay?" Without waiting to hear my answer, he asked the follow up question that changed my life.

"Would you like to know more?"

We made love another two times before morning.

Pity Party

"Are you offering me a pity fuck?" the man asked, his harelip curling in disgust. "I don't want your pity."

I tried to smile pleasantly in return. "You've been cruising me for half an hour, and when I show interest, you change your mind?" I had nothing invested in this hook up, so I wasn't angry at the rejection. Rejections were the way of the world. I just sensed that his defensive wall could be topped.

But the man's lip remained curled. "If you were truly interested, you wouldn't have waited half an hour."

Out of the corner of my eye, I saw Alfonso but didn't turn to acknowledge him. I always made a concerted effort to pay attention to the person I was talking to, especially in French Quarter gay bars where wandering eyes indicated you were really hoping for something better.

"If *you* weren't interested," I replied, hoping a twinkle in my eye might keep the conversation light, "why did you keep cruising *me*?"

I could see Alfonso waving at me from behind the man with the harelip. The one time I'd gone home with him, he'd demonstrated how, with a bit of contortion, he could aim his piss into his own mouth. It was like watching a living fountain with a recirculation system. He grabbed his crotch now and motioned with his other hand as if drinking from an invisible glass.

"Well, *I* was interested." The harelip man folded his arms across his chest.

I shrugged. "If you had *truly* been interested, you wouldn't have waited half an hour before telling me so."

The man looked me in the eyes a long moment and then uncrossed his arms. But now they were on his hips.

Alfonso gave up and walked away.

"You know," I said, "there are chubby chasers out there, and no one accuses them of going after heavy men because they pity them."

The guy with the harelip closed his eyes for a second as if to lessen the pain. "So you're a harelip chaser?" he asked. "I'm supposed to find that more acceptable? It still makes me an object, not a person."

I nodded to try showing I understood. I knew otters who only went out with bears, or young men who would only date older men, or guys who'd only date other guys with tattoos, the type more important than the man himself.

I glanced over to the pool table, breaking my rule of keeping my eyes focused. A tall black guy was competing with a Japanese man of average height. Kenji loved playing a modified eight ball he called "Cueing the Dildo" at a table he'd set up in a spare bedroom in his Warehouse District condo. The two times I had sex with him involved an extra set of "cue sticks"—long, thin dildos called Slim Sevens—that we both had to keep inserted in our backsides throughout the game. Each time one of us prepared to make a shot, the other would need to push the shooter's dildo deeper into his ass simultaneously as he made the shot. If we successfully sunk the right ball in the right pocket, our reward was to have our Slim Seven withdrawn completely and then reinserted to the hilt.

I turned back to the harelip guy. His expression showed he'd noticed my wandering eyes. I was blowing it.

"Does it matter *why* I'm attracted to you?" I asked. "You seem to think I'm so physically superior I couldn't possibly be genuinely drawn to you. But even in all my physical superiority, I'm happy when someone I'm attracted to is attracted to me as well. It's not a given."

"It's not the same thing."

I stood silently looking into the harelip guy's face for a few moments. He didn't look away. "I live in the Marigny," I said. "We can walk." I offered my hand, and after only another moment of hesitation, he reached out and took it.

It was still early, not yet midnight, so other men passed us on their way to the bars, smirking as they saw us holding hands. A few straight couples passed as well. Even when they pretended not to see us, I hoped that subliminally, they were recognizing gay folks as normal.

Not that all of us were. When I turned on the dim overhead lighting in my bedroom a few minutes later, the man with the harelip gasped. "What the—?"

Two framed George Dureau photos hung above my headboard, one of a black dwarf, the other presenting a long-haired white man balancing on his hands because both legs were amputated at the top of his thighs. On the wall to the right of the bed hung a painting I'd bought at an estate sale in the Bywater. In it, an elderly white man, bald, knelt in front of a wheelchair, giving a young Latino wearing an eye patch a blow job.

"I'm outta here," the guy with the harelip said, turning toward the hallway.

"Okay," I said. "I'm sorry this isn't working out." Then I motioned to the artwork with a Vanna White wave. "Can I just show you one more thing before you go?"

The man sighed.

I started to unzip my pants.

"You can't be serious."

I'd seen that level of disgust before. It never got easy to bear, but I pushed on. "I have two holes in my dick." I pulled my flaccid penis out and pointed to the tip of the head, where I, like most men, had a slit, and then to the top of my shaft, to a hole just below the head.

"So you had a Prince Albert. Bully for you."

"I was born with two holes. Piss comes out of one, and most of my cum comes from the same hole, but a little cum also comes out the second hole."

The man's brows furrowed. "Really?"

"I've had guys kick me out of their apartment as soon as they saw it. They think it's some new STD."

"Is it?" The man stepped back an inch.

"Just an abnormality. It gives me a slight risk for a urinary tract infection, but I can't bring myself to have surgery." I watched the man with the harelip staring at my dick. "I mean, if there was surgery to make this guy *longer*, that would be one thing. But just to go in and start cutting and rearranging things? Uh-uh."

The man looked back up at me.

"I'm Caleb," I said.

The man paused another long moment. "Doug," he replied.

I smiled. "I want to kiss you, Doug." I moved a step closer, reached for his hand, and pulled him the rest of the way over. I leaned forward, my pants falling to the floor. I paused for consent and, when he didn't protest, I aimed my lips toward his.

Some men are natural kissers and some aren't. I couldn't even count the number of men who channeled snakes, their tongues flicking through my lips for a second or two before withdrawing and then flicking forward a few centimeters once again. But Doug was one of those guys who could seemingly transfer his entire tongue into my mouth and keep it there. A full complement of another man's tongue filling the empty space in my mouth was just as satisfying as a hefty dick in my ass. I moaned in pleasure.

We ground against each other for the next two or three minutes as we kissed. Finally, Doug pulled away. "I'm not bad at rimming, either, when I get a chance."

"Don't say I never did anything for you." I turned around and leaned over the bed.

Doug knelt behind me and buried his face in my ass, like a man who dives into a cold swimming pool to get the shock over with. Spreading my cheeks with his face, he licked the valley up and down my crack before pressing his mouth against my hole. He kissed it a few times, reminding me of the Miller's Tale, and then started licking the center puck.

Here, most guys usually turned into cats, licking my asshole instead of their paws, but with the same slow, methodical, lackadaisical air. Doug, though, while licking even more slowly, kept his tongue pressed hard against my anus. With each lick, he pressed harder and harder. I could feel my sphincter resisting, but Doug fought back.

Like breaking a seal on a stuck jar lid, Doug pushed past the inertia and found a way in. His tongue penetrated an inch, two inches into my ass.

"Hot damn!" Not many men were capable of tongue-fucking.

Doug reached around my waist and began stroking me. He used a combination of friction and grip, his fingers moving the skin on my shaft so that the skin stimulated the nerves underneath. But he also loosened his grip every few seconds so that the friction instead came from his skin against mine. Then he'd grip more tightly again.

My dick was already so hard it almost hurt, and with that tongue moving back and forth through my sphincter, it wasn't long before I felt a telltale tingling building up front.

"Unh. I'm gonna cum."

Doug swung me around and swallowed my cock without a break in rhythm, the way a trained relay team passed a baton. Within seconds, I shot into his mouth.

Before my contractions finished, Doug rose to his feet and pressed his lips back against mine. He shot a tongueful of cum into my mouth, warm and salty and thick, and we passed it back and forth for another minute. I felt a drop slide down my chin. Finally, he withdrew and swallowed, licking his lips first and then darting forward to lick my chin. I swirled my cum and his saliva around in my mouth another moment, not wanting the moment to end, and then swallowed, too.

"You can't possibly think I considered that a sacrifice," I said.

"But you didn't *know* I'd be any good at sex."

I shrugged. "That's unknowable. It's not as if there are reviews on Yelp. The first time with anyone is a gamble."

He seemed to concede the point with a slight nod.

"I'm having a party this Friday night," I said. "Can you make it?"

Doug's eyes narrowed. "What kind of party?"

"It's a pity party."

His mouth fell open.

"Better close that," I said. "I'm still young. I can cum twice."

"You motherfucker."

I sat on the edge of the bed and patted the mattress beside me. Doug looked as if he couldn't decide if he wanted to hit me or spit on me. Frankly, either would have been okay, though I'd have preferred the spit. He finally decided to sit next to me, though he made sure our legs didn't touch. Then he folded his arms again. He was still fully dressed.

"I threw my first pity party two years ago," I said. "For myself. I'd been in a relationship for years with a guy who made me feel like a freak every day." I wanted to gently touch Doug's lip, but I knew it was too soon for that. "I'd always been self-conscious about the two holes. After four years, he told me he was going to throw up if he ever had to look at my dick again. He took all his stuff and walked out."

Doug's arms remained crossed against his chest. He pursed his lips subconsciously, evaluating my account.

"I'd just turned thirty, and I thought I had no future. So I decided to kill myself."

Doug's arms loosened a bit, sliding apart so that one hand rested on top of the other, both now resting on his stomach. Pity was a powerful force. But he still looked wary.

"I put out an ad asking anyone who wanted to fuck a freak to show up at my place at 8:00 the next Friday night." I shook my head, remembering. "I wanted to go out with a bang, and I thought I might even talk some S&M guy into strangling me."

"Fuck, Caleb."

"Instead, thirteen perfectly normal guys knocked on my door. A few of them had some kind of abnormality, too, a missing finger, an asshole three inches higher up his crack than usual, a severe overbite. A couple were heavy. But most of the guys were average in almost every way. Except for one outstanding male specimen, the hunkiest guy I'd ever had sex with." I sighed.

"And?" Doug asked. "I can tell there's an and."

"Well, most of them were pretty damn good," I said. "Obviously, I couldn't fuck thirteen guys or let thirteen guys give me a blow job. So I either sucked them off or let them fuck me. Two guys did a show with each other for me and then ended by both fucking me at the same time." I chuckled. "No single dick has ever been too much for me after that."

Doug reached down to adjust his pants.

I'd lied about all the party guests being "normal," except that I'd really found the word to have little meaning. One guy, normal enough that night, had later invited me on a camping trip. It wasn't until we were sitting around our camp lantern after dinner that he excused himself for a few minutes, coming back out of the tent wearing ceramic fangs and little else other than a long wolf tail. It appeared to be attached to a butt plug inserted up his ass. The tail clued me in rather quickly as to who was going to be top that evening.

Sure, the sex was odd, and not something I'd talk to Mom on the phone about later, but who was it hurting? While I wasn't particularly into that kind of role-playing, letting the guy howl while he fucked me made him happy.

And he did have a nice dick, so it wasn't as if I was suffering as a result of my service.

"It was a transformative experience," I went on. "Once a month ever since, I've held another pity party, but now I invite guys who consider *themselves* physically undesirable."

"And you're recruiting me?" Doug asked. "I'm still not finding that terribly flattering."

I put my hand on his leg. He looked at it but didn't try to remove it.

"Here's the thing," I said. "All the tension between us tonight is because you do feel inferior. It doesn't matter if you *are* inferior or not, or if *others* think you're inferior. You *think* other men find you inferior or you wouldn't have started arguing the minute I approached you. So why pretend now? You know the situation and I know the situation. Everybody at the party knows the situation."

"Why don't you just hold an Ugly Miss America contest?" Doug suggested, his harelip curled in disgust the way it had been at the bar. "A Special Olympics for the sexually disadvantaged."

I frowned and rubbed my chin, wishing the drop of Doug's cum was still there.

"Fuck! You're not actually considering it, are you?"

I patted his leg again. "It's time for you to take off your pants."

"Dude, you are definitely foreplay-disadvantaged."

"Show me your dick."

His chin jutted out. "I want some Mardi Gras pearls."

Aha, sarcastic jokes now. Things were going to be okay. I knelt beside my bed and pulled out a box from underneath. I reached in and showed Doug a string of purple anal beads. "Will these do?"

"Fuck!"

"I caught these at the Krewe of Wharf Rats parade in the Marigny."

"Charming."

"Drop your pants and bend over."

Doug shook his head but stood and followed my instructions. I lubed up the string of increasingly larger beads and inserted the smallest one first, sliding the entire strand in slowly one bead at a time.

"Agh. Those things are getting a little big down there."

"Two more to go."

"Unh," he moaned. "Agh."

I fastened the ring at the end of the strand to the tip of my penis. "My cock's coming in next." After playing with his ass the last few minutes, it was hard enough to make the attempt again.

"Fuck."

I'd have to teach him a larger vocabulary.

I slid my lubed dick in slowly. It was too soon for me to cum again, despite my earlier boasting. That would take another twenty minutes. But I was hard, and I began fucking Doug slowly.

"You're going to stroke yourself," I instructed as I slid back and forth inside his ass. "You're going to catch your cum in your hand." I pulled my dick out completely, bringing the largest bead at the end of the strand with me. Then I pushed the bead back in and chased it with my dick once more.

"Goddamn."

"Tell me what you're going to do with that cum when you catch it."

"I…uh…I'm…"

"Tell me. What are you going to do?" I pulled out of his ass, taking two beads with me this time and shoving both of them and my dick in without giving him even a second to adjust.

Doug groaned loudly. "You fucker."

"I'm trying, Doug. If I don't get it right, we'll have to try again in a few hours."

"Goddamn."

He sure liked to stick with a word once he chose it.

"What are you going to do with that cum, Doug? I need to know." I almost started singing the song by Marc Anthony, but there was a time and a place for these things.

I kissed the back of his ear, nuzzled his neck, inhaled his scent loudly. I liked the sweat off his shoulder blade.

Doug's body began vibrating as he masturbated more and more vigorously. I started fucking faster to give him momentum. Fifteen seconds later, he shouted loudly, his entire body jerking for another few seconds.

I slowly withdrew until I'd pulled out the last bead. I turned Doug around to face me. "What's the damn verdict with the cum?" I demanded.

Doug's eyes narrowed again and he turned me around once more, forcing me to lean over the bed again. He pressed his hand against my asshole to shove the bulk of his load into my crack, but then he rubbed the mass across my entire buttocks. I smiled. No one had done that before. It would be fun to let it dry there.

But Doug dropped to his knees again and used his superior feline licking skills once more, slowly lapping every bit off every last centimeter of my ass. When he finished, he stood up, and I turned to face him.

"So…Friday at 8:00?" I asked.

"A pity party, huh?"

I shrugged. "It'll be just like tonight," I said, "times ten."

Doug pulled up his underwear in silence and then his pants. He started fastening his buckle.

"Make that eleven," he said. "I know this guy…"

I smiled. "The pittier, the merrier." I kissed Doug gently on the lips. There was no hint of pity as he kissed me back.

Electricity

Working in the gay bookstore near the French Quarter was fun. I only worked there on weekends, going to school weekday mornings and working in a nearby retirement home on weekday afternoons. But weekends at the bookstore gave me time to study Spanish or anatomy between customers and opportunities to cruise when customers came in.

Many men would often slowly walk around the store, browsing the fiction section, the political section, and the biography section, before "accidentally" discovering the magazine racks. Then they'd stay there half an hour before deciding who to take home, the hunk on the cover of *Honcho* or the hunk on the cover of *Men*. The best part of these difficult decisions was that the magazine racks were placed directly in front of the checkout counter. So as the men flipped through the pages, I dutifully checked them out in return.

Two men had just come in wearing tight denim shorts, tight enough for me to see they weren't wearing underwear. The rear seam on one man was wedged in his crack, making him look as if he wasn't even wearing shorts at all but was simply a beautiful, blue-skinned man. The other man had a worn, faded area on his crotch, where apparently the first man often rubbed him, or maybe where he rubbed himself, or perhaps where strangers rubbed him the way pilgrims wore down toes on the bronze statue of Peter in the Vatican. Perhaps it was just where his dick pressed so much against the fabric that the stress of that constant contact had worn down the fibers by itself.

I felt my own shorts tightening now as I watched.

Because the men at the racks were often fully engaged while there, I could usually look as long or as hard as I wanted without the guys realizing it. This was a respectable bookstore, however, so I could never stare in an obvious way. And even when I saw an exceptionally good-looking man alone in the store, even when he bent over to reach a magazine near the floor, even when I couldn't help but see that navy blue handkerchief thrusting out of his back right pocket, I had to resist and simply smile cordially as the man purchased his magazine and left.

"Navy blue is my favorite color, too," I wanted to say, "but I usually wear mine in the other pocket." I never wore handkerchiefs at all, actually, open to whatever developed, but I knew the signals. And I wanted to respond, yet I was at work. It wouldn't be right.

The two men in tight shorts huddled together as one of them showed a photograph to his buddy. Their thighs pressed up against each other. I wanted to go back to the Lifestyle section and rearrange some books, so I could accidentally—and inappropriately—brush past their asses as they stood next to the magazines.

I rubbed my crotch a moment through my jeans and then looked out the window for distraction.

Clouds were gathering. That wasn't unusual for a New Orleans summer afternoon, but these were a little darker than typical. It was so hot in the store, though, with only one tiny air conditioner, that I was glad for the shade. Men would always come in here sweating and keep sweating while they were here. I was afraid they'd leave too soon because of the heat. I wanted to bring a towel and dry them off, or maybe go over and lick off some of that sweat running down their arms. Or maybe…

Well, it wouldn't do to keep thinking of it, so I tried to distract myself by looking at the gay travel section nearby. *How to Pick Up a Man in Ten Languages*. Good grief. Sí, oui, ja. I heard the magazine rack turn and glanced back.

A moment later, the two men came up to the counter with three magazines and a digest. I rang up the purchases and placed them in a bag, avoiding eye contact until my final, casual "Thank you." I acted as if I didn't notice their well-formed chests through their T-shirts, or their nicely developed biceps. I wasn't trying to act stand-offish, of course, only "professional."

They nodded and smiled, walking toward the door, where the man with the wedgie turned and gave me another smile as he left. I wished I could have been the one to give him that wedgie. He could have given me his phone number, couldn't he? It wouldn't be *completely* inappropriate if we met sometime away from work. I rubbed my crotch again and tried to study some Spanish while I waited for the next customer.

Sunday afternoons were slow, though, and no one else came in for the next half hour. As 6:00 approached, I added up the receipts for the day and counted out as much as I could, barring a last minute sale. Then, just before closing time, the sky opened up and the rain began pouring down. I'd be stuck here for God only knew how long because I hadn't brought an umbrella. Damn, and I had wanted to walk through the Quarter before it got dark.

I could almost always pick up someone who was driving down Dauphine as I walked. I enjoyed the immediacy of it. I didn't have to worry about being proper and could follow my hormones. But my afternoon stroll was out of the question now. Sheets of rain fell, and the streets started filling up.

I heard a drip and looked out the bay window behind the counter where I stood. Water was leaking in and splashing on the book display. Fuck.

I quickly grabbed books, wiping them off on my red T-shirt and setting them on the counter. All the dust from the books left black streaks on my chest.

Once I'd dried them all, I ran to the other bay window on the other side of the store, but thankfully that display was okay. The French doors in the back corner, though, were leaking terribly onto the photocopy machine.

A bookcase blocked my view of the machine from the counter, and last month, a guy had photocopied his dick and folded the paper to make it into a card. He'd written his name and phone number inside. What with the paper tray jutting out preventing him from getting too close to the machine, the photocopy testified of a length I was intrigued to investigate, so I did call later when I got home.

I was impressed again with the value of truth in advertising.

Now, of course, my focus was on stopping that leak. There were old wooden shutters that fit into the door on the outside which could then be screwed into place from the inside. I grabbed one of the heavy shutters and ran outside. The balcony from the apartment above leaked as if it weren't even there, and wind blew still more water in from the sides. I had both shutters up quickly, but I was drenched by the time I finished.

Disgusted, I went back inside and was just about to close and lock the door when a man came running up. "You closing?" he asked, his face full of desperation.

"Well, I can't leave anyway. Come on in."

"I'm not going to buy anything," he said. "I didn't bring any money. I just wanted to get out of the rain. Is it still okay?"

"Sure." I let him in, slid the bolt over, and put in the wire mesh to block the glass in the doors, more to protect from vandals than thieves.

Then I finished counting out while the guy wiped water from his arms and stood under the ceiling fan to dry off. At least the temperature was no longer 95 degrees.

As I tallied the figures, I glanced up a few times at the man. He was about thirty, with dark, disheveled hair. He wore a wet T-shirt, white, that showed his nipples. They pointed strongly toward me. He had the smallest overhang of stomach, but his chest and arm muscles made that irrelevant. He exuded masculinity at every breath. I watched his chest rise and fall, the fabric clinging to his skin. Some swirls of dark hair showed through the wet cloth.

His eyes closed, the man's face pointed up toward the ceiling fan, his arms slightly spread apart, while he enjoyed the feel of the wind. I wished I could kneel in front of him before he saw me coming. It was after 6:00, so I wasn't officially at work, especially since he'd only come in to get out of the rain.

I felt the pain of my erection against my shorts, but I knew I had to ignore it. I liked my boss, had fucked him in the back seat of his car once, and didn't want to do anything to harm the store's reputation.

I finished counting out and turned off the lights behind the counter, walking out into the middle of the room to join the man.

"Feels good under this fan," he said. "Come on over and see."

I moved a little closer but still kept my distance.

"Oh, come on." He took my arm and pulled me over to stand directly under the blades as he stepped back a couple of feet.

I lifted my face up as he'd done. The wind brushed my face and chest and arms and even my legs, all damp, and I couldn't help but sigh.

"Yeah," the man breathed. He came a little closer and lifted his face again. With our backs arched slightly, our crotches hovered only a few inches away from each other. I was going to have to walk away or…

A loud clap of thunder shook the building, and we both jumped. Then the lights went out. I instinctively reached out and touched the man's arm.

"No electricity," I said. With the lights out, shutters over two windows, and storm clouds blocking the sun in the late afternoon sky, it was dim but not black in the store. A large bookcase stood between us and the nearest window, though, so the dimness was considerable, especially while my eyes were still used to the bright light. I could just make out the figure of the other man.

He put his hand on my arm in return. "I don't know," he replied. "I think there's still plenty of electricity."

He took a step forward and pressed his crotch against mine. Then he pressed his chest against me. His wet T-shirt clung to my wet T-shirt. I could feel the humidity rise to my face. Then I felt a wetness on my face and lips, and a tongue prying its way through my lips and deep against the roof of my mouth.

I worried about propriety for one second longer and then put my arm across the man's back and pulled him even closer. His tongue probed deeper into my mouth.

I felt a hand groping my crotch and trying to grab onto my dick through my pants. His fingers alternately caressed and grabbed, caressed and grabbed. I reached down and felt a long, hard lump in the other man's pants as well. I could even feel him throb through the fabric.

I reached behind and ran my fingers along the seam which lined the man's crack. Near the bottom, where I knew his asshole would be, I pressed my fingers into the denim.

There was a slight moan, and then the man kissed me even harder.

He reached for my zipper and tugged it downward, reaching through the opening to feel through my underwear. Then he undid my buckle, yanked open the top button above the zipper, and in one motion dropped to his knees as he pulled my pants to my ankles. He buried his face against my underwear, breathed in deeply, and then pulled my underwear down as well.

Was it a good thing or a bad one that the store didn't have security cameras?

As the man's mouth engulfed my cock, I put my fingers in his wet hair and drew him forward. I liked the feel of the warm wetness of his mouth and the cool wetness of his hair. He rocked back and forth on his knees, and I felt myself swelling even further to fill his mouth.

After a few moments, I pulled him to his feet and kissed him, tasting my precum on his lips. I peeled his T-shirt up above his chest and kissed his nipples, licking the sweat mixed with rainwater off his nipples. He pressed my face against his chest and guided my head across and down his torso. I licked as I moved along, and finally, my face was even with his blue jeans.

He wore no belt, so I flipped open the button and pulled the zipper down only an inch. Then I rubbed the hard lump with my face. His dick quivered and forced the zipper down a few millimeters. With my nose, I forced my face past his fly and, digging in still further, I pushed the zipper the rest of the way down. His pants fell to the floor as I reached for his underwear and pulled them to his ankles.

The man had a mushroom cock with an oversized head. I licked the top and then under the edge. The whole thing bounced each time my tongue touched it, so beautiful I just wanted to stare.

Finally, I opened wide and took the whole head in. Thank God I'd had plenty of practice already over the past few years. He pushed forward and shoved his dick to the back of my mouth. It was almost too much to handle, but then he pulled back just enough to let me breathe and pushed forward again. Deep throating was just like learning to breathe while swimming laps, but I'd never been able to swim more than two laps. I took it as long as I could, and then I stood, pulling my pants up with me.

"Hang on," I whispered. I trotted back toward the counter and realized I was going to make a final sale after all, to myself. "I need to get a raincoat." I picked up a bottle of lube and a condom and headed back to where the guy was standing erect in the dim light. The rain still beat down outside and thunder vibrated through the building.

I dropped my pants again and turned the man around. He leaned forward, reaching toward the magazine rack for support.

I dripped some lubricant on my cock and rubbed it to cover the shaft and head completely. Then I tore open the condom package, pulled the rubber out, and unrolled it over my dick. The man turned his head to look back at me as I dropped more lubricant on the condom. "Lube that thunderbolt," he said, a glint in his eyes making the room seem brighter than it was.

I wiped the excess lube still on my fingers onto his asshole and then added a little more as he squirmed to meet my probing digits. Finally, I could wait no longer and pressed the tip of my cock against his ass. I eased forward slowly, letting the head gently enter.

A bright flash outside was followed almost instantly by a tremendous clap of thunder. We both jumped, me forward a little and him backward. My cock shoved halfway up his ass in an instant.

"Oh, God, yes," he breathed. He turned to look back at me again, an expression of both pain and pleasure on his face. "Take me by storm," he said.

All his puns should have taken away from the experience but instead only enhanced it. I shoved myself the rest of the way inside, and without waiting, I began pumping away. He gasped and held onto the magazine rack more tightly. It squeaked as we rocked back and forth.

Lightning crackled outside, and the building shook again with the thunder. I forced myself inside the man a little deeper this time, as far as I could go, and hugged him tightly for a moment before sliding out and back in again.

I moved slowly the next few moments, pulling out gently until just the tip of my head was still inside, and then just as softly easing my way back in. The wind outside blew sheets of rain underneath the balcony and against the windows. A few thumps on the glass told us it was hailing now.

A couple of car alarms went off nearby, and I started sliding in and out faster. A *Handjobs* fell onto the floor, shaken out of the rack. I could hear moans in between the rolling thunder, and soon my moans joined until the air was filled with continual noise. I was usually rather quiet during sex, but now I felt free to let my natural urges take over. I pushed in and pulled out, pushed in and pulled out, hearing the squeaking and the alarms and the rain and the hail and the thunder and the moans. I clung desperately and slid in and out, in and out, in and…

"Aaauuugh!"

I held onto the man, my arms wrapped around his chest, as if trying not to be further swept away by the storm. Drops fell from my brow onto his muscled back. I pressed my face into his neck and kissed him.

After a few moments, I slowly pulled out. But before I could do anything else, the man turned and pulled me to the ground. He sat on my chest, pinning my arms to my side as he straddled me. Then he thrust his swollen cock right in my face and began jacking off. He groaned along with the thunder, and I breathed in deeply to smell his wet, musty body.

"It's gonna rain!" he finally gasped, and I closed my eyes as drops of warm cum splattered across my face.

He sat motionless for a moment, his head tilted backward, and then he slowly looked down at me, his face still contorted from the explosion. He carefully slid down my torso past my abdomen till he was sitting on my cock. Then he leaned forward, his nose touching mine.

The thunder was softening in the distance as the storm finally passed, but the building still trembled softly with the rumbling. The man licked gently at the drops of cum on my face, and then he slid off to lie beside me on his side, nestling his head on my chest. I draped an arm across his back and smelled his wet, clean hair. I kissed the top of his head, and then we lay silently in the dark for another half hour, until the electricity came back on again and we could see well enough to exchange numbers.

Court of Forbidden Love

"Make sure you shower," the stake president told me over the phone, "and wear a clean pair of garments."

"Excuse me?"

"If we decide to excommunicate," President Caldwell continued, "we'll have to ask you to take off your garments." He paused. "And we'll need to verify."

What the fuck? When it had begun to look more and more like I'd be called before a Church tribunal, I'd done a little research to prepare myself. While I knew I'd be asked to remove my Mormon underwear at the conclusion, I figured I'd be asked to do it behind closed doors, not in front of everyone.

What a bunch of pervs. I'd rather get my jollies honestly than through voyeurism.

Though I supposed a religion so focused on proxy work was bound to create leaders with specialized tendencies.

At 6:25, I pulled into the parking lot at the New Orleans stake center. It was also the building where the Metairie ward met each Sunday. I'd been coming here my whole life.

There were only nine cars in the parking lot. Not everyone was here yet for the court.

It had finally come to this. And I'd been so good for so long. As a teenager, I refused to go into detail when confessing masturbation to my bishop before heading off to my mission in Switzerland. Bishop Dixon was on the High Council now and would certainly hear some details tonight. I'd refused to watch R-rated movies both before and after my mission. In Switzerland, I'd refused to look at my first companion's uncircumcised cock even though he offered and I was more than curious.

I turned off the engine and stepped out of the car, taking the building in for a moment before heading inside.

I missed the old mimosa tree that had been cut down to make room for a new HVAC unit.

At the front doors, I peered through the glass into the lobby. This might be my last time inside the building where I'd sung "I Hope They Call Me on a Mission" as a child and memorized Seminary scriptures as a teen. I should have already walked away the moment I realized the doctrine would never have room for people like me. But after twenty-three years of scouting and volleyball and ward socials and Sunday School, abandoning my past wasn't as easy as dying my hair blue and my beard purple.

What was easy was President Caldwell spotting the clues I was gay.

I looked at my watch. 6:29. I strode quickly down the hall to the High Council room. The door was open, and I walked in.

"Good evening, Warren." President Caldwell waved me to a seat with a genial smile. Only one of his two counselors was present and six of the High Council.

But Brother Hebert shut and locked the door behind me. "Not everyone could make it," he said, answering the question on my face.

"I'm not familiar with disciplinary councils," I said, sitting at the foot of the table. I didn't know anyone who'd been ex'ed. Most people who broke major Church rules simply stopped going to services and drifted away without ever facing a trial. Even those who did get called in usually refused to attend and so couldn't offer any details. "What am I supposed to do?"

"This is a Court of Love," President Caldwell corrected me. "No matter what happens here today, we want you to feel our love deeply." He smiled, a thin line of teeth barely visible. "Deeply."

"Uh-huh."

Brother Mandini offered an opening prayer, full of supplication for the Spirit to "open our hearts and souls to each other." I didn't close my eyes but watched the other men in the room instead. They seemed sincere enough. Brother Castillion had his fist to his mouth, concentrating as hard as he could on Brother Mandini's words.

"Amen." Everyone lifted their heads.

"So, Brother Talbert," President Caldwell said, "tell us your story."

I frowned. I thought one high councilman was supposed to speak for me and another against me. This seemed more freeform than I expected. But maybe that would give me a little more power to direct the course of the evening. I surveyed the faces turned toward me. I'd never seen such intensity.

I'd given up most of my power by agreeing to come at all. But they wanted to hear my story.

So be it.

"The first time I suspected being gay was a permanent condition," I began, "was at a regional Singles conference in Pensacola." No one seemed to be taking notes. I wondered if I was being recorded. "The Singles reps always tried to keep the cost reasonable for these events, but part of the way they managed that was by putting four people to a room."

I saw two of the high councilmen exchange glances.

"I'd spent all evening feeling uninspired to find a wife and went to my room early, around 10:00."

"Did you take all your clothes off?" Brother Dixon asked. Brother McKay, sitting next to him, nudged him with an elbow.

"I stripped to my garments and climbed into the bed farthest from the door. I was asleep by the time the first of the others came in. He chose the empty bed, of course."

"Of course," Brother Dixon said, his lip curling a little.

"The last guy came in around 1:00," I said. "I woke up when I felt the mattress shake."

"What happened then?" Brother Dixon asked. Brother McKay gave him a harder nudge this time.

"I was just about to fall back asleep when the other guy in my bed scooted up right next to me. I was on my side facing the wall, and he started spooning me."

"Oh my stars." This time Brother White spoke.

"He pretended to be moving unconsciously in his sleep, but I knew he was awake. When he casually draped an arm across my chest, I pretended to move unconsciously, too, wiggling my ass into his crotch."

I looked about the council room. No one was speaking now.

"Then he knew that I knew, and a second later, I felt him pull down the bottoms of my garments." I took a breath. My first time had been special, even if I never did learn the guy's name. "I was scared, but I wanted him to do whatever it was he wanted to do. I felt a finger searching for my asshole. When the guy found it, he kept his finger there while he worked his cock over."

The high councilors were all leaning forward in their chairs. Did they really want to hear more?

Brother Dixon appeared to.

Pervert.

"I heard the guy licking his hand and then putting spit on his dick, but let me tell you, that's not the most effective lubricant." Brother Mandini smiled. "He had to push really hard to get in. I had to push hard against him to keep his cock from just shoving me off the bed. He held onto me hard and pushed and pushed."

Brother Hebert's huge Adam's apple bobbed as he swallowed.

Did church courts always get these guys horny? I wondered if their wives were at home right now anticipating their return. Or dreading it.

"I remembered feeling my skin might be tearing. I almost cried out, but I didn't want the other men in the room to know what we were doing. It was even harder than keeping quiet while I was beating off on my mission, with my companion in his cot only four feet away." Brother Mandini smiled again. "Finally, after a really long time, the guy was all the way in. He let me rest for a few minutes, which told me this probably wasn't his first spit lube conference, and the pain gradually subsided."

"And then?" Brother Castillion this time.

"Part of me just wanted to stay like that all night," I said. "It felt like an eggplant in there."

Brother Dixon blinked while Brother McKay's eyes widened.

"But I was afraid he might go limp," I said.

"What did you do?" Brother Dixon asked. He adjusted his tie.

"I wiggled my ass again and pressed hard against him. He reached up and tweaked my nipple and then started pumping, still holding onto me as tightly as he could, almost as if he was trying to pull his entire body into me. When he made his final thrust and then stopped and trembled, I thought I'd never experience anything so lovely again."

"But you did?" Brother Dixon asked, his grin overly eager. Really, was the stake president not watching? This guy needed to be pulled aside for a worthiness interview ASAP.

"A couple of months later," I continued, "Sister Porter's house blew up from a gas leak." Most of Metairie was landfill, with houses built on long pilings pounded into the ground. Sometimes, the land underneath settled over time, pulling the gas lines apart.

Kind of like building your life on a foundation of Church teachings.

"So the Elders' Quorum got together to shovel dirt under the stake center. We ordered two truckloads and started shoveling in back." I shook my head at the unpleasant memory. I had felt pressured to volunteer for too many unpleasant tasks by Church leaders over the years. "There was a lot of empty space to fill."

"That was very generous of the elders," Brother Mandini said. "I remember when the elders in my ward came to clean my back yard."

President Caldwell sent a stern glance his way, and he stopped talking.

"The Elders' Quorum president wasn't there that day, so people started acting like I was in charge of the project. Especially Raymond."

"The African-American member," Brother Hebert noted. Given LDS history, there weren't many black members. I couldn't tell if the tone in Brother Hebert's voice had a note of judgment to it or not.

I paused, remembering how tight Raymond's T-shirt had been. He wasn't wearing garments underneath because as a recent convert he hadn't been able to go to the temple yet. "Every single time he scooped up a shovelful of dirt," I went on, "he'd ask, 'Where do you want me to put this?'" So aggravating that I hadn't noticed at the time he seemed to be indicating the wooden handle more than the dirt.

"'Put it wherever there's room,' I kept telling him, but he kept asking with each new shovel of dirt, 'Where do you want me to put this?' 'Where do you want me to put this?' One time, he was absentmindedly scratching his crotch while he asked. I knew he couldn't be sending me an invitation intentionally with all the other elders there to see. And frankly, I was so hot and miserable I couldn't have cared less if he was." Back then, I'd still thought it might just barely be possible to change my orientation.

"I was dirty and sweaty, so as soon as we ran out of dirt, I sent everyone home. Raymond walked off toward the parking lot, too. I sat on the back steps under the covered walkway and tried to cool off."

"Hot and sweaty, huh?"

Brother Dixon.

"I didn't even want to get in my car, I was so dirty." I closed my eyes, remembering the day I buried the last of my hope, the day I uncovered my hope for the future. "A couple of minutes later, Raymond came over and stood right in front of me. He was a good guy, and I always liked his answers in Gospel Doctrine, but at that moment, I was in a grumpy mood and just wanted him to go away."

"But he didn't," Brother Castillion said. It wasn't a question. There was no reason it should be. Raymond had stopped coming to church shortly after that, never giving a reason, though he'd been scheduled to take out his endowments only a month later. I'd wondered if I was responsible, if I hadn't been good enough. Then I'd tried to convince myself he left because I'd been *too* good.

"He offered me his hand without saying a word," I said, "and I took it. He led me to the work area and pointed. 'There's still a lot of room in there,' he said. He told me we should crawl under to find out just how much."

The look on Brother Mandini's face suggested he was reflecting on the close call with sexual disaster he might have had when the elders cleaned his back yard. Of course, he lived in another ward. What was the chance that any of the elders there were gay?

I smiled, remembering the time I'd seen Aaron at the Corner Pocket.

"After what happened in the hotel, I recognized what was going on," I said. "So I crawled under the church with him." I looked at Brother Dixon to see if he was going to say anything.

"What?" He shrugged, looking left and right in confusion.

"There we were, lying on our backs in the dirt—hot, sweaty, and filthy. Raymond reached over to unzip my pants. He pulled out my sweaty cock and started sucking. After I came in his mouth, he turned me onto my stomach and had me pull my pants down. My dick was now in the dirt, but I knew what was coming next, and I didn't care."

"Oh my heck."

"What I didn't know was that he was going to use a mouthful of cum as lubricant. It's certainly better than spit, but silicone's still the best." The room was silent now. You could have heard a condom wrapper drop.

"Raymond lay on top of me for another twenty minutes, his cock still inside me for a while even after he shot until it became too flaccid to stay in."

He'd kissed me then, a faint taste of cum still on his lips.

As we lay in the dirt, Raymond told me I was the only person at church who understood him. I'd found that sad, given I'd never met with him even once outside of our regular meetings. When he resigned not long afterward, I knew I should follow his lead.

But like a chicken, I'd waited until I was called into a court before addressing my membership.

The continuing silence in the council room was odd, considering how vocal some of the men had been from the start. Finally, I cleared my throat. "So am I gay enough to be excommunicated?" I asked.

The councilmen exchanged glances with the stake president and each other.

"Warren," President Caldwell said, "would you step into my office while we deliberate?" He pointed to a door leading from the council room to his office. I nodded and went inside the tiny room, closing the door behind me.

Rear Window was suspenseful no matter how many times I saw it. Waiting in President Caldwell's office was, of course, not suspenseful. It wasn't as if the jury would be out for hours. I'd be on my way to the Ponchartrain on Causeway Boulevard to watch some suburban gay dancers before long. I leaned over like a willow tree and tried to relax all my muscles. I'd need some kind of emotional release when this was over. I stood up and took a deep breath.

There was a tap at the door, and the stake president stuck his head in. "Ready, Warren?" Less than three minutes had passed.

I nodded.

He welcomed me back into the council room, and there I stopped in my tracks. Something was off. The councilmen looked different. They were all standing behind the chairs they'd been sitting in, but there was something else. Brother Mandini had taken off his glasses and set them on the table, but that wasn't it, either. There was something more. There was…

All the high councilmen had removed their suit coats and hung them on their chairs.

Everyone had taken off their ties.

I pulled at my purple beard as I tried to figure out what was happening. They weren't going to try exorcising me, were they? Were they about to pray over me? Beat me?

"Come kneel before us," President Caldwell ordered, closing the door to his office and pointing to the floor in front of me.

I hadn't read anything about this part of the proceedings and wondered just how much went on in secret that the rest of the world, even the members of the Church, never knew about.

These men held no power over me. The priesthood wasn't real. These guys were just small businessmen, a contractor and a real estate agent and a dentist. An associate professor and the manager of a grocery store. Why had I even bothered to come?

"Warren," President Caldwell repeated, more gently this time, "please kneel."

Whatever. If they got their kicks out of bullying people, I could grant them this one last time. I'd drive away soon and never look back. Let them have their power trip.

If they were about to make me wash their feet, maybe I could force myself to throw up on one of these men instead.

Or at least spit.

I knelt on the floor.

Damn this industrial carpet. I should have brought my blow job knee pads.

The high councilmen began unbuttoning their shirts.

"What the hell!" All sorts of possibilities flew through my brain, none of them good. I knew many Church members believed in aversion therapy. These guys might try to gang rape me in the hopes of making me sick of getting fucked.

I started to stand back up.

President Caldwell raised his hand, and everyone stopped moving in mid-button, as if they were playing a game of Red Light and didn't want to have to return to the starting line. "Warren," he said, "you can choose disfellowship and pretend to toe the line, returning to full fellowship within six months, or you can leave the Church altogether. Many young men and women in your situation choose to leave, and we accept their choice. But this was the choice given to us many years ago, and we offer it to you now."

I looked from face to face, wondering if somehow, the stake president had arranged for my court to appear on an episode of *Pranked*. Only Mormons didn't have a particularly good sense of humor when it came to sexuality.

"Whether you stay or go," President Caldwell continued, "we welcome you to join us in an evening of courtly love."

Some people secretly recorded their tribunals. How had they known I wouldn't be one of them? I was radical, after all. I had a tattoo of the Liahona on my lower back, pointing the faithful gay Mormons in town for Mardi Gras and Southern Decadence toward my asshole.

I watched in fascination while everyone in the room, President Caldwell included, removed the rest of their clothing one piece at a time.

They would clearly not be performing at the Ponchartrain anytime soon.

Brother McKay has a small pink triangle tattooed above his right nipple.

Brother Mandini had a string of barbed wire tattooed around his upper left bicep, too high up to see when he was wearing his garments. It looked like just above the barbed wire was the symbol for "paragraph," along with some numbers: ¶ 175.

When the last sock came off, I stood motionless as everyone approached me. I hadn't noticeably consented yet, but I was only a few feet from the door leading to the hallway, and I certainly wasn't tied down.

My eyes darted about as I verified there were no unpleasant props lying about anywhere.

Brother Dixon reached me first. He had a tattoo of a nipple ring on his right nipple. A real nipple ring would be detectable even through a shirt and garments.

I'd worn a white shirt to the meeting but also jeans and no tie. He traced a finger across my chest, slowly, but trembling from the effort of restraint. He rubbed my left nipple lightly through the fabric. I shivered.

Brother Dixon's nipples were flabby and his paunch not the sexiest thing in the world, but I couldn't resist touching his tattoo.

His dick leaped in response like a conductor's baton.

After Brother Castillion helped him remove my shirt and the top half of my garments, Brother Dixon licked my left nipple first and then my right, letting his teeth scrape lightly as he started to bite down, stopping before it hurt.

Brother Mandini glided over and licked the inside of my left ear while Brother Hebert nibbled on my right lobe.

I remembered the talk Brother Hebert had given at stake conference on how the Word of Wisdom predicted the climate crisis by urging us to eat meat sparingly.

"Ow!"

"Sorry," Brother Hebert mumbled. He started kissing my neck. Someone was unbuckling my belt from behind. Someone else began unzipping my pants.

At my best, I never attracted this much attention in even the sleaziest French Quarter bars.

When I was fully unclothed, I looked down at myself. I wiped a drop of my pre-cum off my dick and brought it to my lips. Sweet before the savory.

Brother White gently pushed me back into my chair and lifted my right foot, slowly sucking on one toe at a time. After a moment, he had to lift my leg and pull it to the side when Brother Boudreaux knelt before me and started sucking my balls. No one had ever done that to me before. It felt warm and comforting…and slightly painful and dangerous.

Brother White left my foot resting on the top of a chair he'd pulled over. He moved over to my other foot, pulling that leg up and out of Brother Boudreaux's way, too. I felt like I was caught in a gynecologist's stirrups.

Brother Boudreaux finally moved aside while President Caldwell, Brother Mandini, and Brother McKay stood in single file before me as I sucked them off one by one. Brother Mandini had a sizeable cock. Fortunately, one of my first boyfriends had taught me to deep throat. It definitely took practice. But there was something thrilling about feeling a cock that far inside me through either of my holes.

President Caldwell's penis had a large red birthmark, but I'd learned how to recognize herpes and knew the wine coloring was safe. Brother McKay's dick had what might have been a single wart near the base, but it could have been a colorless mole, too, or a skin tag or something else. In any event, I'd already been vaccinated for HPV. And both Hepatitis A and B. I was also on PrEP. That didn't cover everything, but I accepted that living life was never risk-free.

Brother Dixon knelt beside my chair and insisted I spit out each mouthful of cum into his pubic hair and a small but exceptionally hairy patch on his lower abdomen.

After Brother McKay moved to the side, Brother Dixon stood in front of me until I licked the cum all back off him again.

Lukewarm cum with an occasional pubic hair isn't as sexy as it sounds. But Brother Dixon seemed even happier now than he looked when Fast and Testimony meeting was finally over after a rambling travelogue. People liked what they liked, and sometimes, if it wasn't too disagreeable, I gave it to them. When he kissed me to get the last of the cum into his own mouth, it was kind of fun to see him enjoying himself.

I imagined a game of Telephone where we stood in a circle and passed the same mouthful of cum from one man to the next until we'd made the full circle.

I'd attended one sex party at a bathhouse in the Quarter and another at a private club in the Bywater, but I'd never played with so many eager people at one time. And I *was* playing along with them now. Whatever they were dealing with internally was their problem. I never analyzed the conscience of the guys I picked up at Lafitte's on Bourbon Street, did I? It was all about the moment.

Brother White sat on the edge of the conference table, lying back with his dick pointing to the ceiling. "Lift him up," President Caldwell told the other high priests.

But it was me they were talking about. Brother Castillion slapped some lube on my ass and on Brother White's dick, and together, the group of middle-aged men lowered me down on the erection waiting for me, making sure I remained facing the men standing beside the table.

"Lie back on my chest," Brother White ordered. It was a sexual position I'd never tried, and I wasn't sure how effective it would be.

Until Brother Castillion approached me from the front and lifted my legs, sliding his dick into my ass alongside the one already in there.

"Aahhh," I moaned.

"Aahhh," Brother Castillion moaned.

"Aahhh," Brother White moaned.

Thank God everyone wasn't as big as Brother Mandini. I wondered if doctors could add a second asshole several inches up from the first, creating a dead-end tube seven or eight inches deep. A mangina. I started fantasizing about having three or four cocks inside me at the same time.

While the two men fucked me, the others kissed, nibbled, or licked my toes and fingers and ears.

How could the best sex I'd yet had be with old fuddy-duddies from church?

Brother Mandini leaned over and gently tweaked one of my nipples. "It's starting to get late," he said to no one in particular. "I want to see my kids before bedtime."

President Caldwell, standing behind and to the side of Brother Castillion, nodded. "Let's finish up," he said.

After Brother White and Brother Castillion came, the others helped me off White's dick and stationed me in the area between the table and the wall, facing President Caldwell's office. "There's more?" I asked, spent though I hadn't climaxed yet myself.

President Caldwell stood in front of me while everyone else moved behind me. Someone slathered more lube on my ass, and then I felt a finger go inside. By this point, my sphincter didn't protest very much. A moment later, a second finger entered. Then a third and a fourth. As loose as

I was after being fucked simultaneously by two dicks, by the time the seventh finger went in, I still felt close to capacity.

President Caldwell lubed my dick, slid a condom on me, and then turned around, backing up carefully as he guided my cock inside him. Interesting that mine was the only dick they deemed necessary to cover with a condom the entire evening.

Whatever.

Once I was fully inserted, hands reaching around me from behind pulled me backward a few inches. Then the fingers in my ass pushed me all the way back inside the stake president. They guided me out again. And in again. I felt like a dildo.

Mormon doctrine had it that trees and rocks had spirits. I wondered what kind of spiritual life sex toys might have in the eternities.

"Elder!" President Caldwell shouted. "Bishop!" he called out. "President Carson!"

Our previous stake president.

I was tired and irritated and excited and ready to burst. "I'm cumming!" I groaned. "I'm cumming!"

My body refused any further guidance from the sidelines and took over at its own pace. I heard a Hallelujah shout from the group as I shuddered when I came.

Everyone stood still for a moment, just breathing. Sweat dripped from my brow. Brother Dixon licked something off his hand. Then the councilmen moved back to their seats, pulled out towels from bags I hadn't even seen they'd brought with them, and began cleaning first themselves and then, with additional cleaning supplies, the table, chairs, and in a few spots, the carpet.

No one offered me a towel, and I didn't really want to clean up in any event. I didn't have it in me to live this kind of life, but if it worked for them, it wasn't my place to judge. Not much, anyway.

"Don't say anything to my other counselor," President Caldwell said, "or the other high councilmen. Not everyone is like us."

I felt a tap on my shoulder and turned to see Brother Dixon. "Uh, Warren," he said. "I…uh…I wiped up some of the cum around the room with your garment top." He smiled nervously. "Do you mind if I keep it?"

I laughed. "Please, and take it with you."

He might be a friend of Dorothy, but I doubt he understood the reference. "What about my garment bottoms?"

"Oh, you were never going to get those back." He smiled again, mischievously this time.

I found my pants and shirt and pulled them back on. I often went commando on my nights in the Quarter. I could try it at the Ponchartrain just as easily.

"Thanks for a lovely evening, guys," I said after I tied my shoes and stood back up. I opened the door to the hallway. "You can send my excommunication letter in the mail." I almost wanted to say something cutting, something withering, about their hypocrisy.

But the truth was I understood them. And, well, they were pretty good at what they knew.

So instead, I blew them a kiss and walked away without another word.

A Gaggle of Gays

Cum is an acquired taste, and I'd acquired it by the age of fourteen.

A year earlier, I'd discovered pre-cum, which was sweet and "delicious to the taste." But once I'd shot into my palm, I couldn't bring myself to transfer the load to my mouth. The clear pre-cum had been enticing. The partly clear, partly cloudy-with-swirls cum wad looked just a little repulsive. I tried sniffing it first, then licking it, but it took months of beating off before I could suck the entire load from my hand into my mouth. Another couple of months before I could swallow.

Now, almost two decades later, the thought of going even one day without a mouthful of cum is mind-boggling.

The doorbell rang, and I looked at my watch. 10:15 in the morning. The mail carrier was always on time. I hurried to the front door and got down on my knees. A second later, the mail slot opened, and three or four pieces of mail flew through and landed at my feet. I reached forward and held the slot open. A moment later came the special delivery: the mail carrier's throbbing cock.

I didn't even know the guy's name, and I can't remember now how I'd managed to get him to do it the first time, but we had an almost daily rendezvous at the mail slot between 10:00 and 10:45. I often tried to draw out oral sex with most men, but even with a mailbag to help shield him from prying eyes, the carrier was vulnerable, so I did my job as quickly as possible. I certainly had enough practice by this point to get right down to business.

A few moments later, the carrier's load hit the back of my throat, and his penis quickly withdrew from the mail slot. But I stayed on my knees a while longer, letting his cum roll back and forth across my tongue. I sucked it between my teeth, put it back on my tongue, luxuriated in one of the finest natural experiences known to man.

Then I swallowed.

When I stood up, I unzipped and pulled out my own penis. With my fingertip, I wiped up a single drop of pre-cum and licked it. The perfect chaser.

I returned to my home office and got back to work.

My sexual awakening as a teenager was mostly private. I didn't do anything with another man until my first week at the Missionary Training Center near the Brigham Young University campus. One of the Center's leaders—I can't even remember what his position was—took me into his office for a private interview. In an apparent attempt to draw out any sexual sins from my past, he asked probing question after probing question, but it turned out his ulterior motive was to participate in some decidedly more physical probing. His was the first dick I had down my throat.

Just as one had to build up to swallowing cum, one also had to build up to sucking dick without triggering a gag reflex. This kind mission leader gave me multiple opportunities to start developing that ability during my stay.

It's always useful to have a portable skill.

I served my mission in Germany, but the bulk of my service was to other American missionaries, not the people of Deutschland. I would point out to my companions pretty young women we ran across during our daily work, and then at night just before bed, I would bring them up again, perhaps tell a suggestive story or ask my companion some graphic questions, ask him what kind of things he thought were appropriate within marriage and which weren't. Then at 10:30, I'd apologize for my prurience and turn out the lights like an obedient servant of the Lord.

Arousing guys so that they'd beat off on cue was another skill that took some work to develop. But I was committed and learned the language of sexual temptation even faster than I learned German. Before long, I was getting my companions to beat off in their beds only minutes after lights out.

To be fair, with guys our age, I could have talked about melting candle wax and triggered a response.

No matter how quiet a guy tries to be when in the proximity of other men, he can't be completely silent. I could hear the tiny squeaks my companion's bed made, the slight rustling, and the sometimes all too obvious thumping. When the sound died off, I'd get out of bed and turn the light back on.

"Well, Elder?" I asked my third companion, Elder Woodruff. He was the first one whose cum I managed to taste. "Let me see the damage."

Elder Woodruff sheepishly pulled down the covers, revealing a wet spot in the middle of his Mormon underwear. "I'm so embarrassed."

"Oh, man," I said. "If you go to the bathroom to wash up, the other two elders are going to suspect what happened. You would have taken care of anything routine *before* lights out."

"I'll just change my garments."

I shook my head. "We'd better not take the chance. That might stain. And you know everybody runs around in their garments in the morning."

"What am I going to do?" He frowned. "Maybe I should just throw them away. I can order a new pair."

"Let me think a minute, Elder." I pretended to consider the situation carefully for a couple of minutes, motioning as if I'd figured out the answer but then stopping and thinking some more. Finally, I said, "Take them off and turn them inside out."

"What?"

"I think…" I took a deep breath. "I think if I lick it off, I can get your garments clean without anyone else knowing what happened."

"Lick it off!?"

I took another deep breath and then nodded with an attitude of certainty. "It has to be done, I'm afraid. Now, come on." I motioned for him to get out of bed, and soon he was standing naked beside me. I grabbed his garments and licked off every last drop of cum that I could. My companion paled and turned away, which gave me the opportunity to bask in the pleasure. After a few minutes, I put his garments back on the bed. "I think it'll be okay now," I said.

Elder Woodruff looked at me and shook his head, a mixture of emotions on his face. "You're a real pal," he said.

"Anything for you, buddy."

A week passed before the scenario repeated itself. Then we just openly took care of business every night for the remainder of our time together. He always insisted on turning out the light and beating off in the dark, and we quickly adapted to keeping the light off during my clean up, so as not to alert the other elders by a thin beam of suspicion at the base of our door. I'm not sure if my companion ever realized he could remove his garments altogether while beating off, given that there was no further need to hide his actions from me, but he continued shooting into his garments and then handing them to me.

I was able to keep up the practice with the last six companions I served with.

My love of cum morphed over time into a love of cum and underwear. I still can't get enough of both. I even kept a pair of Elder Montagna's garments covered in dried cum. I had him add a new load every night for the last month we were together without ever licking a single drop off or washing them.

I think he knew I was in love and seemed flattered I wanted to keep them.

He never wrote me even once after he was transferred away.

I still pull them out of my sex box once in a while and look at them even today.

My cell buzzed and I answered. "Hey, Rodney." It was my latest boyfriend. Guys didn't last long in relationships with me. I used to feel bad about it, but I think every one of my relationships benefitted both me and my partner.

It was just that the benefits I could offer were limited, and when we both realized we'd reached that point, I sent them happily on their way, often with a name and phone number to help them get over me quickly. Most of us continued to remain friends over the years. And most of them still contributed semen to me on occasion.

There isn't just one way to do relationships.

"How are you this fine day, Sean?"

"Doing some good work."

"But you'll be at my place by 6:30?" he asked. "It's our one-year anniversary. I have a lot planned for tonight."

Almost none of my previous boyfriends had lasted this long. I was impressed. And I was still enjoying Rodney's company, so I did kind of hope we could make it a little longer, though it wasn't productive to dwell on that unlikely scenario. "I'll be there at 6:29."

"You'll miss my pre-cum if you're late." Rodney was still in his late twenties and could cum at least twice in an evening. He usually came the moment I arrived so he could work back up to cumming again before I left. If it was a night I was staying over, I could expect another load in the middle of the night.

"Then you give me no other choice."

"Most of my other boyfriends got tired of me cumming all the time."

"A match made in our little factories." Rodney was ex-Mormon, too, and understood the reference to Boyd K. Packer's infamous talk against masturbation and homosexuality.

"You always know how to turn me on."

"Well, if you cum before I get there, at least catch it in a cup."

"I keep telling you to freelance for Hallmark."

We hung up, and I got back to work. I made reasonably good money, but the life of an artist was always precarious. Fortunately, I had a dedicated fan in Alex Cannon, the owner of a gallery downtown. His cum was featured in several of my paintings.

My style had come as a revelation. Kirby, a guy I was dating several years ago, was on some kind of medication that turned his cum pink. When he shot onto his pale white stomach one night, I gasped.

"What's wrong?"

We'd recently checked *Pollock* out of the library. I scooped up my boyfriend's cum with one hand and hurried to the other side of the room, where I had a blank canvas waiting to be turned into a great work of art. I flung Kirby's cum against the canvas and watched it trickle down.

"Are you crazy?"

"I'm gonna be famous."

I never did quite achieve fame, but like every other skill, painting with colored cum took a little practice. This dye worked, that one didn't. This angle worked, but not that one. Like Jackson Pollock, I learned that I achieved the best results when my canvases were lying flat on the floor as I dripped cum onto them.

At my first show, when Alex turned on a black light, the crowd gasped. Occasionally, the pigments I'd added would affect the luminescence, but there were always enough bright drips and trickles to make some of the men in the room subconsciously check their zippers.

I'll admit, the phone numbers I received from art collectors was just as rewarding as the money. Rich men always got a little kick out of becoming part of the next masterpiece.

Of course, it would be impossible to create enough work to make a living if cum was my only medium. I used other paints as well. I even painted some mainstream work. But most of my creations depicted men sniffing jock straps or guys having cum deposited on their bodies in a variety of ways. One that sold within minutes showed my boyfriend at the time licking cum out of a friend's navel. While Tom of Finland did drawings, I enjoyed acrylics when I couldn't get the rare material I preferred.

I'd had open relationships from the start, and what was especially gratifying about Rodney was not only his absolute lack of jealousy but also his substantial ability as a photographer. When friends or tricks or escorts came to my place, I'd ask if they were okay with my boyfriend making some permanent memories of the occasion with his camera.

My imagination was pretty solid, but it was easier painting when I had photographic support. I looked through the latest batch of photos now. There was that cute pizza delivery guy shooting onto the pepperoni. A poker pal shooting onto his winning cards. Alex's husband shooting onto the toilet seat in a public restroom.

There was the photo of cum pooling on the asshole of my favorite bartender. He only let his boyfriend shoot on him, but he did let me lick it off his ass. The bartender was a dribbler himself, couldn't shoot to save his life, but he let me lick off the cum that dribbled down around his fingers and dick after his cum oozed out the tip of his penis. The challenge of getting every last drop from every crack and crevice was intoxicating.

I thought back on all the anonymous cum I'd swallowed over the years. My insatiable need to taste it was no match for the insatiable need so many men had to dispense it.

Once, during a flight to Australia, I convinced a total stranger sitting next to me to beat off under a blanket while everyone else slept and then let me lick his hand. The request didn't even seem to faze him, and I was sure he wasn't gay.

No photo of that encounter, unfortunately, but here was a nice shot of my friend Colby, a nurse, dressed only in his scrub tops, his dick hanging down with cum dripping out, directing a spoonful of medicinal cum toward the camera. Yes, that was the one I would work on next. I'd call it, "A spoonful of cum helps the medicine go down."

Corny could sell paintings. Especially if the corny was hot. My most successful painting to date was "Let he who is without sin shoot the first load," two priests in cassocks facing each other as they jacked off.

"The ice cream man cummeth," featuring a load of cum shooting onto a scoop of vanilla ice cream, with a bit of cum dripping down onto the masculine hand holding the waffle cone, might have brought in some good money, but I couldn't bear to part with it. It hung permanently in my office.

By the way, cum and ice cream is an even better combination than ice cream and root beer, in case you're looking for something new.

And have you ever tried a load of cum in a cup of strawberry-flavored protein shake?

I wondered if I should consider coming up with a cookbook. I could even design my own cover. *Cum to Dinner* might have a niche audience, but fans might email me with other suggestions.

Or phone numbers.

I painted steadily for two hours this afternoon. When I started to flag, I pulled out my Squirting Cock and slid it up my ass. I often painted in the nude. Just the presence of the dildo inside me revved up my creative juices for a while, but eventually I needed to squeeze the inflatable bulb, shooting a load of Jizzle Juice up my ass. I always doctored it with some pepper to help me feel more intensely the artificial cum working its way back down my rectum.

When I wanted my Squirting Cock to shoot into my mouth, I put all sorts of other flavors into the cum: almond, strawberry, coconut. But my favorite was asparagus. I sometimes invited five or six guys over for dinner, insisting everyone eat at least three or four stalks of asparagus so that I could have their cum for dessert.

I usually served them cheesecake for their own dessert. So we were all happy.

I sat on a towel in front of my easel, reaching behind me once in a while to rub the oozing artificial cum all around my anus.

I'd even applied for a job several years ago with the company that made the product, wanting to be a taste tester. But I didn't make it past the interview. I think it became obvious rather quickly it would be like hiring a vampire to guard the hospital blood bank. I'd have to find another way to do my part for mankind.

Thank God for Kirby's pink cum.

I went to the bathroom and cleaned up. Then I drank a protein shake with a high concentration of cellulose as a snack, luxuriating in the thick consistency, the only protein shake that came close to matching the texture of the fluid I preferred.

I reached down and wiped a drop of cum off the tip of my penis. I held it under my nose a moment and then licked it off delicately. Thinking about sex all day long, I could reach down almost any time I wanted and get a taste. It was better than having a soft serve ice cream machine in the house.

I looked over at the painting on my wall.

If Mormon men had shared their cum as easily as they shook hands, I'd have stayed in church. The cathedrals I visited now were multi-level bathhouses and the back rooms of bars. Wrapping my mouth around a dick I couldn't see in a dark, musty room, and tasting a bit of head cheese before that fabulous burst of semen, was a more redemptive event than I ever experienced partaking of the sacrament.

I got back to work. It was a privilege to spend my days doing what I loved.

I hoped Rodney would enjoy the gift I was planning to give him for our anniversary. We might not have a second, so this one had to count.

I'd finished a good portion of the new canvas by late afternoon. After putting my paints away, I douched to make sure Rodney had options this evening. Then I jumped in the shower and dressed for dinner. I knocked on his door precisely at 6:29.

"How long have you been waiting out there?" Rodney asked when he opened the door.

"Ten minutes."

"You should have come on in."

"I'm a man of my word." Once inside Rodney's apartment, I removed my shoes and followed him to the kitchen. "Smells good," I said.

"Asparagus."

"You're sweet."

He leaned over and gave me a kiss. Then he put his hands on my shoulders and pushed me gently down to my knees.

"You always have the best hors d'oeuvres."

Dinner was on the table not long after, and we talked about Rodney's day. I never had all that much to say about my own. "I did a really good elbow today" wasn't the most scintillating of comments. But Rodney usually had something to say about his work teaching ESL. Today he went on about a student who came up with a different excuse every day for not doing his homework. "I tell him I'll excuse him if he can explain his reasons in a grammatically correct sentence."

"Does he realize what you're doing?"

"Does your doctor know you wear Secretions Magnifiques when you go in for a checkup?"

"He apologizes every time after he sticks his cock in my mouth. Says he doesn't know what comes over him."

"You could report him."

"He could probably report me."

"Wearing cum-scented perfume isn't a crime."

I sighed. "The crime is that more men don't wear it."

I thought of the times I'd even managed to turn on straight lawn workers and air conditioner repairmen with the perfume I ordered from Paris. They always looked confused when I pointed out their erections tenting their pants, but they usually unzipped without much persuasion, often gifting me with their underwear afterward, if I asked for it casually. Most guys, gay or straight, seemed content with cumming pretty much any time they thought they could get away with it, whether or not I was their preferred sex partner.

Once, I was in Urgent Care after cutting myself when opening a box, and the young man working on me must have been new because his hands shook just a little. "You'll be a lot steadier if I suck you off first," I told him.

I sucked him off, he finished stitching my hand, and then we both went on with our day.

But of all the cummy experiences I'd had so far, my favorites still involved underwear.

Some afternoons, trying to work myself into a painting mood, I'd spread my underwear collection on the bed, drawing each pair to my face one at a time. Most of the time, I could distinguish between the underwear even with my eyes closed. This one belonged to the FedEx driver. That one to the Chinese take-out guy. This other to the Jehovah's Witness who came back without his companion and shot two loads for me, one in the front of his underwear and the other in back.

When we finished dinner, Rodney ushered me to the living room, motioning for me to sit on the sofa. "Are you ready for your anniversary present?" he asked.

I steeled myself for disappointment. My boyfriends usually meant well, but a visit from an escort or even bringing in guys for a three-way or four-way were gifts as run-of-the-mill as ties on Father's Day.

I think that's why I preferred underwear to humans. With people, the imperfections and incompatibilities became apparent all too quickly. With underwear, I could imagine whatever I wanted about the wearer.

Focusing on cum might be objectifying other men, but it was good to accept the reality of one's limitations. Perhaps I was on the spectrum.

Or perhaps I was emotionally stunted because of the time my dad caught me masturbating at thirteen and rubbed my nose into my bedsheet like he was training a dog to be housebroken.

Only I didn't feel stunted by that. I'd been intoxicated.

I might have stayed in the Church if there were a way to store a year's supply of semen. Cum-flavored Jizzle Juice. Secretions Magnifiques perfume. If only there were a way to store the real thing in liquid form, not merely as paint splats on a canvas.

Rodney retrieved a medium-sized box and placed it in my lap. I smiled when I saw that the wrapping paper had dried cum spots in three places. His attention to detail was impressive. I tore off the paper, recklessly tossing it aside, and opened the box.

The smell was overwhelming. I got a hard-on almost instantly. I picked up the first item. The spot where the cum had soaked in was still damp. I put it against my face and inhaled.

"It's fifty different pairs of underwear," he said.

"Fifty!"

"I've been working on your gift for a couple of months. The newest ones are on top."

I dug through the box. Briefs, boxers, boxer briefs, cotton jock straps, leather jock straps, thongs, underwear of almost every variety and color and size and pattern. A pair of those funky Chinese underwear with a tube in front for your penis. A plus sized pair of pink bikinis. Mesh briefs, free range briefs, underwear with padded front and rear pouches. And the most astounding aspect of the collection was that—

"I've been looking through everything you own already," Rodney said. "I made sure to get things you didn't have yet."

That was no small feat. And it must have been stressfully expensive for someone on a teacher's salary. My mouth dropped open.

"Hold it right there." Rodney whipped out a turkey baster he'd hidden under a sofa cushion and squirted something into my mouth. "I asked some of the guys at work if they would jack off at the end of the day so it would still be fresh when I got home." He smiled. "You know, the ones who've already approached me at some point, so I knew they wouldn't go straight to HR."

I'd rarely had so much cum in my mouth at one time. Before I could swallow, Rodney leaned over and kissed me, his tongue reaching into my mouth to pull some of the cum back into his and then push it back into mine again. We kissed for almost two minutes and then swallowed together.

I only realized at that moment he was wearing semen-scented perfume especially for the occasion.

"And now for the pièce de résistance." Rodney pulled out another package, a small velvet box, too large to hold a ring but the right size for…a bracelet? A necklace?

I pried open the lid, and a wadded up piece of stained white fabric leaped out. I spread it on the sofa between us and sucked in a deep breath. A one-piece pair of Mormon garments lay before me. Every inch of it covered in dried cum.

"Oh my God."

"Don't take the name of the Lord in vain." Rodney playfully wagged a finger at me.

"What you did was not in vain." I could hardly breathe.

"I asked all of my friends and all of your friends to help. I asked guys on their way to the fertility clinic to make an appointment with me later. I put an ad online." He smiled. "There are two hundred and fifty loads on that piece. From guys of pretty much every age and ethnicity."

I stared at the pair of garments for three or four minutes, lightly caressing the embroidered markings I knew were hidden under the cum, and the seams around the coated dick slit in the front. The vision was lovelier than anything I'd ever painted.

"What did you get for me?"

My face flushed with sudden warmth. I wanted to stop time and run out to get him something better.

"Come on. Hand it over."

I reached into my underwear and pulled out a velvet box of my own, this one small enough for a ring. Rodney smiled and opened the box. But he frowned as he pulled out two steel cock rings.

"One for you," I said, "and one for me." I reached over to take the smaller of the rings. "They're engraved." I stood and dropped my pants, motioning for him to do the same.

He did so, a little reluctantly. As we slipped them onto each other, I said, "I may need more than just your cum, but I don't need anyone else but you." It wasn't what I'd originally planned to say, but it felt like the right thing now.

If we made it to our second anniversary, I might get him an engagement ring.

Perhaps for his birthday in a couple of months, I could offer to start counseling. Or get us into couples counseling so we'd both be better at navigating what would always be an unconventional relationship.

Rodney smiled. "Happy anniversary," he said again. I could tell that wasn't what he wanted to say.

"I love you, too," I told him.

He hugged me for a long moment, kissing the side of my neck once, twice, three times. Then he led me to the bedroom, where six of my exes were waiting for me. Rodney took out his camera and began shooting.

Getting Inside

I've managed for almost forty years not to think about that remarkable day in Rome, the one time in my entire life I had sex with anyone other than the woman I married a year and a half later, the day I lost my virginity to the only man I've ever loved.

But now that my grandson has come out as gay, I can't keep those memories buried in my mind. They play over and over, first in English and then in Italian.

Kids come out of the closet so young these days, don't they? Devin is barely fourteen. But I guess if that was old enough for Joseph Smith to become a prophet, it's old enough for a young man to know the gender of the person he wants to have a relationship with.

I was nineteen when I served as a missionary in Rome with Elder Porter. He was my senior, out a year longer than I'd been. We'd been together a couple of months, our first day as companions April 6. "Merry Christmas!" he'd said when he greeted me at the door. 99% straight, I noticed he was good-looking but thought no more about it.

Over the next several weeks, we worked hard together, always getting in our full hours, while some of the other elders in the apartment fudged their numbers. We studied together, had a good Companion Inventory once a week, and even did our cooking as a team. Everywhere else in the mission, the elder assigned to cook for the week usually did all his cooking alone.

But we liked each other's company. Elder Porter sometimes questioned basic Church rules, like why *every* young man had to serve a mission, why we needed to go to church *every* Sunday, or why we *all* had to have large families. Some of his questions shocked me, but I was pleased he was willing to share his feelings, since most missionaries never talked about any of their doubts. I felt special.

Late May now, the day was proceeding normally when Elder Porter suddenly suggested we hop on a bus and try Spirit Tracting.

I don't think he had any ulterior motives. It just turned out that way.

"What's Spirit Tracting?" I asked.

"Really, Anziano Brewer? Your other companions never did it?" He laughed. "What kind of trainer did you have?"

Elder Porter always had a genial laugh.

"You just go along until you feel prompted by the Spirit to go inside somewhere," he continued.

"Does it work?"

He shrugged. "On a regular day, you know we can knock on a hundred doors and not have any success, but I've never gone Spirit Tracting without getting inside to connect with at least one person."

"Do they get baptized?" I pressed.

"Our goal is to make a positive difference in the lives of others, whether they choose to live as Mormons or not."

I wasn't sure I agreed but decided to let it pass. We did need to try something different. *I* needed it. "I guess we don't have anything to lose."

We lived on Giovanni Maggi, but we never wanted to tract in our own neighborhood. Elder Porter had explained it was like dating someone from work. "Could be awkward if you had to keep running into them later."

I'd never dated at all, not anyone from school or church or anywhere. I saw no point since I couldn't get married until after I finished my two years as a missionary. My parents only let me participate in group activities. And I'd never held a real job. My dad insisted I put all my efforts into my studies. I was considering engineering, though I'd also wondered about air conditioning work or even computers. Something manly enough to attract a woman, given my rather average looks.

"Have you dated many people from work?" I asked.

"Mmm. A couple."

"Have you…have you ever kissed a girl?" Elder Porter stopped and gave me a look which made me feel foolish. But I pressed on. "My mother said she never kissed my father until they were married."

My companion stared at me another long moment. "There are a lot of things you can do besides kissing."

I felt a little thrill to be in the company of someone so experienced, not recognizing at the time my crush had already been developing for weeks. I knew of two other elders in the mission who'd needed to talk to General Authorities before they were allowed to enter the Missionary Training Center. That almost always meant some kind of sexual transgression had to be waived.

I was out in the world now, interacting with worldly people, even worldly Mormons. In only fifteen months, I knew I'd be back in St. George, ready to begin looking for a righteous girl, marry her in the temple, and finally start doing some of the things I'd only dreamed about.

One didn't need experience, or even much accurate information, to fantasize. Maureen would later let me know, on our wedding night, just how little I understood about female anatomy.

Elder Porter pushed the buzzer to signal the driver we were getting off the bus. I wasn't even quite sure where we were. I'd been staring out the window without focusing on street signs. I thought I remembered passing the tiny white pyramid near the old city wall, but I didn't recognize where we were now.

"This way." Elder Porter pointed, and I followed after him.

Almost all of the palazzi in Rome were locked. You had to push a call button on the citofono out front to have someone let you in. That was usually easy enough. It was only the palazzi with portieri that were impenetrable. But we had a stretch of four buildings with no doormen, so we were happy.

Not that we got inside any of the apartments anyway.

A missionary's life was filled with unending frustration. Catholics in Rome were not tempted even slightly to become members of a church headquartered in Utah. Most weren't rude about it, simply disinterested. Last week, though, a man had spit in my face and slammed his door so forcefully our ties fluttered in the wind.

"Hold still," Elder Porter had told me gently.

I stood with my eyes closed, feeling the spittle trickling down my eyelids and cheeks. Then I felt my companion wiping my face with his handkerchief. He wiped slowly and deliberately, his touch soothing, like that of a familiar barber.

"Okay," he said. "You're all better now."

I opened my eyes and was surprised to see Elder Porter's face coming quickly toward me. He smacked his lips against mine and grinned.

"My saliva's better," he said.

My first kiss would no longer be over the altar in the temple's sealing room. I was almost angry. But not quite. I liked the twinkle in his eyes when he looked at me.

"We've tracted a whole block," I said that fateful day we went off script.

"You can't rush the Spirit, Anziano."

We turned the corner then, and I stopped in my tracks. Maybe six or seven blocks away stood the Coliseum. That meant we were on the very edge of Rome One. We weren't allowed to cross certain boundaries.

"Beautiful, isn't it, Elder Brewer?"

I wondered how something with such a history of decadence and sin could be so breathtaking, but my companion was right.

He clapped me on the back. "We're getting inside in the very next building," he announced. "I can feel it."

We entered a tiny courtyard, the "front" door on the side of the apartment building. A hydrangea next to the entrance was covered with bright blue flowers. When I'd first arrived in Italy, I'd understood the word "palazzo" to simply mean "apartment building." It wasn't until later that I learned the literal definition was "palace."

I tried to imagine what living a fairy tale life in Rome might be like.

I looked over at my companion.

The front door was ajar, so we didn't need to buzz anyone to get inside the foyer. We stepped into the tiny elevator and pressed "5" to take us to the 6th floor. We always started on top and worked our way down.

The elevator rose slowly, jerking a couple of times. After one large jerk, I gripped Elder Porter's arm. He smiled reassuringly and I relaxed a bit. I hated elevators to begin with, and those in Italy often only held maybe three people, four if they were all skinny. In some of the older or poorer areas, the palazzi might not have an elevator at all. I liked those buildings best.

The elevator continued jerking upward, the lights flickered, and suddenly the car stopped altogether.

But we weren't on the sixth floor.

"Uh-oh," I said.

Elder Porter pushed the 3 and the 4, but the elevator didn't move. "Let's just pry the doors open," he said. "We can either crawl out the top or the bottom to the nearest floor."

"Mannaggia."

I helped my companion pull the doors apart, but the sight before us made my stomach lurch. A solid wall. There was no way out.

"Oh, my goodness," I said. "Oh, my goodness. Oh, my goodness."

How was I ever going to convince a woman I was manly?

Elder Porter put his hand on my shoulder. "It's going to be okay, Anziano. It's—"

The lights flickered again and then went out completely.

I reached over and hugged my companion like I used to hug my teddy bear. He hugged me in return, one hand cradling the back of my head. "It's gonna be okay," he whispered. He pulled me tighter against him, gently rubbing my back, the way my father used to do when we went camping and something growled close by during the night.

I felt protected and vulnerable at the same time.

"What are we going to do?" I asked.

"The elevator will probably start up on its own soon. Maybe when one of the tenants presses a button outside. We'll wait a bit and then start yelling if we have to."

"Do you think it was booby trapped?" I asked. "That only tenants have a special key to insert somewhere?"

"I've never—"

"What if the cable breaks? What if the elevator falls? What if we die?"

Manly, right?

Those two years helped me grow in so many ways.

"We aren't going to die, Elder." He patted my back like I was a baby.

"You don't know that. I—I'm not ready to die." I didn't want a father now. I wanted…I wanted…

I didn't know what I wanted, only that I wanted it desperately.

Elder Porter placed his cheek against mine, the touch offering a hint of the reassurance I needed, but it wasn't quite enough.

"I don't want to die before…"

"Before what?"

I felt stupid and sinful and immature. I opened my mouth three times without saying anything. And then finally I blurted out, "I don't want to die before I've had sex." Embarrassed, I pressed my face into my companion's shoulder. I wasn't sure why, since he could hardly have seen me blush in the dark.

He held me quietly, rubbing my back softly. "During the terremoto in Napoli," he said, referencing an earthquake that had occurred near Potenza before I arrived in the country, "our apartment in Castellammare was destroyed."

We'd all heard about it. The elders were right in the middle of baptizing a convert in a portable font in the living room they used as a church, when suddenly the ceiling and walls of their place started crumbling.

"We slept on the beach that night. It was cold, the end of November." He fingered the short hair on the back of my head. "I was really scared."

"How awful," I mumbled against his chest.

"I'm going to do something for you that my companion did for me then." He pulled away, turned me around in the dark, and then pulled me against him again, my back to him now. I felt his hand on my stomach sliding down slowly.

"Oh, my goodness." We were only supposed to speak Italian to each other while we were out of the apartment. I needed to obey the rules. Breaking them led to all kinds of sin. "Per…per caritá," I corrected myself.

My companion caressed my crotch through my suit pants, and I felt both thrilled and mortified to realize I was growing hard. "Is this okay?" he whispered.

"Elder…" I knew what he was doing was wrong, but I didn't want him to stop. What if this was the only chance I'd ever have?

Of course, I'd lived a pure life, and I'd have a better chance of reaching the Celestial Kingdom without this sin added onto my resumé, but then, I'd get extra points for dying while serving as a missionary.

So…

Elder Porter reached around me with both hands and unfastened my belt. He pulled my zipper down slowly and pushed my pants to the floor. I could feel my companion rubbing his fingers against the wet spot where the tip of my penis was straining against my garments.

Those were the old days when Mormon underwear still came in one piece, kind of like a union jack. Elder Porter reached through the slit in the front of my garments and wrestled my penis out into the open air.

He stroked it gently.

"Anziano Porter…" I could feel him fumbling for a moment with his own pants. After a loud clunk on the floor let me know they were down around his feet, I heard him freeing his own penis as well. He reached forward to grab my right hand and directed it behind my back to rest on his penis.

My hand didn't rest long. I hadn't even touched myself in a sexual manner since the day I entered the MTC in Provo. But his penis felt good, warm and hard and slightly curved.

Elder Porter was still fumbling about. I heard some clinking, too, as if he were fiddling with his key chain, which should have been down on the floor in his pocket at this point. He took my hand off his penis. "I'm putting some olive oil on my dick," he said.

Such a crude word.

And such a blasphemous act. That consecrated oil we carried in vials on our keychains was to administer blessings to the sick.

What if we were struck down?

I felt my companion pulling apart the slit on the rear of my garments. "Per caritá."

"Is this okay?" Elder Porter's wet finger rubbed my anus for a few seconds, and then I felt the tip of his penis touching me. He dragged it up and down my crack. Pressing it up against my hole, he reached forward to kiss the back of my neck as he pushed his way inside me.

I didn't understand how something could hurt and give such pleasure at the same time.

Was it like being both wrong and right simultaneously? Hadn't Joseph Smith said something about that once?

"Anziano Porter," I said.

"Elder Brewer," he whispered in my ear. "Elder Brewer. Elder Brewer."

I didn't know much about sex talk, but it was working for me. I felt alive in a way I never had before.

"Do you know how to say this in Italian?" Elder Porter patted my behind.

"Sedere?" I suggested.

"Culo," he whispered, rubbing first one cheek and then the other. "I'm inside your culo."

I closed my eyes. Not that it mattered, since we were still in total darkness.

"Do you know *what's* inside you?" he asked softly, pushing himself in as far as he could go.

I gasped. "Tuo pene?" I asked.

"É mio cazzo," he said. "Il mio cazzo sta dentro il tuo culo."

"Mannaggia." Speaking Italian didn't seem to be the solution.

"Ti piace?"

"Yes," I said, so softly I wondered if he could even hear. "I like it."

"And do you know what me putting my cazzo in your culo is called?"

I did! I'd heard someone use the word in my last area, and I'd asked an Italian elder in the district to explain.

"Scopare," I said. "Stiamo scopando." I paused. "Scopiamoci?"

Elder Porter chuckled, that friendly, friendly laugh of his. "It's not reflexive," he said. "And that word's okay, but here's a better term." He pulled all the way out, pushed the tip of his penis just in and then barely out of my anus several times over the next few seconds, and finally slid all the way in again. "Stiamo facendo l'amore."

"Oh, Anziano."

I felt a burning in my rear, along with wet, sliding pleasure. I didn't want him to stop. Every second of that glorious experience seemed to last an eternity. Given our age, when I look back, I expect Elder Porter was finished in three minutes. But it was a life-changing three minutes.

"Aahhh!" Elder Porter stopped moving and hugged me tightly for a long moment. I obviously hadn't seen him ejaculate. I couldn't even feel his semen inside me. But just knowing such an incredible thing had happened felt the way I imagined receiving the gift of the Holy Ghost must feel for our converts.

I'd received the Holy Ghost when I was eight, so I didn't really remember.

Elder Porter and I were Spirit Tracting.

After holding me tightly another few moments, he slowly pulled out, turned me around, and kissed me full on the lips. He pushed his tongue deep into my mouth. I let him inside.

My companion was a man, and we weren't married, but that day I tasted exaltation.

"It's your turn now," he said softly. "Get your keychain and put your cazzo in my culo."

I reached for my pants crumpled up on the floor around my ankles.

"Say it," he demanded. "Tell me what you're going to do."

"I'm going to—"

"In italiano."

"Metteró il mio cazzo nel tuo culo."

"Fallo," he commanded. "Fallo!"

I didn't want to use my consecrated oil. What if we did crash to the bottom of the elevator shaft, and I had to give Elder Porter a blessing? "I have a little bottle of hand lotion in my pocket," I said, as if he needed to know.

"Good," he said. "I get a little tight after I come."

How many times had he done this?

And with whom?

I wondered if his senior from Castellammare was still in Italy. I knew one of the assistants to the mission president had been stationed there during the earthquake, but that district had four elders.

There wasn't much room to maneuver in the tiny elevator, and thankfully, my hormones were raging so strongly I didn't even consider what might happen if the elevator suddenly moved again and the doors opened. I rubbed some lotion on my pe—on my cazzo. Then I took an extra dab and felt around for my companion's anus. As I applied the lotion to his opening, he reached back and guided my fingers.

"Slide your finger inside me," he said, pulling it into him. "Feel me."

He was warm and wet. And tight, as he'd said. My finger felt like it was trapped in Chinese handcuffs. I'd heard a character on TV once make a remark about bondage. This must have been what he was talking about.

"Metti dentro due dita," Elder Porter said.

"Davvero?"

"Due," he commanded.

I squeezed a second finger in next to the first. His anus felt tighter now, naturally, almost uncomfortable, but my companion took my hand and pulled my fingers in deeper until they couldn't go any further.

"Wiggle them around," he said softly. "Pull them in and out a little."

I did as he said, and somehow the nerves being stimulated on the skin of my fingers made my penis so hard it hurt.

"I have to use my cazzo now," I told him.

"Please," he said. "Per favore."

I pulled out my fingers, made sure my penis had plenty of lotion on it, and aimed it right back at the same spot. "This is the place," I whispered, immediately sure this additional blasphemy would be the end of us both.

The opening felt a little looser now, so I hoped I wasn't hurting him. I was thicker than he was. He moaned, and the sound made me go deeper faster. He moaned again, and instinct kicked in. I pulled out and pushed in, again and again, faster and faster.

In the darkness, my other senses were magnified. I listened to the shluk, shluk, shluk of my penis sliding back and forth, to Elder Porter's panting, to my own panting. I heard his tiny grunts, the pop when I slipped out, and Elder Porter's moan when I pushed myself back in.

I felt sweat on my forehead and the skin on my penis tingling as if it were covered in hot sauce.

The tingling became burning, my penis a stick of dynamite with a fuse flaming down too quickly to prevent an explosion. I needed to stop before my companion was hurt.

Instead, I kept trying to go deeper and deeper. I *had* to go in completely, get my sack inside him, too, get *me* inside. I shoved myself forward as hard as I could, over and over. We were both going to be annihilated. I never wanted this moment to end. But after only a few more seconds…

"Porca la miseria!" I shouted. If having him climax inside my rear had made me feel more alive than ever, climaxing inside him made me understand what the eternities must be like.

I held onto Elder Porter as hard as I could, my arms wrapped around him so tightly I wondered if he could breathe. "Sorry about the language, Anziano," I whispered.

"You sound like you were born here," he said. It didn't sound condescending. He turned back around and gave me a peck, and then we dressed in the darkness. We'd never removed our shirts and ties, so it didn't take long.

We were still trapped, of course, but I no longer felt any fear. Elder Porter stood beside me and held my hand. I was aware of its soft warmth which signaled I was standing with another living being sharing this experience, separate and foreign but real to me now in a way he never had been before. It wasn't until the lights came on that I let go. The elevator jerked a couple of times, and I braced myself against the rear of the car. We rose slowly one more floor and stopped.

The doors opened, and my companion gently urged me onto the landing first.

"Non c'é nessuno," I said. I thought someone else had finally done something to reactivate the elevator.

"Let's go take a walk," Elder Porter suggested.

I nodded. We walked down the stairs in silence. Out on the street, my companion pointed toward the Coliseum. "It's out of our district," I said.

"We won't go in. We'll just walk around it and come back."

We slowly walked the next fifteen minutes in silence. But the words in my head were echoing and rebounding all over the place. Just as we returned to the next palazzo to begin tracting again, I knew I had to say something.

"We're going to have to repent," I said. "Confess to the mission president."

"That we walked around the Coliseum?" Elder Porter put his hand on my shoulder. "Some rules really aren't that important, Anziano."

I shook my head. "We need to tell him what we did in the elevator."

Elder Porter frowned. "We didn't do anything in the elevator, Anziano, except sing hymns while we waited for the elevator to start up again."

"But…but…"

"I think you might have been hallucinating at one point," he said. "Some of those lyrics you were singing…"

"Lyrics?"

"Elder Brewer," my companion said, looking directly into my eyes, "you don't have to repent of thoughts."

"Thoughts?"

"We all have thoughts." His smile was so gentle, barely there but sweet enough to taste.

I knew perfectly well he was lying, and yet I was willing to take the out he was offering. In an instant, I didn't even feel guilty anymore.

Except for the guilt I felt over not feeling guilty.

But I'd had years of practice closing off parts of me I didn't want to deal with.

I was made senior during the next transfers, my first junior a greenie from Pocatello. We worked hard in Sassari in northern Sardinia, but we never baptized anyone.

Elder Porter ended up going home two months early. Voluntarily, it appeared. We were all rather shocked. Back in those days, almost no missionaries left early unless they were sent home in disgrace.

I wrote him one letter, but he never responded, and I never tried again. I wondered if he were even alive now. He'd gone home right as AIDS was exploding across the western world.

I wondered what kind of future lay ahead for my grandson.

I typed Elder Porter's name into the search bar on my computer screen. His first name was Wayne, wasn't it? He'd only told me once, but I was sure I was right.

A man his age with his name showed up living in Sacramento. I looked at the phone number next to the name.

Could I have reached out this easily any time I wanted?

I needed Devin to have good people in his life.

I punched Wayne's number into my cell phone and waited.

"Wayne Porter. What can I do for you?"

I didn't know if I could say it.

"Hello? No? Okay, I'm hanging up now."

"Anziano," I said, "voglio il tuo cazzo nel mio culo." I wasn't even bisexual really. Did 1% count? "Voglio…voglio…" My voice trailed off.

This time there was a long silence on the other end of the line.

"It's Elder Brewer," I said. "Are you doing okay, Wayne? Are you good? Are you happy?"

I wanted to tell him about the extra-virgin olive oil I used to masturbate, how that smell still made me think of him.

How I opened a bottle every time I looked through my mission photo album.

I heard a heavy sigh, and it almost broke my heart. "I've thought about you often," he said, "but I didn't want to disrupt your life." His voice didn't sound as jovial as I remembered.

"Maureen died last year," I said. "Breast cancer."

"Mi dispiace." I could tell he meant it.

"Are you married?"

"Bill left me for a younger man a couple of years ago. You know how it is."

I still never watched R-rated movies, so I probably didn't know as much as I should have. All I said was, "When can I come see you?"

Wayne chuckled, though the sound still seemed a bit muted. "April 6th?"

"You always did like Mormon Christmas," I said, "even though no other Mormons ever celebrated on April 6th."

"I always did Mormonism my way, didn't I?"

I laughed. It felt as if forty years hadn't passed since we'd last seen each other.

"I think I should tell you, though," he said in a serious tone, "I live on the 11th floor of my building. Are you okay taking the elevator?"

"I'll have you know," I replied, "that among other things, I'm an elevator repairman." I smiled. If only I hadn't waited so long to call him.

Though I could hardly have divorced Maureen. I had loved her, too.

And yet, what might have happened if I'd left my mission and gone home with him all those years ago?

"I've missed you, Elder," he said.

"I'm a bit larger now than I was last time you saw me. Thank goodness American elevators are bigger."

Wayne chuckled again, and this time I heard the sound I knew from our days in Rome One. The whisper of the Spirit telling me what to do next sounded the same, too.

And this time, I'd listen.

Porn Store Sleepover

Folks in Seattle were grabbing everything they could, the Safeway in Rainier Beach embroiled in a chaotic riot. Four inches of snow were forecast for tonight, on top of the eight we'd already received over the past two days.

"That's mine!" a middle-aged white man hissed, grabbing a package of Atkins protein shakes out of my hand.

You'd think the mayor had announced our entire city was following the Donner party into the Sierras. I picked up the last pack of strawberry cream shakes and held it like a football, keeping my other arm outstretched before me to ward off frantic shoppers as I headed for the registers.

I wouldn't have minded letting Negasi tackle me, though. A good-looking Ethiopian immigrant, the cashier gave me a wink every time I chose his checkout line. I could never tell if he was merely practicing a friendly East African custom or inviting me to write down my phone number.

"Thank you, Mr. Tate," he said. I noticed he hadn't needed to read my name off the receipt.

"Call me Jim, Negasi," I said, handing him my "business" card. His smile widened a little as he took it, our fingers touching for just a moment. I wondered if he was a top or a bottom. He winked yet again before I picked up my shakes and nodded a goodbye.

Maybe the wink was merely a tic.

In any event, I hoped he'd call. Opportunities to meet men weren't plentiful, despite my job at the adult video store in White Center. My boss, Stefan, had made it clear three years ago when I first began working for him that he'd tolerate no sexual intimacy with our customers, either in the store or away. I'd seen two of my coworkers fired when a customer let slip a casual mention of their trysts.

I transferred from the 107 to the 60 in Georgetown. A burly Latino plopped into the seat next to me a few stops later. Even in the cold, he emitted an odor not entirely unpleasant, a hint of masculine sweat from unwashed clothes. The sun had yet to come up, so I didn't know if he was going home after working all night or just starting his day without a shower.

When I was twelve, one of my friends asked me in front of several other boys, "Would you suck my dick if I washed it first?"

I couldn't believe my luck. I'd dreamed about this for months. "Sure!" I said. "You don't even have to wash it."

Bill looked at me in disgust. "It was a joke," he said. "You were *supposed* to say no, and then I was going to say, 'So you're a *dirty* cock sucker!'"

The 60 slid just a little going over the South Park bridge, and the Latino grabbed my leg in fear.

I put my hand gently on his. The man stared at me in terror and jerked away. But he kept his eyes fixed on mine in the dark bus, and a moment later returned his hand to my leg. He looked about nervously, but none of the other passengers paid the least attention. It was still only 6:30. Most of us weren't really awake yet.

The man kept his hand on my leg till we reached the stop for the transfer station, where people brought extra trash and yard debris that wouldn't be picked up at their curb. He gave me a last confused, questioning look and stepped off the bus.

I had another card. Why hadn't I given it to him?

During my two years as a Mormon missionary in France, I'd given my card to lots of folks. Most people seemed far less interested in contacting you about church, though, than for sex. I'd vowed to abstain even from masturbating while volunteering for missionary work, but two thirds of the way into my stay, I ended up with a particularly difficult companion. During one of our weekly Companion Inventory sessions, he changed the course of my life.

"Elder Tate, we're both really stressed out," Elder Peck told me. It was dark out, we'd been tracting door to door for hours, and we were mentally exhausted from three months of zero success. "We've tried to talk out our differences, we've prayed, we've asked the zone leaders for help." He took my hand. "I think we need to take a more radical approach if we want to work together in a unified way." He placed my hand on his belt buckle.

We were able to duck into an alley. The only lubricant we had was the olive oil we carried on our keychains to use during priesthood blessings.

He consecrated my ass first, and then I consecrated his.

I didn't often think about Mormons anymore, except when a DVD featuring a religious fetish came into the store. Or a guy wearing a cross, or a taqiyah, or a Star of David walked up to the counter. A Sikh came in once. Watching a man in a dastar walk back and forth between the theater and arcade with his pants unzipped and the head of his penis peeking out isn't something you forget easily.

Normally, I asked guys to zip up while in the front part of the store, but there were times I simply couldn't bring myself to do it.

The 60 slid again on the ice as we headed across the overpass at the far end of South Park. By the time we reached the Olson Meyers Park-and-Ride at the bottom of the last, steep hill before reaching White Center, only a few passengers were still aboard.

"I need to take a break for a couple of minutes," the driver said. The Asian man stepped off the bus, put one hand on his chest while wiping his brow with the other, and headed for the bathroom.

I instinctively jumped off and rushed to catch up. "Scary driving on these roads, isn't it?" I said. The Park-and-Ride was next to a senior housing complex, so the sidewalks had all been salted, cleared, and resalted.

"I am so stressed," he admitted, "and I just started my shift." He unlocked the bathroom. "I thought the coffee would help me keep more alert, but…"

"Anything I can do to relieve some of that stress?" I asked with the friendliest smile I could muster this early in the morning. "You're out here serving us. I'm happy to serve you if I can." I let him see my eyes glance down at his crotch for a second.

The driver froze with his hand two inches from the bathroom door. I realized I might be coming across a bit stalkerish. But you couldn't just assume someone was going to say no, could you? You had to ask to find out. I'd always taken no for an answer.

The driver remained motionless for two or three seconds and then seemed to decide I might be a mystery shopper testing his professionalism. "I—I'm married," he said.

"Well, I certainly don't want to increase your stress," I told him. "I wanted to *relieve* some of it." I glanced at his crotch again. "Can I do that better by getting back on the bus, or…?"

Propriety was important, and there were folks who weren't interested in anyone other than their spouse. Some weren't interested in sex at all, with anyone. But I'd learned that a great many guys spent hours every day hoping for opportunities they didn't dare seek out themselves.

The driver pulled me into the bathroom and shut the door. "Oh my god," he said. "I don't know what in the world I'm doing." He *seemed* to know, though. It didn't take him two seconds to unzip and whip it out.

His dick was medium sized, the Goldilocks ratio for blow jobs. Too small and it would slip out of my mouth. Too large and I couldn't take it all. I licked the head, wrapped my lips around the top, and then grabbed the driver's ass and pulled him toward me, forcing his dick the rest of the way into my mouth.

"Oh my god."

I pulled back and then forced him forward again. He got the hint and began rocking back and forth on his own, fucking my face. "I've gotta get back on the bus," he said, pumping away. "I've got to drive up that hill." He shoved his dick forward more forcefully. "Then I've gotta go back down the hill." Shove. "And back up again." Shove shove. "And back down." He grabbed my head and pulled me forward as hard as he could while ramming his dick as far down my throat as he could, mad and happy and frustrated and needing release so, so badly.

"Unnh!"

I swallowed, pulled my head back, carefully licking the last drops of white from the tip of his penis.

"Oh my god."

"I'll get back on the bus now."

"I—I—"

"It's gonna be okay." I gave him a friendly pat on the shoulder and left him in the bathroom to recover. We hardly needed a distracted driver on a snowy hill. Now that we'd set the precedent, though, perhaps we could repeat the experience in better weather. I sat back in my seat and watched a few flakes drift down outside my window in a brief flurry.

A few minutes later, we reached 15th and Roxbury. I exited from the rear so as not to make the driver feel any more uncomfortable. I couldn't resist glancing into the front door as I passed, though. His face was impassive, but he gave me a swift thumbs up, his fist close to his chest so the passengers behind him couldn't see. He was the regular morning driver. I wondered if tomorrow would be too soon to repeat today's experience.

Of course, I still hadn't cum yet, so the quickie had only been partially satisfying. And now I'd be at work interacting with horny men all day long. I ran the reports, counted my till and the safe, and emptied the trash cans in the arcade and theater. The soft scent of stale cum permeated the back rooms.

I'd asked my boss to order some cum-scented cologne to sell as a gag gift, but I thought I honestly might like to try it myself. Put a dab on my neck and wrists to see if an indeterminate something might draw the right stranger on the bus to me. Stefan said he couldn't find anything in the usual catalogues. He ordered plastic salt and pepper shakers in the shape of black and white penises instead.

"We've got a lot of bondage equipment that doesn't sell," I told him. "Maybe we should just stock simple knee pads."

Sometimes, Stefan took my advice, and sometimes, he didn't. I was a lot happier making suggestions than making decisions, so that worked for both of us.

Straightening the DVDs was my last morning task before unlocking the doors. *Whack Job*, directed by Stormy Daniels, was one we'd just put out. I set it next to *You Rub Me the Right Way*. I turned on our neon sign and plopped down in my office chair behind the counter. Directly in front of me was a wall covered with dildos. Looked like a new color had been added during my days off. Dark red.

I thought back to a PBS documentary about intricate bird dances coded by DNA. I wasn't entirely happy with every piece of my DNA, but I appreciated the segment that coded for recognizing the beauty of the human penis. Some days, as I watched the men in the arcade flit from booth to booth, I wondered what kind of Nature documentary aliens might make describing the mating rituals of straight human males whose only sexual access was to other men who might be straight, bi, or gay.

I liked starting the morning off quietly and resisted turning on the radio. Unfortunately, that meant the sounds of men and women being fucked onscreen in the theaters kept banging against my eardrums.

"Unh! Unh! Unh! Unh!"

"Unh! Unh! Unh! Unh!"

"Unh! Unh! Unh! Unh!"

Okay, radio it was.

Adam Levine kept yelling that he was an "Animal." Jason Derulo sang "Want to Want Me." I couldn't tell if he meant someone else wanted him or if he was simply attracted to himself. One nice thing about being gay was that even if I didn't turn on anyone else, I could always rely on my own generosity in getting my reasonably attractive penis to devote its sexual attention to me.

The back door chimed as a customer walked in with his hood covering half his face. "Turn up the heater, Jim!" he barked playfully.

"What are you doing out in this weather?" I asked. Nathan hadn't missed a Sunday in all the time I'd been working here. An Asian-African American in his early forties, he worked at Boeing as an engineer.

"Coats and gloves are all right for other people," he said, "but I've always found the best way to generate warmth is the friction of skin on skin."

"You'll want the theater then?"

He nodded.

I collected $8 and wrote the time his ticket expired with a green Sharpie on the back of his receipt. When he walked over to the gate leading to the theater, I pressed a button and buzzed him in. I looked at my watch and waited. Two minutes later, right on schedule, Nathan called out. "Can you come in and adjust the volume?"

I went on in past the straight and fetish theaters to the gay room where I knew he'd be. In the flickering light from the monitor, I could see Nathan leaning forward with his hands on the back of a blue plastic chair, his shirt pulled up, his pants around his ankles, and his ass facing the back half of the room like a Venus flytrap waiting hopefully for a juicy insect.

"Up or down?" I asked, part of our ritual.

"In and out," he replied.

I hit the volume button and lowered the sound one notch. "That better?"

"One day," Nathan said wistfully. "One day. Fortune favors the prepared."

I lingered a moment longer than necessary. Nathan's trap beckoned, but I didn't want my fly to get fired. I looked up at the screen just as a hunky older man started to press his dick into the backside of a tattooed college student. Half a second after the older man's penis touched the younger man's ass, the film cut to a new angle, with the older man's dick now fully inserted. As he pulled out a couple of inches, I could see his penis was now covered with a condom.

Porn rarely showed actors putting on condoms. Even after all these years, it was hard to make condoms sexy. Some of our regulars bought two or three every time they came into the store. Others grabbed small bottles of silicon lube and went in back without even glancing at condoms. Perhaps they'd brought their own, though most guys used water-based lubes with latex.

Felipe, a stunning teller from the bank around the corner, always brought a jar of petroleum jelly with him on his lunch break. Some condoms worked just fine with silicon, but petroleum jelly meant intentional barebacking.

I looked again at Nathan's ass. He was an überlube man. I wanted to put just a dab on my finger and slip it half an inch inside him, feel his sphincter tighten around me.

Condoms always pinched and pulled at my ass, so I preferred bare skin myself. Of course, that was how I'd ended up with HIV sixteen years ago. But only six months into treatment, my viral load had become undetectable, where it remained to this day. Taking the pills was a bit of a bother, as were the regular blood tests, but for the most part, I didn't even think about being positive.

"You still there, buddy?" Nathan asked without turning his head.

My prostate was so primed, I was sure I could slide my dick inside him, pump for thirty seconds, and be done before Stefan would notice on the surveillance video I'd been gone from my post too long.

But how fun would a quickie that quick be?

"One day," I said. "One day. Successful people create their own fortune."

"How successful are you, Jim? Do you want me to give you a raise?"

I pushed a button beside the gate and buzzed myself back into the public area, shaking my head briskly to clear the testosterone fog enveloping my neurons. The rest of the morning proceeded as usual. A handful of other regulars trickled in, but far fewer than usual. Nathan's carnivorous ass finally got the meal it wanted, and he waved goodbye on his way out of the store. Stefan stopped by for a few minutes to make sure I had enough ones and fives to get through my shift. "You need anything else?" he asked as he opened the back door to head home again.

Permission to be human?

Stefan had once confided that he'd been faithful to his wife the entire twenty-three years they'd been married. "I used to need variety," he said, "but ever since I met Cindy, I've never needed anyone else."

Was monogamy like left-handedness? It clearly existed among humans but did not seem to be the predominant trait.

"Just keep me posted on the weather."

Stefan didn't allow employees to use the internet either on a work computer or our phones. That kind of distraction was too tempting for shoplifters. Even going to the bathroom left the store vulnerable. I could only imagine what would happen if there was an incident while I was in the theater "adjusting" the sound.

I sat behind the front desk, staring at the men's underwear on a nearby rack, listening to Lauren Daigle encouraging us to "believe." She had to compete, though, with a movie in the arcade a customer had ratcheted to its highest volume. "Oh, yeah...oh, yeah...oh, yeah…" every few seconds through her song and the next and the next.

Even mainstream sex videos featuring no fetishes at all were often the equivalent of water torture porn.

Randy, a thirty-something white bank teller, dropped some used DVDs on the counter. Various forms of bestiality, which we refused to sell. Randy viewed his online purchases a dozen times and then donated them to us. Stefan in turn donated them to a video store owner from another state whenever the guy came to town to visit. "Those wild boars," Randy said, tapping one of the DVD cases, "they shoot two whole cups of cum."

"I appreciate that bit of information," I said. "I never know when I might get a chance to play on Jeopardy."

Larry popped into the store around 1:00. He was a light-skinned black man with noticeable lipodystrophy and completely unconcerned about his appearance. I loved how he winked at me as he entered the arcade. He'd never propositioned me, was probably not even interested, but I did fantasize about him when I saw the red light above his door. Sallow cheeks and shoulders carrying a huge lump of fat could still be a turn on. At the very least, not a turn off.

He sometimes exited the theater with a spray of cum across the back of his shirt. Actually walked out of the store like that.

Was that intended as a conversation starter?

One day, I thought, repeating Nathan's mantra. One day.

A woman came in a few minutes later. We were lucky if we had one female customer a week, so I was surprised she'd ventured in on such a nasty day. I could see through our one tiny window above the front door that the snow was coming down thickly. The heavy stuff wasn't supposed to start till after my shift was over at 4:30.

"I'll get these two eggs," she said, placing them on the counter. The eggs contained thin rubber sleeves men could wrap around their dicks to assist in masturbation. They were not a popular item. Men who wanted masturbators usually bought the heavy-duty ones that cost much more. I rang them up. As I put them in a bag for her, she confided, "My boyfriend wants me to lay an egg for him on his birthday." She rolled her eyes.

"Men," I said.

She nodded wearily.

"We also have strap-ons," I said. "Have you ever tried pegging him?" I explained the term, which seemed to intrigue her. "Now you have something you can ask for on *your* birthday."

The next half hour passed without a single customer. When the front door finally chimed again, I jumped up eagerly. "Hi, Mario." I waved.

He returned two DVDs he'd rented. *Neither Snow Nor Rain Nor Cum* featured a man in a mail carrier's uniform getting a faceful of cum. *Ricochet Jizz* showed a man spitting out a stream of cum from his mouth onto a man's firm abdomen. "How far can you shoot?" Mario asked as I checked in the DVDs.

"I've never measured."

"You'll have to come over to my place sometime so we can play Dick Darts." He motioned to the floor. "I set a dart board on the living room floor and we see who can shoot best to get the most points. Standard rules apply. And it's where the *first* part of your load lands that counts."

If the store was nearly empty, some of the customers tried anything they could think of to encourage me to visit them after work. One non-stop talker always went on about how I should join him for some nude blackberry picking.

To quote Dana Scully, "There are hits and there are misses. And then there are misses."

"What does the winner get?" I asked.

"The right to put their dart anywhere they want. I'm trying to set up a league, but I've only got five people committed to Monday nights so far."

I tried to imagine the playoffs.

Mario couldn't find anything new to rent and so headed back out into the snow. Another twenty minutes passed quietly, only the radio keeping me company. American Authors told me about "The Best Day of My Life." Today certainly wouldn't count in my own memoir, unless I found a way to follow Bachman-Turner Overdrive's advice and begin "Takin' Care of Business" before much longer. Taylor Swift suggested that it might be possible, if I was "Delicate" enough.

Good grief, was I bored.

Thankfully, Carlson stomped in a few minutes later, trying to shake the snow off his shoes. I started processing his theater ticket before he even reached the register. He liked to spend hours in there, sometimes all day. "It's not very active today," I warned him.

"All it takes is one."

"Really?" I said, laughing. "Just one?" I handed him his receipt.

He shrugged. "If 'one' refers to 'one large group of horny men.'"

Handshakes, pats on the back, group sports—nothing created a camaraderie among men like fucking.

I buzzed him past the gate. I heard some banging about and wondered why Carlson felt the need to rearrange the chairs. Five minutes later, a man I'd completely forgotten about exited, zipping up. I heard a little more banging and one loud whump against the side of the wall. Several minutes after that, yet another customer I was sure had already left came out through the gate. He went into the bathroom and turned the water on in the sink as he washed up. Then he left through the back door with a slight wave directed back over his shoulder.

"Stay warm," I called out.

On my next walk thru of the arcade, I found a movie still playing in a booth a new guy had vacated only a moment earlier before hurrying out of the store. The man had also dropped several one dollar bills on the floor. I loved finding money when it was impossible to tell who'd left it. If I knew who'd dropped any money, I always returned it.

Once, I'd returned two twenties to a police officer I recognized from my own neighborhood. He barely nodded an acknowledgement. The least he could have done was give me a thank you grope. It would have been the courteous thing to do.

Reaching down to pick up the dollar bills on the floor now, I could see from the flickering light of the TV monitor that the top bill was covered with a spray of cum. I reached over for a paper towel from the dispenser. Before I could wipe the bill, the man in the adjacent booth poked his cock through the glory hole. He moved it around slowly through the opening like a fisherman dangling a hook. I could see his veins, the skin just barely noticeable as light brown in the dim light.

On the monitor, I watched as a burly man in work boots lifted his legs into the air. Another muscular, hairy man ripped off his plaid shirt, knelt down under the raised legs, and dug his face into the first man's hairy ass.

The screen turned dark as the former occupant's last payment ran out.

I'd tarried too long as it was. Stefan couldn't see from surveillance video what happened inside the booths, but he could certainly tell how long I'd been inside. I wiped the top bill, put them all in my wallet, and closed the booth door before returning to the front desk.

The computer screen showed the time as 3:21. It was going to take forever to get home in this mess. And then I'd have to go straight to bed so I could get up again at 5:00 and head right back. Ugh.

A trim, middle-aged white man in a business suit came in fifteen minutes later. He looked about the place slowly. It was often difficult evaluating newbies. Some needed a friendly chat with the cashier to loosen them up. Others were too skittish and freaked easily. This guy's suit was expensive, so he probably had a good deal of standing, at least in his own circle. Would that give him confidence? Or make him feel he had more to lose if he were found to be frequenting such an establishment?

He passed right by the lingerie, lingered a moment beside the vibrators, and finally stopped at the penis pumps.

Carlson poked his head over the gate. "Send another load my way!"

The man turned in surprise. He was going to run off for sure.

"I'm just following medical advice," Carlson explained to the businessman. "My doctor says I need three semen suppositories every day. He said capsules were okay, but the best method was direct injection."

Horny men were nothing if not tacky, I thought. I saw it all the time. The funny thing was that if you were horny, too, these things didn't sound tacky at all.

The other man dropped a penis pump in perfect synchrony with his lower jaw. He looked at me nervously, turned back to Carlson, and then headed for the back door. He paused by the bathroom, and I could see even from behind that he was adjusting his pants. He opened the back door, stared out at all the snow blowing by, and then marched back in and up to the counter.

"Theater," he said in a disinterested tone. He didn't look me in the eye.

"It's okay," I said, hoping I wasn't violating any boundaries. "We're here to provide an essential human service."

The man frowned as I handed him his ticket. Then he shook his head and chuckled. "The bank where I work closed early today and sent everyone home."

I smiled. "Some things are more essential than money."

I buzzed him past the gate and then turned the volume down on the radio. Could Carlson maintain his enthusiasm for a third go around? Within a couple of minutes, I began to hear the increasing sounds of success. "Yeah," Carlson shouted, "that's the way! Deeper! Harder! Yeah, that's it! More! More! Don't stop! Give it to me!"

So cliché, but I had to adjust my pants, too.

Just once…

I turned the volume up on the radio again. Charlie Puth assured me that help, or even love, was just "One Call Away." A moment later, the businessman pushed the gate open and headed directly for the exit. I could see even more snow blowing past. I wished Blake would get here for shift change early before it became too difficult to get home. I walked over to the front door and looked out into the street.

At least three and a half inches of new snow covered the sidewalks. The street was almost entirely white, with only two thin grooves showing evidence of the few vehicles still out and about. I could only hear a couple of cars on neighboring streets, so the snow had less and less competition every minute.

Carlson came out of the theater. "Guess I'd better call it a night," he said. "You have far to go when your shift's over?"

"Rainier Beach," I told him.

"I'm just half a mile away. You can spend the night at my place if you like."

"Uh..."

"Here's my number." He plopped a paper towel from one of the theater dispensers on the counter with his cell phone number.

"Thank you."

He gave my hand a squeeze and then left the store. I adjusted my pants again and started counting my till. I always counted the coin first since it was the most trouble, and the vast majority of transactions involved trading larger bills for smaller ones or charging for the theater, neither of which involved coin. Then when my evening relief came, it only took a few seconds to count the bills.

4:00. Way too early for Blake to come in. This was the period when I hated hearing the door chime. I didn't want anyone to come buy something that forced me to count all my coin again.

4:10.

4:14. 4:15.

4:16.

Soon I'd be home, taking a warm shower, two fingers up my ass while I stroked myself with a handful of suds.

Well, maybe not "soon." On a good day, it took ninety minutes to get home. God only knew what it would be like tonight.

4:20.

The phone rang. Uh oh. I could see on the Caller ID it was Stefan. I took a deep breath and picked up.

"Blake can't make it," Stefan said. "His bus route from Burien was canceled. I looked up the 60, too. It's shut down for the rest of the day."

Fuck. "Maybe I can take the 120 downtown and—"

"Buses aren't going up any hills in Queen Anne or Rainier Beach or Skyway."

I wondered if under the circumstances it would be okay to call Carlson.

"Can you stay on the clock a few more hours?" Stefan asked. "You can close early at 9:00, and I'll come get you. Cindy's already told me we should have you sleep in our guest room tonight."

Ack! That would almost be worse than sleeping on the street.

Said the man who'd never had to sleep on the street.

But spending the night at Stefan's place was a boundary I didn't want to cross. "Can I sleep on the sofa in the gay theater?" I asked.

Stefan didn't answer right away. "I guess so, if you feel comfortable doing that. I can bring a blanket over for you."

"Oh, I'll just wipe down the sofa before I go to bed."

"I meant to keep you warm."

I laughed. "You keep this place at 70 degrees. I'll be fine."

"The heater goes off at midnight."

"Oh." But I had my coat. "I'll be okay." That meant no nasty commute tonight *and* no nasty commute first thing in the morning. Plus, I'd be getting extra hours. And the crowd couldn't possibly be too heavy. "You guys cuddle up and have a good evening."

"Thanks, Jim."

I hung up and looked around the empty store. I was finally going to get a chance to watch a movie in the gay theater and beat off at work. Not a very respectable ambition for most people, but then, who wanted to be respectable? If well-behaved women rarely made history, the Ward Cleavers and Mike Bradys of the world rarely did, either.

I wanted to be Goldie Hawn in *The Banger Sisters*. I wanted to be Cate Blanchett in *Bandits*.

I wanted to be Al Parker.

Lucas Hedges might never star in a movie about my life, but really, I was happy enough being me.

At 5:05, a customer I'd never seen before came in the store and bought a blue dildo. He was in and out within two minutes. By 5:30, no one else had come in. I peeked out the front door. It was dark now and quiet. I couldn't even hear cars on nearby streets, and the snow was still coming down steadily.

By 5:45, I began feeling guilty. I enjoyed getting paid, but if the store wasn't making any sales, it seemed unfair to stay on the clock. At 5:55, I called Stefan.

"You okay?" he asked.

"We haven't had a customer in over an hour." It was only a slight exaggeration.

"Okay, go ahead and lock up. You sure you don't want me to come pick you up?"

"I'm good. Can I use your office computer to check my emails?"

Right after we hung up, the lights flickered. I turned off the Open sign and locked the front door. The breaker box was right there, so I turned off the spotlights by the entrance. On my way past the register, I turned off the main lights, though two remained on at all times so the person opening in the morning could see enough to make his way to the alarm box.

The lights flickered again. It would be just my luck to spend the night in a porn theater and not be able to watch any porn. I stuck the Allen wrench hanging from the store keychain into the bar on the back door. Just as I was about to turn it, the door opened outward, and I almost fell over.

"Sorry, Jim, didn't know you were there!" Philip was about sixty, a former Marine, the "former" being the most accurate part of that description. He had quite the pot belly now but was completely unselfconscious about it. Some guys, no matter how unattractive they might be, seemed to think every woman or every man was always after them. That wasn't self-confidence. It was narcissism. But Philip simply seemed comfortable with himself.

Like most gay men, I was usually attracted more to guys who were fit, but Philip exuded sexuality. So did one of our regulars with a stiff prosthetic leg, as did a short Latino bicyclist who looked good in Spandex despite his man-boobs, and a down-and-out guy missing one of his front teeth, who still always smiled in such a genuine way that I tried to save half-filled lube bottles guys had left in the arcade and give them to him when he left the store. He certainly couldn't afford our lube prices.

"We're closing up early, Philip. I'm afraid I can't let you in."

"Fuck. I gotta pee. Can I at least run into the bathroom?"

I motioned him inside and finished locking the door. Thirty seconds later, the lights flickered. Ten seconds after that, they went out.

"Hey!" Philip shouted from inside the bathroom.

"Electricity's out," I called back.

I heard a flush, and then the bathroom door opened. The building was pitch black. Philip fumbled his way toward me, and we walked the last couple of feet toward the door. When I opened it, there was a faint glow from lights still on in other parts of the city, but the immediate neighborhood was quite dark.

"I'm not driving in this mess with no streetlights. Can I stay here a while to see if they come back on?"

Damn. But I could hardly kick the guy out in these conditions. I closed the door. Then I realized several things at once. There was only one chair behind the counter, so we couldn't really wait there. We'd have to sit on a sofa in the theater. What would happen next was inevitable. No one had that much self-restraint. But the security cameras wouldn't be able to record us going past the gate, so it was possible Stefan would never know.

In any event, it was happening.

I took Philip's hand, and we began walking slowly to where I knew the gate was located. Fortunately, I'd left it ajar as part of my closing procedure. Otherwise, I would have had to crawl under, and I wasn't at all sure Philip could have managed it. Once inside, I made sure not to close the gate completely, and I led Philip to the gay room. I didn't suppose it mattered which one we sat in since no movies were playing, but it felt like the appropriate place to be.

"You hussy," Philip whispered. With no other sound in the building, the words echoed in the tiny hallway.

"Okay, here's the sofa," I said. "We can sit here and wait for—"

Philip took off his coat and threw it on the floor. I could hear him pulling off his shirt as well, so I began pulling off mine. Philip's shoes came off with two loud thumps, and then I heard his zipper. I followed his example, and soon I was naked, too. We stood in the silence a moment, and then I felt a hand groping for me in the dark. Philip touched my chest, his fingers fumbling their way down my stomach to my crotch.

"Ha!" he said. "You're already hard."

He gently tugged the skin back and forth over the head of my penis. I reached out until I found his dick and did the same thing. I wanted more than a hand job, though. I wanted *him*. I pulled him closer until his protruding stomach bumped up against me. I put my both hands on his stomach, rubbing slowly, migrating north to his nipples, going around back and pulling him in even closer. I felt his hands reaching for the back of my head as he drew my face toward his.

I sensed his warmth before I felt his cheek brush against me.

After his lips found mine, Philip thrust his tongue into my mouth. How wonderful that he didn't just insert the tip of that sexy muscle half an inch inside. It felt as if his entire tongue filled my mouth.

He'd had corn chips in the past half hour. The subtle remainder felt comforting.

"Mmmmm," I moaned. Philip shoved his tongue in even farther.

I hoped he wouldn't trigger my gag reflex going in so deep.

"Let me get some lube," he whispered. I heard some rustling on the floor, and a moment later, Philip found my hand and put a small bottle in it. "It's silicone," he said. "I'll lean over one of these chairs."

"I don't have a condom," I told him. In the current atmosphere where consent was mandatory both legally and—finally—morally, I wanted to be sure I wasn't assuming anything.

"Find my hole and get your dick inside it," he commanded. I could hear the Marine in his voice.

I squirted some lube in my hand and rubbed it all over my dick. With the rest of the lube still on my hand, I reached forward. Philip grabbed my wrist, guiding my hand to his asshole. I rubbed some lube around the opening, around and around in a circle. I wished I could see it, but somehow the absolute darkness enhanced the sensation, the way some restaurants served dinner in the dark.

I slid my index finger half an inch past his sphincter.

"Don't worry about loosening me up," Philip said. "I always prepare with a butt plug before I head over."

I stroked myself a few seconds to get as hard as possible, followed my hand back to his hole, and pressed it against the opening. When I was sure I was in exactly the right place, I slid myself forward slowly until my head was past his military checkpoint and paused a moment.

Military checkpoint. Good grief.

Testosterone seemed to disrupt the normal functioning of the frontal lobe. It must be why sex talk, and even sex thought, was so simplistic. Every time I entered someone, I imagined myself going through Stargate into another world. A primal, liberating, yet somewhat intimidating leap into the unknown. Since Philip's sphincter had offered little resistance, I inhaled deeply and kept sliding my dick in all the way to the hilt.

"Aahhh!" Philip breathed.

"God, you feel good."

Now fully inside Philip, I wrapped both arms around his large body. Could men with firm asses be Rubenesque? I pulled out a few inches and pushed back in. Then I did it a little faster. I'd wanted Philip for so long. It was too bad several of my favorite regulars hadn't been trapped in the store along with us.

Making "love" with a partner was all fine and good, but what I enjoyed most was the sheer friendliness of sex.

I wondered whether if God existed, he would welcome us into heaven with a hug, a handshake, or a fuck.

"I love your slippery ass!" I moaned. I kissed the back of his neck and kept pumping.

"I beat off before I came to the store," Philip panted, "and squirted my cum up my ass."

Personal lubricant took on a whole new meaning. "I want to stick my tongue in there and lick it up."

Was it felching if you were lapping up someone else's cum? I kept pumping away. Every time I had sex, it was like a revelation, a discovery that sex was better than I remembered.

If only it could last an hour. Two hours, three.

I slid all the way in again.

"Pull almost all the way out slowly," Philip commanded, "but shove yourself back inside as hard as you can every time." I complied, groaning heavily. "Do it!" he said more loudly. I shoved myself back in again hard and fast. "*Do it!*" he shouted. I wondered if he'd ever been a drill instructor.

It was difficult not to pull out as quickly as I was going back in, but I soon adjusted my rhythm. It was a tease for both of us, over and over. I wasn't sure how long I could last under these conditions. I slowed down for a few moments to delay, but Philip reached behind and pulled me toward him roughly at the same time he was forcing his dick backwards.

All I could think about was my dick inside him, covered in his cum, lathered in it, some of it sneaking into the head of my penis, some of my pre-cum mixing with his semen. I wanted to taste his cum and then my cum and then our cum mixed together to appreciate the subtle differences.

Who the fuck cared about subtlety?

A tingling started and grew stronger and stronger. I imagined Zachary Quinto or Simon Pegg being beamed off the Enterprise and into my cock. I felt like my dick was being possessed, that another living being was materializing inside it. I held onto the sensation as long as I could, like pulling back a string on a bow.

I released my arrow. "Aauuggghhh!"

Philip stopped moving. "Leave it in for a minute." Even his whispers were commands.

I did leave it, my face pressed against his back. He was sweating. I gently licked the skin and inhaled deeply. Sex smelled good before, during, and after. But especially after.

Finally, the former Marine pulled forward until I slipped out. He reached about on the chair he'd heard me place the bottle of lube on, and in seconds, he'd spun me around in the darkness. He must've had night vision lenses inserted into his eyes while in the military, as he didn't even have to feel about for my asshole. He just grabbed me and drove in without the slightest warning.

I groaned loudly, not entirely in satisfaction. I had *not* butt plugged myself ahead of time. But Marines were all about decisive action, not comfort.

"It's like stepping into a cold pool," he said. "If you have to go in unprepared, it's best to get the pain over with so you can start enjoying yourself faster."

I noticed he didn't pull out slowly with each thrust, as he'd asked me to do, so I didn't entirely buy his reasoning. It was in and out as fast as possible, giving my sphincter no time to relax.

"Unh," I groaned. "Unh. Unh." I gritted my teeth, the pain stronger than the pleasure. He didn't need to turn this wonderful memory into a negative one.

"The great thing about being sixty-three," he grunted, "is that it takes me a *long* time to cum." He pumped and pumped, shoving harder and harder each time. The chair in front of me skidded forward a few inches. He pulled me away from the chair and spun me to the side, pushing me two or three feet toward the wall. He slipped out for just a second, but the moment I slammed into the wall, he rammed his way back inside, his aim still perfect.

One experienced a certain gratification when a basketball swooshed through a hoop without touching the rim.

He must have been a marksman in the Marines. I'd have to ask him sometime. I hadn't fully agreed to the roughness, but I hadn't refused it, either, and there was something satisfying in knowing that Philip was enjoying himself, even if I wasn't.

But the pleasure slowly began to return, lagging behind the pain a bit longer, then running neck and neck, and finally overtaking it.

My last boyfriend had called me The Philosophical Fucker. He still called me up sometimes for a late night fuck, demanding I act as a commentator from start to finish. I didn't realize for quite some time he was posting videos of us on the internet. Further evidence, if any were needed, that sex turned us all into idiots.

One had to wonder about the evolutionary advantage in linking procreation to an abandonment of rational thought.

I constricted my sphincter as tight as I could.

"Aaahhh!" we both said in unison.

Philip's dick had to be close to seven inches long, but with each shove, I willed it to grow even longer. And wider. What had seemed too much to handle Ten minutes ago wasn't quite enough now. I wondered if there were dildos which could be enlarged once inside you. I'd have to ask Stefan to look for it in his catalogs.

"Harder!" I hissed at Philip. "Harder!"

Philip began pulling me away from the wall with each partial withdrawal and shoving me back against it with each forward thrust. Thump! Thump! Thump!

Then he began pulling almost entirely out each time so that he had to go back in past my sphincter with each and every new thrust forward. His impressive weight could have been intimidating, but he was fucking me with a controlled frenzy, a controlled mercy.

Two minutes more. Three minutes. Four minutes. He wasn't kidding. I realized now why so many guys liked older men. I'd always thought it was for their looks.

Philip pushed so forcefully over and over that I was surely being bruised both in front and in back. Despite the silicon, my asshole was starting to burn, but it only served to make me more aware of how wonderful it felt to have another man's cock inside me. Straight men really didn't know what they were missing. Even those pegged by their wives probably didn't last this long.

I relaxed, letting Philip push and pull and ram me as he pleased. The abandon only added to the pleasure. I tried to memorize the stimulation of every nerve ending.

Was this one of the reasons men went into the porn industry, I wondered? Whenever I listened to the recording I'd made of me singing "Adon Olam," I remembered every wonderful moment of my first anniversary with Chayim.

"It's coming!" Philip shouted. "My big load is coming!"

To my surprise, he pulled out all the way, pulled me from the wall, and pushed me face first over the edge of the sofa. Reaching down to support myself, my hand pressed against a sticky spot on the cushion. I could tell from the texture it was a mix of lube and cum, maybe an hour old. As I wiggled my fingers through it, I felt a warm, heavy splat all along my spine.

"Oh, man! Oh, man!"

I continued to lean over the arm of the sofa and felt a tiny river of thinner fluid trickling down from the thick mass of cum. It dripped into my crack. I recalled H.G. Wells's *Island of Dr. Moreau* and wondered if humans would ever be able to splice any genes from wild boars into ours.

Philip pressed up against my ass and started nuzzling my back, rooting and sniffing until he found the cum. He licked up the main glob and then turned me around again to face him, pulling me fully to my feet. He pressed his face against mine, found my lips, and shot his tongue into my mouth.

At first, I was disappointed he'd already swallowed, but we kissed for almost two minutes, and the taste of his tongue alone was all I needed. Finally, he pulled back, and we both sighed. I wasn't sure what hormone triggered melancholy, but I felt a flash of after-Christmas blues.

Philip grabbed my head again to give me one last peck, and then I heard him fumbling around for the paper towel dispenser on the wall. He pulled several sheets out and handed them to me before grabbing several more for himself.

"How long do you think the electricity will be out?" he asked.

"I don't know. All night? Five minutes?" I cleaned up as best I could and inched over to the trash can under the paper towel dispenser.

"Let me get your back."

I turned around and felt Philip dabbing and wiping the rest of his cum off me.

"Maybe we should go stand by the door for a while," I said. "That way, once the surveillance cameras are recording again, it won't look like we've been back here." Though really, if I had to, I thought I could make a reasonable argument for leniency.

"I only live half a mile away," Philip said. "I lied about not being able to get home."

"Fucker." I laughed.

"Damn right. Fuckee, too. I'm glad you're versatile."

His stomach bumped up against me, helping me estimate where to wrap my arms around him. We hugged for a few minutes, but finally, it was time. "We'd better get dressed."

It took a moment to figure out whose clothes were whose, but soon we made our way out of the theater and to the back door. I cracked it open. Even without streetlights, we could see that the snow was still coming down, though a little less heavily now.

"We can't do this at the store anymore," I said. "But if I'm going to get in trouble for having sex with a customer, I want to make it count. I'll have to come to your place after work once in a while."

"Next Sunday good for you?"

He took a dollar bill out of his pocket, scribbled his address and phone number, and tucked the bill into my underwear. We pecked goodbye, and I closed the door after watching him disappear down the alley in the dim light.

I didn't expect Ben Stiller would be starring in *Night at the Porn Store* anytime soon, but I was sure I could recall tactile sensations from the past hour even if I wouldn't be able to conjure up many images.

The rest of the evening went well. I found the flashlight I used to patrol the arcade and kept it by my side while I dozed on the sofa. Around 4:00 in the morning, there was a huge crash somewhere in the store.

Without the alarm system, I was a bit frightened. Then I saw a ceiling tile had fallen in the straight theater. Ugh. A leak in the roof. Fortunately, most of the water fell right into the garbage can.

When the power came back on an hour and a half later, I cleaned up the remaining mess and then emptied all the other garbage cans in the store to get ready for opening.

Stefan arrived just before 7:00. "Sleep okay?" he asked.

I almost replied, "Like a baby," but that wasn't quite accurate. "Like an eighteen-year-old," I said. I gave him a quick, edited version of the evening's events.

He gave me an odd look and then handed me a gift card. "Cindy insisted," he said.

The card was for a hundred dollars. "Wow, Stefan. Thanks." I reached for my wallet and slid the card inside.

"You've gone above and beyond the call of duty," he said.

"My pleasure."

He nodded and then smiled. "After you run the daily reports, you should probably go in the bathroom and wash that cum stain off your shoulder before we open."

My mouth fell open.

"Thanks for the offer," he said, "but I'm good." He chuckled and clapped me on my other shoulder. Then he walked away, but I saw him adjust his pants before he closed the door to his office.

Visiting Hours for Smoothies

Judgment Day had come and gone, and my husband Dwayne and I were shipped to the lowest degree of heaven after having our genitals removed. Our Ken doll lumps in front were created with tiny holes for urine, which meant we could no longer piss standing up as we had during our mortal existence.

But the fact that we still ate and drank meant we still had complete digestive systems—Jesus couldn't get rid of our assholes. Now that our poop came out in little clean balls like rabbit pellets, Dwayne and I could at least still share some degree of physical intimacy.

Rimming had never been our favorite pastime back on Earth, but we took advantage of the body parts we still had, making love out of the remnants of our sexuality.

"Hey, Kyle," Dwayne whispered this morning when he saw I was finally awake, "can you dildo me? I'm feeling especially horny today." Most of that had to be in his head, of course, since the only testosterone we could produce these days was from our adrenal glands.

I yawned and propped myself up on my elbows. "Morning, sweetpea." I stretched over to kiss him. No morning breath in the Telestial Kingdom. No oily skin. No morning crust in our eyes. "Which dildo do you want to wake up to?"

"The plorange one."

After the Millennium was over, after the final resurrection, we finally had a word that rhymed with orange.

Life wasn't all bad on the outskirts of heaven.

"Ah," I said, "the double-headed one."

Dwayne reached for his bedside table and plopped the dildo and a bottle of lube on the bed between us. We'd decided on our first day here—was that ten years ago now?—that if we were to be denied God's presence for eternity, then we'd make sure every single day to give each other as much love as we could. Usually, that meant reading books aloud to each other, swimming in our backyard pool, and going to live concerts.

It didn't take long to discover that most of our favorite musicians and singers had been assigned to the Telestial Kingdom, too. Freddie Mercury wasn't a surprise, of course. Or Gwen Stefani. But Josh Groban? Really? Well, whatever he'd done to get here, I was glad he did it.

But the most important commitment Dwayne and I made was to include something sexually intimate at least once a day. If we started off this early, we often made love once or twice more before the day was done. Just like in the old days when we first started dating at BYU.

Dwayne wiped some lube on my ass, letting his index finger push gently past my sphincter a couple of times as he did so. I returned the favor but added a second finger as well, as he'd always preferred bigger dicks.

Back on Earth, we'd never been able to find a double-headed dildo with one end of the dildo larger than the other. But a good many artisans ended up in our little corner of heaven as well.

Our genitals were gone, but Heavenly Father could hardly prevent us from living on a planet with natural resources. No sex allowed? Then we'd choose to make dildos. I also had a nipple ring. Dwayne had a stainless steel ring inserted through part of his Ken mound.

Within a few months of our mass arrival, several enterprising folks here had the beginnings of a smoothie porn industry well under way. Of course, days and months and years weren't the exact equivalent of time measurements on Earth, but Telestial years weren't like dog years. Everything was maybe 1.3 or 1.4 times longer. No one seemed to care enough to make any calculations. We had what we had.

I inserted the larger end of the plorange dildo into my husband's anus. "Oh god, that's good!" he moaned. "Deeper," he commanded. "Deeper!"

I slid it in six inches and then turned around on the bed to position my ass near his. I put the tip of the smaller end of the dildo against my own anus, carefully positioning the head past the opening.

"Here it comes," I said. With that, I backed up as forcefully as I could toward Dwayne. I was so tight that my dildo could only advance slowly while my weight shoved the larger end deeper into my hubby.

We both groaned until our ass cheeks were touching. On all fours facing away from each other like giant love bugs, we started rocking slowly back and forth, forcing the dildo to shift forward and backward in our asses.

"Faster!" Dwayne commanded me.

We rocked faster.

"Faster!!" he shouted.

We kept at it almost ten more minutes. The problem, of course, was that without a prostate or testicles, we could never orgasm. In some respect, our sex was the kind I sometimes had before I met Dwayne, when I'd pick someone up in a bar, go to his place, service him, and then be sent on my way without the other guy addressing my own need to cum at all. But Dwayne and I had learned how to make the unending lack of a payoff part of a monumental session of foreplay.

One day…

The Telestial Kingdom housed a good many scientists and physicians, with plenty of free time for other residents to go to school to join their ranks if they chose. We didn't get sick here, of course, but biology was fascinating if nothing else, and medical research was good for other things, too.

Because our incomplete bodies were "perfected" now, the same techniques used on Earth to treat transgender men and women weren't as successful here. But science was universal, and every day, we were closer to restoring our genitals. Dwayne was already designing the new and improved (i.e., larger) dick I'd have one of these days.

What was God going to do about it? The judging and punishing was all completed. There was no Second Judgment Day.

After we pulled the dildo out, Dwayne turned me around and shoved his ass in my face. "Lick off the lube!" he ordered.

I rooted happily between his cheeks. I couldn't quite make out the flavor, though. He was always searching for ways to stump me. I pulled back a moment. "Leather?" I asked.

"Try again."

I licked as deeply as I could and pulled back once more. "*Sweaty* leather?"

"Ding! Ding! Ding!" Dwayne laughed. "Oh, Kyle, you're getting too good at this. I'm going to have to start mixing flavors. Forty percent sweaty leather and sixty percent clean skin with a dash of marijuana…"

"And sommeliers think they're so gifted."

Dwayne rotated toward me, threw me on my back, and lifted my legs. "Let's be fair," he said, "we're developing new grape varieties and fermenting methods every year. Sommeliers need to stay on their toes, too."

"I prefer staying on my back."

Dwayne dug his face into my ass and licked off every drop of lube he could. When he was finished, I pulled myself into a sitting position and he sat on the bed beside me, issuing a long, happy sigh.

"Time for breakfast?" I asked.

"Grilled cheese sandwiches and maple syrup, please!"

I hoped to order that flavor of lube before his next birthday.

Dwayne and I shared a casual morning, catching up on Anne Frank's latest novel. A bisexual, she was also here in the Telestial Kingdom, though a few levels above us. She always made sure the rest of us could get copies of her books if we wanted them. In *Breaking out of Telestial Detention*, she described a fictitious group of characters who dig a "tunnel" through hyperspace to reach freedom.

Joseph Smith once said that if we understood how beautiful the Telestial Kingdom was, we'd kill ourselves to get there.

Even a beautiful cage was still a cage.

After lunch, Dwayne and I usually gave each other several hours to do our own thing. "I'm off to play pool with some friends," he said, giving me a kiss. No onion breath, either. There were definitely nice aspects to this place.

I missed semen breath.

Dwayne would be gone at least three or four hours. I pulled out my latest embroidery project, a portrait of us on our wedding day a few years before gay marriage was criminalized in America, not long before the start of Armageddon.

I worked two days a week now on a farm just a few miles outside of town. It wasn't difficult, since we always had the right amount of rain, with no weeds or pests. All the bugs and harmful bacteria had filled the measure of their creation back on Earth, so they all ended up in the Celestial Kingdom. They were all nice bugs these days, but they were still bugs.

So I enjoyed my time on the farm. Sometimes, I spent a few hours as a line cook at a local restaurant, and once in a while, I drove a food delivery bike, but since no one needed money here, no one had to slave away at any job just to survive. I had lots of time to follow other pursuits.

I was trying to master the clarinet so I could play klezmer music, and I was gaining a basic competency in Russian because I hoped one day to read some of the classics in their original language. But I had hand embroidery down pat.

Quite nice to have 20/20 vision again.

My watch beeped just as I finished Dwayne's left eye. I put the tiny defect back in his iris that had been eradicated during the resurrection.

"Vaughn!" I exclaimed, looking at the hologram my watch was emitting.

"Hey, old buddy. ¿Cómo estás?"

"Missing my old amigo," I replied.

"I got a day pass," Vaughn said. "I can use it any time. You okay if I pop in for a while today? What works for you?"

I laughed. "Slumming it again?" Vaughn was the only person from my mortal past who'd ever visited me once he made it to the Celestial Kingdom. My parents had never come to see me. None of my siblings had.

Those in the higher kingdoms were permitted to visit folks in the lower kingdoms if they chose, but those from the rough corners of heaven could never venture into the gated kingdoms above.

I'd been good friends on Earth with one niece, even after most of my other family relationships faded. She was probably too busy popping out spirit babies now and keeping up with her new family to worry about her old one.

Not a single royal from Dwayne's family had ever visited him. He said he'd made peace with their emotional abandonment back on Earth. Of course, it hadn't been true then and it wasn't true now.

So I recognized the value in Vaughn's occasional visits. He'd been my favorite companion when we worked as missionaries in Bolivia.

"No puedo esperar," I said.

"Be there in a jiffy."

Sixty seconds later, there was a flash from the front porch, and then Vaughn knocked on the door. He walked in and hugged me tightly the moment I opened for him. "It's been too long," he said. Of course, time in each kingdom was slightly different. Even time zones among the different levels of the same kingdom needed to be taken into account whenever someone traveled.

"Almost six months." It was impossible not to consider what might have been if I'd chosen to stay in the Church. But since my orientation hadn't changed at death or later during the resurrection, what good would living in the Celestial Kingdom with even a wonderful woman do me? Or her?

"What's new, buddy?"

I deliberated briefly on how to respond but then decided to be honest. Telestialites rarely lied. It wasn't because we were forced to tell the truth in heaven. There was just little point in lying. "I got a new tattoo. Wanna see?"

"A tattoo, Kyle? Really?"

"We can erase them any time we want, you know." No one would care to look at the same tattoo for a thousand years, after all, much less five million.

"Okay, okay." Vaughn laughed. "Show me. Then we'll do some real catching up."

I unzipped and dropped my pants without another word. Vaughn took a step backward, emitting a little gasp.

"I'm hardly going to rape you, am I?"

"Sorry. I'm just used to chastity."

"Are you afraid of seeing my…nothing?"

Vaughn frowned. He'd never asked to see my mound, but I showed it to him now, since that was where my new tattoo lived.

"You…tattooed a penis on…on…"

"Dwayne drew it. He remembered every detail."

Vaughn looked at me, closed his eyes for a moment, and then slowly opened them again. "I'm so sorry, Kyle."

I pulled my pants back up and motioned to the sofa. Vaughn sat only inches away from me. "Are you planning to make the same rules on your world?" I asked.

He frowned again. "I don't know. We have so many classes before we get to that point. So many certifications." He sighed heavily. "And my wives and I need to make a few million more spirit babies first."

He had that wistful look I'd seen in his eyes the day he learned he'd be transferred away from me to another small Bolivian town.

I risked a question. "Are you happy?"

My companion hesitated, but only a moment. "Yes, I am." He put his hand on my arm. I remembered the time he'd rubbed my chest when I was laid up in bed with a bad cold. "It was worth every sacrifice."

I nodded. "I'm glad." Even if Judgment Day had been a full decade ago, I still felt my new life had only just started.

But then, I'd felt that every day of my thirty-two years on Earth with Dwayne.

At least we had the bodies of twenty-five-year-olds for eternity.

"Remember on our mission," Vaughn said, smiling, "whenever I saw a pretty girl, what was the first thing I'd say?"

"'She has a nice ass,'" I quoted.

He laughed. "I'd never even kissed a girl yet."

"Were you able to ask any of the ones you admired in La Paz to marry you after Judgment Day?"

He shook his head, wistful again.

"Are you still an ass man?"

He smiled but looked away. "My love of asses followed me straight into the Celestial Kingdom. It's taking us longer than the others to reach our quota of spirit babies so we can get our planet started." He looked back at me out of the corner of his eye.

Suddenly, I was struck with a revelation.

Dwayne and I didn't have genitalia, but Vaughn did.

"You know," I said, "if you're going to be doing this outreach to me, the least I can do is some inner reach."

Vaughn's eyebrows furrowed.

"Take you inside as deep as I can."

"Kyle…"

"You're already a god," I said. "You can't be demoted."

"Oh, Kyle, it's been nice seeing you again." He stood up. "But I think I'd better go."

"How many times can you cum in a row?" I countered. "With so many wives, and so many spirit babies to make…"

Vaughn looked down at his feet. "Seven is the magic number," he said. "For all of us."

I took a deep breath, marveling at the possibilities. What would it be like to fuck Dwayne seven times over the course of an hour, each load lubricating my dick more and more, to keep at it till he was overflowing with my cum?

My mound was incapable of twitching at the thought.

"You'll fuck me first," I said. "Then I'll suck you off while we reminisce about the old days. And then when Dwayne gets home, you'll fuck him, too."

"Kyle, please."

"And on your next visit, we'll have a three-way."

"Oh my heck."

I smiled. "And on your next visit after that, I'll get five of our closest gay friends over and you'll do us all. Our old branch president from Yacuiba will be glad to see you again."

Vaughn shook his head sadly. "A straight god having a gay orgy?" he moaned.

I'd only participated in three-ways and group sex before I met Dwayne. He hadn't made me give those activities up. I'd just had no reason not to.

But now?

"You can't get demoted for that, either," I said. I took his hand and led him to the bedroom. He didn't even pretend to resist. I grabbed the sweaty leather lube and handed it to him. I could see something growing in his pants.

The sight was almost painful.

Vaughn unbuckled his belt and pulled his pants down to his knees.

"You don't want to get in bed?"

He shook his head. "Drop your pants and turn around. I don't want to see your face. I want—I want—"

I did as he said, wondering why it had taken me a goddamn ten years to think of this.

Better than five hundred, I supposed.

I could hear Vaughn slathering lube on his dick but noticed he didn't apply any directly to me. No matter. I would take his dick completely dry if I had to. I felt him press the head of his penis against me. He pushed with about five ounces of strength and then stopped without going in. He pushed with six ounces of strength and then stopped.

"I've been resurrected," I said. "You know my ass is perfect."

Vaughn pushed the tip of his penis inside me with a quick jab. He hesitated only a moment and then slowly, ever so slowly, kept sliding in deeper and deeper, a centimeter at a time, till he was in as far as he could go. While I wasn't as particular about the circumference of cocks as Dwayne, I found Vaughn's penis a tad less robust than I preferred. Still, I wasn't about to look a gift dick in the shaft.

Vaughn sighed. "I was so relieved to find out anal sex with my wives was allowed," he said.

"You make the rules now. You can allow whatever you want."

He paused a few moments, and I could feel him flexing his dick inside me. Fascinating how the lining of my rectum could tell the difference between a plorange dildo and the real thing. The lining tingled. It triggered some kind of euphoria. I had a fleeting image of my dog running around my parents' home in ecstasy the day I came back from Bolivia.

"I can't believe I'm doing this." Vaughn gave no hint he was going to stop. "Extramarital gay Telestial sex."

"Oh, yeah, talk dirty to me."

Vaughn stopped pumping and laughed uncontrollably for a few moments.

"Loud laughter, too, huh? With a god, it seems all things are possible."

Vaughn pulled almost all the way out, sliding rapidly back and forth a couple of centimeters, letting his head tease my sphincter. He'd definitely done this before.

"You're the first man I ever wanted to enter," he said, slowly sliding all the way in again. "There've only been a handful." He pulled out five inches and then slowly slid in again. "You were the only companion I ever truly loved."

He pulled almost all the way out, rubbing my sphincter rapidly with the head of his dick again for several seconds before going in two inches, pulling out, and going in two inches again, pulling out, and sliding in to the hilt once more. "I remember watching you change clothes." He started pumping faster. "You had such a beautiful ass."

I knew Vaughn wasn't bisexual. Not terribly, anyway. Even if that had been part of his orientation he'd never acted on while on Earth, it would have come out on Judgment Day.

My ass was burning in a way it couldn't from encountering just fingers or dildos. I wished Vaughn could reach around and grab my cock. I wished I could grab my own cock.

I wished Dwayne was here.

"I…." Vaughn began. "I…" Then he stopped talking and fucked me harder and harder. "My wives don't like it hard," he said. "But sometimes…"

That slender dick seemed to transform from Bruce Banner into the Hulk. It didn't change size, of course, just intensity. I never liked anger before, and I couldn't tell which of us it was coming from. I'd never once been unfaithful to Dwayne. I felt like I was breaking the longest fast I'd ever attempted.

What kind of fast offering could be equal to this?

"Please," I said. "Please."

Vaughn then pulled all the way out, and without missing a beat, shoved himself all the way in again. Then he did it another time. And another. A lot of guys were curved just enough that they sometimes missed when making the attempt, but Vaughn had no problem. His proprioception was on target. All the way in. All the way out. Like a needle on a sewing machine going into a piece of fabric. Over and over while I closed my eyes and thought of Dwayne and what image of him I might want to embroider next.

With a final lunge, Vaughn collapsed against me, lying motionless for a long moment. I breathed in the scent of sweaty god. When he finally pulled out and sat on the bed beside me, I turned onto my back without sitting up. "Thank you," I whispered, squeezing out some of his cum into my hand and raising it to my face.

No one ever forgot the smell of Grandma's cookies or Mom's apple pie.

The smell of semen transported me back to a cruel, difficult world where I'd still enjoyed the freedom to express my love as I chose.

Maya Angelou was right about the caged bird.

I put the cum in my mouth and moaned the way I had when Vaughn rubbed my chest all those years ago. I felched another bit of cum and then sat up beside my former companion. He leaned over and kissed me on the forehead.

"It'll be a couple of hours before Dwayne gets back," I said.

He nodded. "Shall we talk about our old mission days while we wait for him?"

I shook my head. "I want to hear about the plants and animals you're going to make for your planet," I said, "the vistas and waterfalls and rainbows." I let one hand rest on my tattooed mound.

"No," he replied, placing his hand on top of mine. He leaned over to whisper in my ear. "Tell me what kind of world you're going to make right here instead."

Subversion Therapy

The men held me down, binding my arms with padded leather straps to the arms of the chair, pulling the straps tight. Someone bound my ankles to the legs of the chair. Burly arms strapped my torso to the back. Then my head was placed in a vise, forcing me to look forward while locking me in place, like a routine eye exam turned into a horror movie.

I heard the blades of scissors scraping across each other and felt brief contact with cold metal as someone, or two someones, cut off my shirt, my pants, even my Mormon underwear.

"Don't worry," Dr. Penfield said. "We learn from pain." He patted my shaved head. "We grow." He stood in front of me, leaned down, and spit into my face. "It's the Lord's way."

The TV monitor in front of me flickered, bursting into life. A blond-haired man ejaculated on the face of another man with dark hair. He then turned around and leaned over, at which point the second man pressed his face into the first man's ass, rubbing it all around, trying to transfer the lines of cum into his ass. He stood, wiped the last of the cum from his forehead onto his dick and then shoved that dick into the first man's asshole.

I felt fingers reaching through the hole in the bottom of my chair and applying lube on my own asshole. A second later, a silicone object pressed past my sphincter, its size making me gasp.

The man on the screen pumped the ass in front of him as hard as he could.

The object entering my rectum pushed its way farther and farther inside. I tried to brace myself, but there was little I could do. I'd been sentenced by my bishop to aversion therapy as a cure for my homosexuality, and the first electric shock was about to be delivered.

My sphincter tightened around the object, trying to protect me.

"I'm going to press the switch now, Luke," Dr. Penfield said. He motioned to someone on the floor beneath me, and I suddenly felt deep vibrations in the core of my body. My ass quivered all over, inside and out.

"We found that cattle prods were a little too extreme," Dr. Penfield went on. "People are so litigious these days. But we use the largest vibrator we can find to make sure this is still an unpleasant experience."

I thought about the nine-inch dick my first boyfriend sported. "If you can handle this," he'd told me on our first date, "you're going to do just fine once you come out of the closet for good."

He'd only fucked me thirteen or fourteen times the one month we dated before the guilt became too overwhelming and I confessed to my bishop. Bishop Atkinson had insisted I register for a month-long ex-gay summer camp between semesters. We were too far from Utah for me to attend a Mormon facility, but the bishop assured me the evangelicals running this one knew what to do.

I'd be straight by the time I resumed studies for my Art degree.

The vibrator hummed away while I continued looking at the screen in front of me. A different scenario had begun, a line up at a police station, with a row of seven cocks jutting through holes in a partition. "Which of these was the weapon used against you?" an officer demanded the witness beside him.

The witness walked along the row of dicks, peering closely at two of them, lightly fingering another. "It's hard to tell just from looking," he told the officer. "I was facing the other way most of the time. I might need to feel them inside me to be sure."

"Okay, okay." The officer sighed wearily. "I just don't want to see you to suffer any more than necessary." He reached into his pocket. "The department requires I always carry some lube with me for emergencies. Let's have you try Dick Number One."

Something pinched my right nipple hard.

"Ouch!"

Something pinched my left nipple.

"Dagnabbit!" I said.

"Nipple clamps make sex unpleasant," Dr. Penfield said from some point outside my line of vision. "We have to make sure you start associating homosexual arousal with a need to stop thinking about men."

I watched as the police witness got fucked by Dick Number Two and then Dick Number Three.

My own cock throbbed, desperately seeking physical contact to release it from its torment.

I felt a hand applying lotion to my head and shaft, and I sighed. These guys weren't monsters, after all. They were therapists.

"Oh," I said, my brows furrowing. "Ow. Hey! What gives!"

The hand was no longer touching me, but whatever they'd applied to my dick was burning like jalapeños.

"We find that a regular warming gel isn't good enough," Dr. Penfield said. "We use a hot gel."

"Oh my god!" I said. "Do something!"

"We want you to understand what burning for an eternity in hell is like."

Someone abruptly pulled the vibrator out of my ass. I hoped they hadn't pulled out half my colon with it. Without the tiny bit of pleasure the vibrations had provided, the pain from my dick became overwhelming. I watched as the police witness was fucked by Dick Number Four.

Someone pressed the vibrator back against my ass. Before I had time to worry if this one was going to have ribs or spikes, the guy shoved the vibrator all the way back in.

"Oh my god!" They'd used the hot gel as lubricant this time around.

"Do you want to go to heaven?" asked Dr. Penfield. "Or do you want to go to hell?"

"*You* go to hell!"

I watched in agony as the police witness was fucked by Dick Number Five. He then dutifully backed up onto Dick Number Six.

"I think…" the witness said a moment later, "I think this might be the one."

"Great," the officer replied. "Let's wrap this up."

"Well, I want to be sure," the witness said, holding up a hand. "We don't want to send an innocent man to prison."

The officer looked at his watch and let Dick Number Six finish.

"I'd better try out the last one in case it's a close call."

"Here," said Dr. Penfield, "sip." He pressed a large straw to my lips. "It's thick and soothing and will help you get through this. Remember, you're here voluntarily. You can leave at any time."

I took a tentative sip, physically unable because of the vise to avert my face from the screen to see what I was drinking. The officer was now looking at the witness's dick while the witness was getting fucked by the last man in the lineup.

"Yeah," the witness said. "It isn't this guy. It was the last one. But I want this guy's phone number when we finish with our paperwork today."

The officer touched the witness's dick. "You know, if you're just having fun with Number Seven…" He kneeled down and took the witness's cock in his mouth.

I swallowed, realizing instantly Dr. Penfield was serving me cum. The taste was unmistakable.

My cock burned. My ass burned. I watched the fucking and sucking onscreen and took another sip.

"Drink up," Dr. Penfield said. "It's a whole cup. We make it artificially, but it's been taste-tested by many of our patients. We need you to create unpleasant associations with all aspects of gay sexuality." I heard the smile in his voice and took another sip. "They treat alcoholics this way, serve them all the liquor they can drink and then give them an emetic. And cum is so disgusting to begin with. Don't you just want to gag?" He chuckled.

I could hear loud suction a moment later as my straw scraped against the bottom of the empty cup. I'd been dreaming about swallowing that much cum all at one time ever since I had licked another student's palm clean after we beat off next to each other in a lightly frequented university bathroom in the math building.

As my eyes focused on the police officer's dick while he beat off onto the witness's ass, I suddenly realized two things: I had a bucket list of sexual fantasies I wanted to fulfill before I committed myself to a lifetime of hetero marriage, and I might be able to cross a couple of those items off during my month-long stay here.

Fulfilling just that one cum-chugging dream might make the rest of what I'd need to put up with today bearable. Maybe I could pretend I really hated cum and they'd make me drink more of it. That was how I'd gotten my first missionary companion to let me wash his feet every day.

It wasn't much, but at least I'd been able to touch skin for a few minutes just before bedtime those first three months.

"I *am* gagging, Dr. Penfield," I said. "I need something to wash that down. Please."

He put another straw to my lips. I sipped, got another mouthful of cum, and started humming Train's "Drops of Jupiter."

But that one brief moment of pleasure didn't last. Someone wound the nipple clamps tighter as the next scene appeared onscreen. I wasn't sure how long the session could continue. The reparative therapy camp was supposed to go on for a month, but they could hardly subject me to this kind of intense treatment eight hours a day, could they?

Two hours later, my leather cuffs were unfastened, and I was directed to walk naked down the hall to a large bathroom. Three of the attendants had left at some point while I was bound to the chair. The facility treated up to fifteen patients at a time. Only two young men in their mid-twenties stood beside me as Dr. Penfield pointed.

"You can't be serious," I said.

"I'll only be present during some of your sessions," he replied, "but I like to make sure your first day goes well."

It was the Christian thing to do, I supposed.

I stared at the tub.

"Bend over," one of the attendants said. I did, and he slid something long, wide, and cold quickly up my ass.

"An ice suppository," Dr. Penfield said. "We find it helps with the pain." He motioned to the tub again. "This will help even more."

I stepped into the mass of floating ice cubes. It burned more than the gel had, but I sat down, and within moments, I didn't feel anything at all.

I remembered how surprised I'd been to learn that almost no one drowned when the Titanic went down. 1500 people had instead frozen to death.

Most guys found Leonardo DiCaprio the sexiest man in that movie. But I'd always paused the scene where David Warner handcuffed Leo to a pipe, beating off while staring into David's face.

After a few minutes, the two attendants helped me out of the tub. I dried myself off and dressed in a loose gown. They led me down a hall, up some stairs, and down another hall. I never saw any of the other patients. One of the attendants pushed open a door and ushered me inside.

My room was small, but I saw a TV on the wall. There was a window on another wall, and while it didn't have bars, the panes had been replaced by another monitor. I could just make out a naked man running through a meadow.

"You'll be confined to your room the rest of your first day," Dr. Penfield said.

"But it's only 3:00!" I was guessing, really. There were no clocks anywhere, and my watch had been confiscated when I checked in this morning.

Dr. Penfield picked up a pitcher from the bedside table and poured me a glass of water. "Drink up," he said. "This is a stressful program. You need to stay hydrated." I wondered what he'd put in the water. Nothing was simple or straightforward here. I drank but stopped with half a glass left. "No," he said, "the whole thing." I forced the rest down.

He pointed to the bed, and I sat down.

"On your back," Dr. Penfield commanded.

I lay down.

"Spread your arms and legs."

And I had thought being bullied on my mission was bad. The one time I'd been caught masturbating after lights out had resulted in a sound spanking from my district leader. It had seemed so juvenile. Weren't we adults?

The attendants fastened my wrists to the top bedposts and then moved down to my feet and cuffed them to the lower bedposts. It wasn't until that moment I realized there was another monitor above my bed.

I hoped we didn't have an earthquake.

"Just a few more sips," Dr. Penfield said, holding another glass of water before me and slipping in a straw. I drank what I could and then shook my head.

I had a sudden realization. "Uh, how often are you guys going to check on me?" I asked. "Because…"

"No worries," Dr. Penfield said. He directed one of the attendants, who approached me with a long, thin tube. "We're going to catheterize you every night."

"What!"

"You must learn to hate everything associated with your penis."

I closed my eyes and gritted my teeth as they inserted the tubing.

"We'll start with a 16 French," Dr. Penfield said, whatever that meant. "Ethan will stay here and read you a bedtime story. And then you'll be alone to contemplate your eternal fate the rest of the evening." He and the other attendant left, while Ethan pulled a chair closer to the bed, reached into the bedside table, and pulled out a digest.

He cleared his throat. "The first story is 'Jack Off of All Trades.'" As I listened to his baritone voice read the salacious words, I could feel my dick stiffen, making the tubing pinch. Ethan put the book down when I made an involuntary noise. "That must be uncomfortable," he said. "I think maybe I can help."

Thank God. I thought I'd detected a glimmer of humanity in the man, something completely lacking in all the others.

God could not look upon sin with the least degree of allowance.

Ethan put his hand gently around my penis. I wasn't sure what he was up to, but his touch only made me stiffen more quickly. He pulled his hand away and opened the drawer in the bedside table again. My eyes widened when I saw him take out a metal cock ring. With spikes pointing inward.

"It's how Victorian mothers kept their sons from getting erections while they slept," he said.

Suddenly, the pinched tubing didn't seem all that bad.

"But why don't I just jack you off instead so your dick can relax?"

I frowned. Was he going to use that hot gel again?

He reached for my cock once more, grasping it gently and pulling upward. Then he let the skin down and pulled upward again.

He was going to give me a dry handjob. With the catheter still in place.

He pulled down harder and pulled up again harder, too. He increased his pace second by second, reaching climax speed well before I was ready to climax.

"Ethan!" I said. How could I ask him to stop? I'd given my consent to whatever therapy they deemed necessary when I signed all those papers during registration. "Ethan!"

With his free hand, Ethan reached into the drawer and pulled out a rubber ball on a leather strand. He popped it in between my teeth. "Mmnnngh!" I shouted.

Two torturous minutes later, I came, my penis burning more than it had at the height of the hot gel application.

Ethan fastened the gag more securely and put the digest away. "I'll see you in the morning, Luke," he said. He placed the metal cock ring with spikes around my penis. It had a little latch to keep it locked. He pushed a button on a remote, and the screen above the bed came to life.

He kissed me on the forehead. "We all love you, Luke. Remember, you can leave at any time."

"Nnnmmnfgh."

At the door, he looked back over his shoulder. "You know, in hell you can never orgasm. The devil will make you think about sex all the time, but you'll never be able to do anything about it." He walked out of the room. I heard his key in the lock before he headed off down the hallway.

I closed my eyes and tried to sleep, but the sound on the monitor above the bed was turned up too high for me to ignore. I watched four movies over the next several hours. *Like Stepfather Like Stepson*, *Inside a Priest's Ass*, *Lusty Leather Love*, and *Deep Esophagus*.

I was hungry, the cupful of cum long since moving on past my stomach.

I could feel a plastic bag lying against my thigh filled with warm piss that slowly turned cold.

I eventually fell asleep.

In the morning, Ethan and the other attendant assigned to me came to wake me up. "We have a big day planned for you," Ethan said cheerily. He pulled out the catheter and removed the bag of piss. He didn't remove my gag, though.

The other young man rolled two tall poles over so that they rested beside the lower bedposts, transferring my heels to positions high up both poles. "Tea or coffee?" Ethan asked brightly.

"Mmnnmmffgh."

"Coffee it is." Ethan directed the other young man, who inserted a tube up my ass. I felt a sudden influx of cold liquid.

Were coffee enemas against the Word of Wisdom?

"Keep it clenched," Ethan told me after the other man pulled out the tube. But I noticed he placed a tub right below my ass. "Let's start the morning off with a prayer. Jeremy, will you offer it?"

The other young man bowed his head and began speaking so softly I could barely hear him at first.

It felt like a live creature was twisting about in my colon.

I hoped they hadn't sent a gerbil up there.

"And please change Luke's soul so he can live in your presence for eternity."

I couldn't hold it any longer. A flood of coffee and other debris shot into the tub at the base of the bed. The two young men looked completely unfazed. Jeremy carted the tub away while Ethan cleaned me up.

Who could be embarrassed at this point?

"Ready for breakfast?" he asked.

He pushed a button, and the upper portion of the mattress moved forward until I was at a forty-five degree angle. Awkward, of course, with my hands still low while both feet hung high in the air. Another movie played overheard, but I could no longer see it, so Ethan pushed a button on another remote, and the TV against the wall began to show a new movie.

Offering a Helping Hand...or Mouth...or Ass.

Ex-gay Christianity was all about turning the other ass cheek, I supposed.

Ethan removed the gag from my mouth, and I slowly worked my jaws. Damn, they were sore. He pulled a small wheeled cart over that he and Jeremy had brought with them this morning and lifted a lid from a plastic container, revealing scrambled eggs. "Open wide." Ethan scooped up a spoonful of egg and placed it in my mouth.

Cold. With no salt or pepper.

"Wash it down with this," he said, holding a straw to my lips. The coffee mug was opaque, but the first sip revealed another cupful of artificial cum.

Bryan Cranston was selling the wrong stuff.

Ethan applied nipple clamps to my tits, winding them tighter until I winced. Then he caressed my balls. And squeezed them until I winced again.

My mother's chemotherapy regimen hadn't been this extreme. I knew she was in Paradise now, waiting for Judgment Day when she would be welcomed into the Celestial Kingdom.

Ethan fed me another few spoonfuls of cold scrambled egg with the cum chaser.

When Jeremy returned, he brought a washcloth and basin and gave me a bath in bed, taking an inordinately long time with my dick and ass.

"Is it Picture Day for the yearbook?" I asked.

Jeremy smiled. "Something like that."

When I was finally uncuffed, I stood and tried to work out all the kinks in my muscles. I was only too happy to walk under my own control back downstairs to one of the treatment rooms. One day down. Only twenty-nine more to go.

I wondered if anyone had ever died here. Moral busybodies always seemed to kill an occasional charge in wayward teen camps or Indian Boarding Schools or homes for unwed mothers.

This time, I was positioned lying prone on a kind of massage table with a hole cut out for my groin. My arms were cuffed in place, my head held again in a vise pointing downward to a TV screen flat on the floor below me. Ethan and Jeremy spread my legs and cuffed them in place.

"Dr. Penfield isn't coming today," Ethan said. "Here's a couple of pills for you." He reached down and pushed three pills into my mouth, followed by another straw. I sucked deeply and quickly, the position quite awkward for swallowing pills. The liquid this time tasted like coffee.

Fresh, I hoped.

"So we gave you two ED pills," Ethan explained, "and an ibuprofen."

"An ibuprofen?"

"Relax and enjoy the movie, Luke. We'll take care of the rest."

I watched as *Well-Hung Jury* began. The deliberations looked quite intense. Here in the treatment room, the combination of gravity, Viagra, and porn soon had my cock engorged. Some of the jurists onscreen tried their best to convince the others to vote their way. "How do you vote?" a man with an unbelievably large cock demanded.

Was that CGI?

"Guilty!"

The man thrust his cock inside the jurist. "How do you vote now?"

"Guilty!"

The man had to be convinced by several more jurists before he changed his tune. But he looked as if he could be singing a cover of Jason Mraz's "I'm Yours" every time he looked back at that CGI cock.

My dick was throbbing. I'd heard of men being able to cum just by emotional stimulation, but I still seemed to need physical contact. I was primed and ready to shoot but couldn't without some tangible help.

The first movie was followed by *Two Holes in One*, detailing the escapades of a golfer and his caddy who together kept taking advantage of the golfer's mouth and anus. I felt someone pressing an object against my ass again.

After a month here, I thought with a grim smile, I should be able to accommodate any man I went home with.

Except I wasn't going to go home with men ever again.

"Unh." The object had gone past my sphincter too quickly.

"It's a golf ball," I heard Ethan say.

I felt another ball follow it, and another, and another. Ethan didn't stop until he'd shoved ten golf balls up my ass. How often would I ever have to accommodate such a thing even if I did come out permanently?

"And now to associate the proper unhappiness…" Ethan's voice trailed off. I heard someone fumbling on the floor beneath me, and a moment later, Ethan spread the damn hot gel all over my penis again.

I watched the caddy lube up one of the golf clubs and slowly insert one end into the golfer.

Ethan stood up and smacked me sharply on the butt. He dug around for the last golf ball inside me and pulled quickly, ripping all ten golf balls out at once, all of them apparently tied together.

I shouted.

"Do we need to gag him again?" I heard Jeremy ask.

There was no audible answer, but a moment later, someone popped a round gag into my mouth.

One of the two men wiped my ass carefully while the other reapplied the nipple clamps. I couldn't see who was doing what, and it distressed me. I wanted Ethan to be attending to my ass. The door opened, and another man walked into the room wearing paper footies over his shoes. He pulled a chair up beside me and turned on a bright overhead light.

"What's your favorite kind of sex?" Ethan asked. Was he talking to me?

"Nnnmmph."

A moment later, the movie changed. *Filthy Garbagemen* began playing in the trash, using various objects on and in each other.

I felt hands on my ass. Was that Ethan?

"Gghh!" I shouted. "Sshhhmmngh!"

"A permanent tattoo is part of the therapy," Ethan said. "Relax and watch your movie. We did give you an ibuprofen, you know."

The tattoo artist began drilling on my ass again, starting at my anus and working outward. I'd never felt such pain before, never believed it was possible.

"He's tattooing flames," Ethan whispered in my ear, "so anyone who sees your ass will be reminded of the eternal fate that awaits them."

"Phhhrrgh!"

"He's going to include a couple of little screaming faces and maybe a few waving arms."

I thought I was going to pass out. I'd had so little nourishment since arriving. But lying down made it difficult to muster the forces necessary to willfully lose consciousness.

"I'm sorry this is so hard for you," Ethan whispered again. "It gets better, though, really." He paused. "Let me see what I can do to help." He walked away, and when he returned a moment later, I felt a sharp sting against my back. "I'll flog you for a little while," he said. "It'll take your mind off the needles. Kind of like a TENS unit."

He whipped me with a leather flogger for the next fifteen minutes. I could tell he wasn't drawing blood, despite the pain. He wouldn't leave any scars. But I could feel my skin becoming raw.

"Jeremy, he needs something more."

Oh my god.

I could hear Jeremy scrambling on the floor beneath me and felt his hands on my chest. He removed the nipple clamps and wiped my nipples with a cloth.

Maybe the relief would help me channel my energies to the other battles.

My penis was still burning from the gel, my ass was burning with the constant jabbing of needles, my back was burning from the flogging.

I watched as the garbagemen found some used condoms and slid them onto their dicks.

"Mmmnnffph!"

"Decadent gay men get nipple piercings," Jeremy said from below. "We'll keep this clean so it heals quickly. Hopefully, you'll be cured before we have to resort to piercing anything more sensitive." He flicked my cock with his finger. It felt like a bullet wound.

I was a wrung out cum rag by the time the movie ended almost three hours later. The tattoo artist continued for just a few more minutes and then declared his work finished. "It is done." His chair screeched across the floor as he moved it back toward the wall.

After giving me another ice bath, Ethan and Jeremy both attended to my ass, making sure it was sanitary for the time being, applying some kind of sticky film to both cheeks. Fried prairie oysters with yet another cup of artificial cum was my only meal for the remainder of the day. Ethan rubbed some lotion on my inflamed back.

Desperately thirsty, I drank the two glasses of cold water he gave me as fast as I could, and then he and Jeremy tied me back to the bedposts, still only mid-afternoon.

There was no catheter this time. Was I supposed to lie in my own urine half the night?

"See you at Bible Study," Jeremy said to Ethan, waving as he walked out the door.

"Later."

Ethan turned back to me. "Do you want the gag again or are you going to be quiet this evening?" He looked at me a moment and then nodded. "Good."

He pulled an unfamiliar device out of the bedside table. From my position, I could barely see what he held in his hands. It looked like a stainless steel tiger, maybe six inches long. He leaned over and set the device on my crotch.

"What are you doing?"

"You said you were going to be quiet."

Ethan slid the tiger over my dick so that the raging fangs hung just millimeters over the tip of my head. The body of the tiger covered the rest of my penis, and there was some sort of base that he clamped around my balls. He pushed a leather strap under me and pulled it up around my waist. I heard a small padlock click shut.

"It's a male chastity belt," Ethan explained. "No one can suck you, you can't fuck anyone, you can't beat off." He handed me two more of the ED pills and let me sip another glass of cold water.

Twenty-eight more days. Plus whatever was still left in store for me this evening.

Ethan inserted another catheter through the tiger's open mouth. "22 French tonight," he offered casually. He turned on the TV facing downward from the ceiling. When a load of cum shot across a man's back, he froze the picture and pulled out the digest he'd been reading from the night before. "This Little Piggy Cried Wee Wee Wee All the Way Home," he read. A story about a middle-aged man committed to pig urine followed.

I did not get hard, even with all the erectile chemicals running through me.

Ethan looked at my tiger, frowned, and began another story. "Go Fuck Yourself." A scientist created his own clone so he could have the kind of skilled sex only he could provide.

I'd often wished I could suck my own cock.

The catheter tubing pinched. Ethan smiled. "I can't beat you off tonight," he said, putting the digest down. He unpaused the image on the TV above the bed. The man who'd just cum wiped the other man's back off with the palm of his hand and then made the second man lick his hand.

I wish I'd gotten that other student's name.

The tubing pinched again.

I closed my eyes and gritted my teeth. My dick felt like a snake trying to shed its skin. Surely, my cock couldn't stay confined in its current physical space. I needed additional skin.

"The best I can do…" Ethan's voice trailed off as he stood beside the bed and took off his pants. He applied some of the hot gel to his dick, gasping in pain, but he kept steadily stroking himself without any hesitation. He climbed onto the bed and kneeled between my legs, giving me a clear view. Not CGI but close enough. He stroked himself slowly at first and then faster and faster.

He began groaning and aimed his dick right at the gaping mouth of the tiger.

His cum splashed across the head of the tiger and into its mouth, across the head of my penis, a little of it trickling down the shaft. I didn't think about catheter hygiene. I just wanted to fuck Ethan, with or without my chastity belt on. "Oh Lord!"

Ethan climbed off the bed and put his face down close to mine. "You can never cum in hell," he reminded me.

He moved back down to the foot of the bed. "But I won't leave you like that all night." He applied more of the hot gel to his fingers and reached for my ass.

After all those needles…

I cried out as the heat seared into my overstimulated nerves. Ethan pushed two fingers deep inside me, felt around for a moment, and then pressed hard against my prostate.

"Aaahhh!"

The tiger was a wet, sticky mess both inside and out. Ethan stood, making no effort to clean either my penis or my ass, the tattooed flames feeling transformed into reality. "Enjoy the rest of your movies," he said. "I'll see you in the morning."

Before the week was out, I had a demon tattooed on my dick, my other nipple had been pierced, and I was sporting a Prince Albert. Dr. Penfield stopped by on occasion to spit on me. I'd been tied to a St. Andrews cross, had a silicone hand inserted into my ass, hot wax dripped onto me, and been flushed with both a tea enema and a piss enema.

Was a piss enema against the Word of Wisdom?

Twenty-one more days to go.

"You know," Ethan told me again one evening after applying hot gel to both of my recovering nipples, "you can leave at any time. Just say the word. You're not a prisoner." He fastened my ankle cuffs.

"Can I…" I struggled to find the words. "Can I…?"

"Can you what?" Ethan squirted some hot gel up my ass.

"Can I…stay here forever?"

Ethan stopped with the bottle of hot gel poised over my catheterized dick. I was up to a 32 French now. "Forever is a long time." He dripped the lube onto me. "Forever is eternity."

"You've been trying to show me what hell is like," I said. "And I'm fine with what I see."

Ethan stood and shook his head sadly, looking as if he'd just had to put his dog to sleep. He pulled over the two poles that were resting against the wall and transferred my bound feet to them, lifting them up and back as he rolled the poles halfway up the length of the bed. He climbed onto the bed and kneeled before me.

"It's no good, is it?" he said, his tone full of melancholy. "My father's a pastor. Doing this work is the only way I can atone for disappointing him." He caressed my abdomen for several moments. "But the fear of God can never match the fear of missing out on love."

He unzipped, pulled out his cock, and slathered hot gel across it, wincing a moment, and shaking his head to get beyond it. Then he pushed himself inside me too fast—not nearly fast enough—and fucked me as hard as only years of frustration could inspire.

When he finished, he lowered my legs to the bedposts and lay on top of me all night. His weight made it hard to breathe, but I sang Maroon 5's "This Love Has Taken Its Toll on Me" to him as a lullaby until he fell asleep.

Ethan left the facility with me the next morning. After a few years of hard work and study, I was eventually crowned Mr. Mormon Leather. Ethan earned a Master's in Counseling, and with my work designing slings, we got by well enough, tying each other up painfully ever after.

My Mormon Rumspringa

The zombie's cock was so huge that every time he thrust forward, I lost my breath. His dick may only have gone as far as the end of my rectum, but it seemed to push my other organs upward against the bottom of my lungs. I could only briefly catch my breath when he pulled back a few inches before thrusting again.

All those zombie movies and TV shows growing up hadn't prepared me for this. I'd always lusted after the breathing characters. Though there'd been a couple of vampires on *Buffy* I wouldn't have minded entering me. Maybe a demon or two from *Charmed.*

But demons were alive, of course.

The zombie stared at me with dead eyes. There were three clawed slash marks on his neck, pustules across his forehead, mucus dripping from his nose. The skin high on his right cheek was peeling back. A fly rested on the tip of his left ear. He kept staring at me, no expression on his face as he shoved his dick inside me again as far as it would go.

How the hell did I end up in this position?

Well, I liked being fucked face to face.

"Unh," I said, my voice vibrating as I rocked back and forth on the hood of the zombie's car. "I absolutely love those tattoos."

Patrick wiped his brow. It was hot in his garage. "Joshua, if you're not ready for something this bold," he said, grunting as he got closer, "you can at least start out with vampire fang marks on your neck."

Something that could be concealed if I buttoned my shirt to the top and put on a tie.

I thought about Angel from *Buffy* again. And Spike.

I still remembered the day I heard about the Revelation of the Prodigal Son. My parents and I watched the press conference on the BYU channel, where we could hear the entire thing. The Prophet had already announced several changes to missionary work over the past few years, lowering the age for both male and female missionaries, allowing brief "two transfer" missions, and making other such adjustments. Too many Mormon youth these days were refusing to go on the missions their parents expected them to.

In my grandfather's day, foreign missions had dragged on for three long years. Now it was hard to get young people to go at all.

The latest revelation announced yet another variation. Young men who didn't want to serve a proselyting mission could instead do an eighteen-month "prodigal" mission, go out and live in the "real" world and see for themselves how unfulfilling worldly pleasures could be. Parents still paid for those missions like always, but the hope was that this avenue for "safer sin" would help the Church retain a larger number of rebellious youth.

The program was only open to young men at this time, the Church spokesperson had said, "but we're awaiting word from the Lord to see if this opportunity will eventually be offered to the young women as well."

"It's like the Amish rumspringa," my mother said as the spokesperson laid out more details of the change.

My father shook his head. "No, that's Satan's plan. This is Heavenly Father's plan. The prodigal missionaries still need to attend church at least once a month. That's more than some young Mormons do who aren't in the program." He'd glanced my way.

Zombie Patrick was still pumping like there was no yesterday. He'd had pustules and stab wounds tattooed all over his arms and chest as well. I'd seen his dick before he slipped the condom on. It was covered in pustules, too. He wiped a drop of sweat now from his pustuled brow. Another dripped onto my abdomen. His water-based lube was losing its slickness, starting to chafe as it grew stickier.

"Sorry," he said in response to a grimace I must have made. "It doesn't usually take me this long."

"Live bodies not as big a turn on?" I asked with a smile.

He nodded, slinging another couple of drops my way. I'd met him at the butcher counter in the grocery store, after all. "It's better if you don't bathe first," he said, "or wear deodorant." I'd already figured out that body odor was part of his persona. He kept pumping, and my ass was no longer just burning but downright hurting.

"You okay?" He didn't stop grinding away.

"I'm a Mormon," I told him. "We're taught to endure to the end."

"A Mormon?" He paused just a second, his eyes lighting up for the first time. He seemed to catch a second wind.

"I'm a missionary."

Along came a third wind, so I kept talking. "I have to report everything to my mission president once a week."

"Fuck!"

"And those emails get preserved in the Church archives."

"Oh, fuck!" he shouted again.

"They'll probably use excerpts when they compile a history of the missionary program one day."

"Aagghh!" Zombie Patrick screamed like a man being split in two as he came. But I was the one who was going to have a hard time walking back to the bus stop. He closed his eyes and rested a bit with his dick still inside me. I considered beating off before he pulled out, but instead I looked about his garage, with a shelf for everything and everything in its place. Patrick was one well-organized zombie.

I didn't think I wanted to have sex on the hood of a car again, though, not even Patrick's which had just been waxed. But that's what my mission was for—to see that a normal life was better than decadence.

Zombie Patrick finally pulled out, peeling off the condom and dropping it in a bucket near the wall. "God, I love when people talk holy."

Excellent, I thought, the Holy Ghost whispering in my ear. I wouldn't have to beat myself off, after all. "Get on your knees and pray!" I ordered. He dropped without thinking, and I slid off the car, pointing my dick in his face. "Take. Eat. This is my body."

Over the next couple of minutes, I got the best zombie blow job of my life.

After I washed up, Patrick gave me an odorous hug that would require washing up again later, and I headed back for the bus stop almost a mile away. Patrick was a suburban zombie with a large house and manicured lawn, living in the kind of neighborhood I'd grown up in.

And yet he still wasn't the zombie-next-door type I could bring home to my parents. I wasn't sure of his job title but assumed he did much of his work from home. I couldn't see him as a bank manager.

Or plastic surgeon.

I supposed I needed to start thinking of my own future. I was nearing the end of my eighteen months, and it only now occurred to me I should have been doing more than having fun and exploring my sexuality. If I didn't have a boyfriend, or better yet a fiancé, by the time I went home, I might have to go back into the closet for the rest of my life.

I'd taken a couple of basic courses at a community college here, things that could be easily transferred to another institution. But I insisted on keeping my load light. I didn't want my mission to be as miserable as those of the proselyting elders.

I'd followed one of my instructors into a staff bathroom one afternoon and sucked him off to lighten *his* load. I'd met with another instructor after mid-terms and asked if there was "anything" I could do to raise my grade from a B to an A.

"I'll even have your baby," I told him, "if you want to try getting me pregnant."

He tried four times before the end of the semester.

When I showed him the negative pregnancy test results after our last encounter, he laughed and said, "Okay, now *that* will get you an A."

I hoped my parents wouldn't make me attend Brigham Young University after my mission. I expected pee sticks wouldn't help my GPA much there.

I passed a couple of retired folks puttering around in their yards as I neared the bus stop, but it was early on a Tuesday afternoon, so most of the homes and yards were quiet.

I'd have to look up what percentage of Rumspringa kids went back to the farm.

If I chose not to return to the Latter-chaste fold, the leaders might find that too many youth were leaving permanently. They might terminate the prodigal mission program, and I knew there were plenty of other young Mormons who could benefit from it.

"It's like when Jesus went into the desert for forty days," my mother had said.

"Only Jesus never succumbed to temptation," I'd replied, "and you know I will."

"Oh, Joshua, you could never fall into *too* much sin." She smiled sweetly. My father had given me a glance revealing he knew otherwise. But they'd both agreed to let me put in my papers.

I knew a good many Mormons became engaged within a month of their first date. I could manage it in the time I had left.

I worked the evening shift at Earl's Sandwich shop three nights a week. I didn't technically have to work while on my mission, any more than I needed to take college classes, but it was boring not to have *any* structure, and it wouldn't be easy to explain the gap on future job interviews. I could hardly say, "Oh, I took eighteen months off to fuck around for my church."

Well, perhaps I could if I applied at whatever company employed Patrick.

I wondered what a zombie would look like after the resurrection.

The job at the sandwich shop was made easier by the proximity of Ass in Boots four blocks away. Supposedly a leather bar, it catered more to the Levi and plaid shirt crowd. Since I liked butch guys, I spent a couple of hours at Ass in

Boots after every shift. I'd need to focus these last few weeks on seeking out marriage material rather than Last Calls. A lot of gay men, I'd discovered, didn't even want to be boyfriends, much less husbands. Fuck buddies or plain old anonymous hookups seemed to be the norm.

One of the lessons I was supposed to learn out here?

I did go home with three guys a few days later. As a Mormon, I certainly wasn't opposed to polyandry. But these guys weren't looking for a fourth. They had me take off my underwear—Calvin Klein, to be clear, not the kind my parents had made me stock up on after going through the temple. Levi Guy #1 shot into my shorts. Levi Guy #2 followed suit. Leather Vest Guy #1 then added his load. The three men took turns jacking me off into my underwear as the climax to our tryst.

"Now put them back on," Levi Guy #1 said.

"We're going back to the bar together," Leather Vest Guy #1 explained.

"And we'll stay with you till you pick up another guy in your cummy undies," Levi Guy #2 concluded.

It worked out okay, as a guy in chaps came back to my place and licked what little cum he could still extract from my underwear before depositing his own wad in the back pocket of my jeans.

Were straight people this weird?

I thought back to the endowment ceremony in the temple and the prayer circle just before going through the veil, with eight men and women pawing at the air like cats.

The guy I hooked up with on Grindr a few days later seemed cut out of the same Naugahyde, wanting us to reenact the famous scene from *There's Something about Mary*. We both ended up with cum combed into our hair. His smelled like rosemary.

I wondered what my parents giggled about in their bedroom on Saturday nights.

As four weeks dwindled down to two and a half, I tried one of the bathhouses in town, mostly an observer this time. I wasn't bad looking, but I certainly didn't find a willing sex partner every time I sought one. There was a lot to see at the bathhouse, of course, even in the dim light, and that could be almost as fun as participating. I mostly watched sucking and fucking, but one group in the porn room tried something I hadn't seen before.

The main guy sucked off one of the other guys, normal enough, but then walked over to a third man who was kneeling and let the cum in his mouth dribble into the third guy's open mouth. The main guy then sucked off a different man and returned to the kneeling guy who'd taken the first transferred load, dribbling that load into his eager mouth, too. I watched as the main guy deposited yet another mouthful of cum into the mouth of the guy on his knees.

It was like watching a mother bird feed her chick.

Or a father bird.

Did the leaders in Salt Lake realize exactly what we prodigals were experiencing every day?

Sheesh. Did those elderly men play around like this with their elderly wives?

Well, if they wanted to, why shouldn't they? Elderly men played around with me all the time.

I wondered if I could ever marry a Molly Mormon after what I'd experienced as a missionary. And would she have any desire to marry an RP?

Returned Prodigals was already what we were being called, despite the leaders ordering members to call us RMs when we completed our gig, just like the other Returned Missionaries.

The night before reporting to the mission president for my exit interview, I tried one last time to find the man of my dreams. The only leather I could afford was an armband to put around my upper left arm, but I also found a pair of tattoo sleeves that made it look like my arms were tattooed, and I wore those as well.

My watch covered the lower end of the left tattoo sleeve, and I just hoped in the dim barlight no one noticed the blunt lower end of the right sleeve. If they did, it was no big deal. I wasn't really pretending, just playing, but I wanted the costume to look reasonably realistic.

The trick was in not putting anything too incredible on my arms that would draw closer inspection. I ended up with a snake wrapping itself around each arm. I would have splurged for some kind of condom tattoo sleeve and put a dragon on my dick, but if such a thing existed, I was unable to locate it.

Other than that, all I wore was a white T-shirt and a pair of black jeans.

I stood near the pool table and looked at men's butts when they leaned over to make a shot. When a guy in jeans and a harness leaned against the wall next to me to wait for his turn at the table, I tried a line from a commercial I'd seen.

"Want to taste my beer?" I asked. I showed him the bottle and then took a sip. I lowered the bottle to my side and tilted my face toward him just a degree or two, hoping the implication was clear.

If it was, he wasn't interested, glancing at me a moment like I was a fly that had just settled on his hamburger.

Or a crab that had just settled on his balls.

I was lucky crabs were the worst thing I'd gotten out here. In addition to the usual vaccinations a missionary had to undergo before entering the mission field, I'd gotten the HPV vaccine and both hepatitis vaccines as well. My parents' insurance covered PrEP, and with my relatively consistent attempts to be careful—notwithstanding my algebra instructor—I'd never contracted anything else, as far as I knew.

I walked out onto the back patio, completely unlit except for whatever thin beams struggled over the walls from the surrounding neighborhood. Someone bumped into me in the dark. A hand grabbed my crotch.

How the guy knew exactly where to reach based solely on the sensory input he received from bumping into me, I didn't know. Maybe in addition to gaydar, some guys used echologaytion.

"Will you piss for me?" he whispered.

"Uh, no, I don't think so." Should I thank him for the offer, I wondered? I still hadn't completely mastered gay etiquette.

Too bad prodigal missions weren't a full two years.

The man squeezed just a little too hard in parting and moved off. I backed up against the rear wall of the bar to stay out of the mingling zone while my stomach settled. I heard lots of other whispers around me, perhaps other attempts at echolocation.

"Are you sure you won't piss for me?" the same voice in front of me asked.

Was the guy still around? I supposed etiquette required a more direct answer. "You should probably move on to yellower pastures," I whispered back. But perhaps that wasn't direct enough, either.

A moment later, I heard an odd pattering noise. Was someone else pissing for him? It didn't sound like a normal urine stream because it was hitting something other than water or porcelain or pavement. It took me another second to realize the pisser was aiming in my direction, hitting the crotch of my jeans.

"Hey!" I shouted.

The guy moved off, and there'd be no way to figure out who the culprit was, even if the bar manager turned on the light. I walked back through the bar, out the front door, and headed home.

I was a little subdued during my interview the following day, still subdued when I met my parents at the airport that evening. "I cooked a pot roast for you!" my mother said cheerily, giving me a tight hug. My favorite meal. "I can see on your face you're ready to leave that life!"

Dad seemed to sense the real reason for my mood. "Let's get you home, son. Have you thought about what college you want to attend?"

At least he understood I needed other options besides BYU.

"I want to take a shower," I said when we walked into the house. Not quite as clean as Patrick's, I noticed. My mother remarked that wanting to be physically clean showed I wanted to be morally clean, too.

While I felt no compulsion to correct her, the truth was I needed to ease myself back into Mormon family life, and a long, hot shower gave me a few minutes to relax before picking up my shield again.

Garments. Ugh.

"This pot roast hits the spot," I told Mom a little later. "And you cooked these carrots just right."

She beamed at my father.

"Were you able to learn how to cook for yourself these past eighteen months?" Dad asked me.

I shrugged. "I can tackle the basics." I'd learned how to make a pretty good lasagna, experimenting over and over till I got it right, but that wasn't something you could eat every day. Thankfully, Earl had taught me that even sandwiches didn't need to be boring.

"I made your favorite dessert," Mom said. "Lemon meringue pie with Cool Whip instead of egg whites, covered with sprinkles!"

I forced a weak smile. I wasn't a child anymore, unsure if I could generate my previous enthusiasm for innocent pleasures.

One guy I'd played with my first month in the field had sucked on a pacifier after we went to bed for the night. He'd had it specially designed in the shape of a two-inch penis. "It's to keep me from grinding my teeth in my sleep," he explained.

At least he hadn't put on a diaper.

I wondered if I was suffering PTSD. I hoped I wasn't going to experience these kinds of reactions from now on over every innocent remark my family and the other Mormons in my life made.

I enjoyed the rest of the meal, only taking a small slice of pie, as I wanted to be *able* to find a nice, sexy man, even if I didn't go out and *do* it.

Three days later was my first Sunday back in my home ward. I was scheduled, of course, to give a short talk on "Sin Is Never Safe." I figured I could get through ten minutes whether I believed what I was saying or not.

And really, I simply didn't know what I believed yet. Perhaps I needed a few months or a year of obeying every commandment and then compare the two experiences. After all, I could hardly claim to have been all that obedient before my mission.

As the organist played the prelude music, I thought back to the evening I watched *Trick* with the first guy who ever fucked me.

When Brother Odom offered the opening prayer, I thought about the Iraqi war vet who liked me to fuck him through a hole in the seat of his fatigues using a camouflage-colored dildo.

This just wouldn't do. I needed to make more of an effort. I directed my full attention to Bishop McFadden when he spoke before the organist began playing the Sacrament hymn and the young priests got ready to bless the bread. He looked a lot like the bartender who'd served me my first rum and Coke. I turned away.

I saw a man in the congregation who looked a lot like Patrick.

"Take," I thought. "Eat."

I surveyed the sparse crowd and saw my mother and father gazing back at me, Mom smiling brightly, Dad looking a little sad.

A priest I didn't recognize blessed the bread, and then the deacons lined up to take their trays to everyone in the pews. There probably weren't even eighty people here today, and that was saying something, given that three families alone had brought nineteen children with them.

I was glad to be an only child.

But I knew the heartache that not having grandchildren would bring my parents. With the right amount of dedication and commitment and luck, I might be able to maintain celibacy, but I was never going to take the chance of ruining a woman's life.

Hell, as trashy as I'd behaved the past eighteen months, I'd probably ruin a man's life just as easily.

I watched as the deacons passed the trays down each row.

I wondered what everyone else here was thinking about. On the few occasions I'd sat on the stand, I was struck by how few congregants were paying attention.

Brother Ulrich, presiding over his brood of four, looked a great deal like the guy who'd brought me to his apartment to explore his treasure map. He'd had it tattooed across his lower back and ass, a giant, red X needled into his flesh right across his anus.

That must have stung.

I'd dug and drilled and plowed for treasure three times that night. We hardly got any sleep. The next day had been one of the Sundays I was supposed to attend church to maintain my official active status. I'd sat at the back of the chapel, the back of priesthood meeting, the back of Sunday School.

But today I was up on the stand, three seats over from the bishop. Good Latter-day Saints were supposed to use this time to reflect on the Savior's atonement and our recommitment to following the gospel.

But things didn't get any better when the deacons started passing the water. The trays reminded me of a guy who'd picked me up at a bus stop and brought me to his place to help him prepare for a friend's birthday party. He had me piss in an ice tray to make little penis-shaped yellow ice cubes that he planned to serve with fresh, chilled lemonade. "Everyone likes a little thrill at a party," he told me.

Only a handful of the gay guys I'd ever met were into piss, but boy, those few were really into it.

I'd left before the party started.

"Sin is never safe," I told myself as I took a tiny paper cup of water from the tray that had been passed to me. I didn't want to live like some of the men I'd met. I simply wouldn't do it. I was home, in church. Partaking of the sacrament was a weekly reset button.

There was so little I hadn't done these past few months. That was the whole point of a prodigal mission, of course. And the Prophet had said it was okay. Surely, all the gay sin was out of my system now. I could still live in one of the "many mansions" inside Heavenly Father's kingdom.

There was more to life than sex, after all. More to eternity. And it wasn't as if even twenty-year-old men with raging hormones never thought about anything else. Gene and I had first met for sex but ended up being movie friends, watching *12 Years a Slave, Gravity*, and *Blinded by the Light*. Darren and I ended up hiking buddies, taking long walks together through a nearby state park. And Clarissa, a young woman I shared a table with while drinking my first latte, invited me to join her book club. Most of the books did little for me, but I'd rarely read outside of church or class assignments before, so the experience was almost as eye-opening as Ass in Boots.

Shobha Rao's *Girls Burn Brighter* was more memorable than anything the brother of Jared ever said.

I rubbed the cover of my leather-bound Book of Mormon softly.

The first speaker today was Sister Cook, who talked about how she'd helped a neighbor suffering from guilt over having won a thousand dollars in the lottery and putting most of it toward her mortgage. "I told her to refinance and then give a thousand dollars to a charity of her choice if she wanted to turn ill-gotten gain into something positive. I suggested the Family History Center. Her new interest rate is half a point higher, but I helped her accept that as God's reminder to always do the right thing the first time."

A couple of minutes later, it was my turn.

"Brothers and sisters," I began, "it's good to see you again after eighteen months away as a missionary." I knew I didn't have to specify which kind of mission I'd served. Every single adult and half the kids there knew the category exactly. "Most missionaries talk about how they've just experienced the 'best two years' of their life. But I can't say that."

And not just because prodigal missions only lasted eighteen months.

"Sin is never safe," I said, wanting to get the required phrase out of the way as quickly as possible. "But obedience is never safe, either." My father's eyes looked directly into mine. "Chastity is never safe." Mom closed her eyes. "The truth is that nothing in life is safe. You make the best choices you can and learn to live with them."

I thought back to my first Christmas in the field. A few weeks previously, I'd hooked up with a guy who showed me his large dildo collection. We took turns over the next couple of weeks using them on each other. The German shepherd dildo was the biggest one I could take, but Andrei liked the donkey dong dildo and the Brahma bull dildo best, and there were lots more.

He didn't own a dog, thank goodness, but he did have a doggy door leading to his back yard, and he loved for me to fuck him doggy style through the doggy door. For Christmas, I'd given him a blow-up Billy goat doll.

Even though his straight friends and his straight sister were present, he hugged me for a good two minutes because we both understood it wasn't a gag gift, no matter how much the other guests laughed.

"Joshua?" I felt a hand on my shoulder. "You okay?"

"Oh, excuse me, Bishop." I looked out over the congregation again. My parents both looked back with their brows furrowed. I leaned into the microphone. "I say this in the name of Jesus Christ. Amen." I sat back down three seats from the bishop. He jumped up and gave an impromptu talk to take up the unexpected free time, and then he turned the mic over to the last speaker, an older man somewhere along the spectrum.

Brother Batts had never married and talked for several minutes about how animals—ferrets, specifically—were going to the Celestial Kingdom because they filled the measure of their creation. We all needed to be kinder to animals, he said, just like Androcles had been, because they might hold our fate in their paws.

One of the best Sacrament talks I'd heard in a while.

As we exited the chapel later, my mother squeezed my hand. "You'll get used to giving talks again soon." My father squeezed my shoulder but said nothing.

I sat in the back of the room during Gospel Doctrine and again during priesthood meeting. As soon as class let out, I headed for Bishop McFadden's office. "I've been expecting you," he said.

"Oh?"

"I'm not stupid, you know."

"I...uh..."

"You're here to start getting your papers ready for a second mission. It used to only happen once in a great while with the proselyting elders, but it's happening a lot these days with the young men who've served prodigal missions."

"Bishop, I..."

"Of course, with all the different types of missions these days, we can't have you just repeat yourself."

"I'm not—"

"The Church is starting a new pilot program. We're not ready to roll it out publicly yet, so you'll need to be discreet about this."

"Bishop…"

"This time you'll serve the entire two years, and this time, you'll live with the proselyting elders."

My heart felt like it might stop beating. I was never going to get to live my life. My missions would last *three and a half years*! That was even worse than the old foreign missions.

I'd come to ask if he could recommend a Church physician to prescribe some kind of anti-aphrodisiac.

"We'll send you somewhere where the elders live four or six to an apartment. You'll do the cooking and cleaning and laundry and shopping for the other elders, but you won't have to do any proselyting."

"I'm going to be a maid?" There were already members who weren't impressed by an RP. I didn't think this would raise my status any. But maybe the M for maid would erase my current stigma.

"Of course, your primary calling will be to service the other elders."

"Excuse me?"

"You don't realize how stressful it is to knock on doors for two years. Those poor elders need something to relieve that stress. It's a win/win for everyone."

I stared at him.

"It'll be considered a service mission, not a prodigal mission."

I opened my mouth, but nothing came out.

"The Church is considering opening this service opportunity to sisters as well. At the very least, it should help more of them to marry in the Church, but for now, the pilot program is just for elders."

"That's…something I'll need to think about. Fast about."

"Let me email you the application." Bishop McFadden stood and thrust out his hand. "The Lord knows how to make every member feel important," he said with a smile he seemed to think was warm. "Because every member *is* important."

We shook hands.

"We all love you, Joshua."

"Thank you." I walked out the door and joined my parents in the foyer. Mom was chatting with Sister Dupre, one of the elderly single women in the ward. A woman who'd never married.

She seemed happy enough.

Dad was looking in the display case where a map was dotted with pins showing where every missionary from the ward was serving around the world.

Mom fried some chicken for lunch. We'd barely finished when the phone rang. Dad still used a landline. He answered and then handed it to me.

"Elder Preston," a male voice said, "this is Elder Bradley. Elder Coatsworth and I are the two missionaries assigned to your ward."

"Yes?" They weren't going to ask me to teach an investigator with them, were they? I did *not* want to be a stake missionary while waiting for another full-time call.

"Bishop McFadden told us you were putting in your papers for a second mission." He laughed. "That's so cool."

"Did you need something, Elder Bradley?" I asked, already tired of the conversation.

"Well, it's just…my comp and I haven't been having much success with the work lately, and we've been feeling a little stressed…"

Heavenly Father had a place for me in his church.

"I'll be right over," I said. "And I'll bring the lube."

Mom was in the kitchen washing dishes and hadn't heard. Dad simply took the phone back and then looked at me a long moment. He stood silently another moment before reaching forward to shake my hand with a terse nod.

I brushed my teeth and quickly bathed in a few strategic places. After donning my black jeans and white T-shirt, I borrowed Dad's car and headed off for my first splits with the local missionaries.

I finally understood how lifeless zombies felt.

I wanted the resurrection.

I'd go to school part-time while on my second mission, maybe learn another language, and still keep an eye out for Mr. Right.

I could make *myself* come alive.

Two blow jobs and one fuck later—Elder Coatsworth's stress levels required that he cum twice—I drove downtown instead of going back home. I parked near a bar I'd only dreamed about frequenting before my mission, calling Dad to inform him I'd be a little late. Then I walked through the door and ordered a drink.

Perfect Stranger

I like anonymous sex. There's something *je ne sais lagniappe* about transitioning from the complete absence of knowledge regarding another person's existence to deep intimacy with him after only a few minutes. It must be close to what race car drivers feel going from zero to a hundred miles an hour in eight seconds.

To be clear, I don't care for *dangerous* anonymous sex. No public sex in parks or Lowe's bathrooms. No private sex with a total stranger who wants to tie me up. I must admit, though, I almost regret not having sex with the guy who propositioned me at a bus stop on the corner of St. Roch and St. Claude, the year before the storm.

A bipolar friend of mine had fallen and been hospitalized for a concussion, but at 4:30 in the morning she'd decided she wanted to go home and called me to accompany her. Afraid to hire a taxi, she wanted to walk from Charity Hospital to her apartment in Mid-City and needed my "protection" to get past the projects. So I threw on some clothes and headed for the nearest bus stop.

With a friend, you could decide when to help and when to be too busy. With a partner, you always needed to be willing and available. Anonymous sex seemed better than a relationship in almost every way.

It was pre-dawn that morning and the streetlight nearest the bus stop was broken. A black man in his early twenties approached me with a blank yet still intense expression. I admit, given my internalized biases, I was nervous, even more when he leaned toward me and whispered.

"The **88** won't be here for another five minutes. Can I fuck you while we wait?" He moved behind me, pressed up against my ass, and reached around to unzip me.

Two cars and a Hubig's truck whizzed by.

"You know," I said, "that's very generous, but I think I'd rather do this indoors." I moved his hand away.

"It's only fun if you might get caught."

Nope. No Parish Prison for me. No Spirit Prison, either. I'd chosen not to live the rest of my life with the constant threat of discovery and excommunication. Bishop Brooks only knew I was gay because I went to his office and told him to remove my name from the records of the Church.

Brother Garcia, whose apartment I'd helped clean after a kitchen fire, never spoke to me again. Sister Bertrand, whose lawn I'd mowed probably a hundred times as a teenager, sent my parents a "Sorry for your loss" card. None of my missionary buddies even responded to my emails. Once my parents disowned me, there were no more emotional bonds, either.

Still, the guy at the bus stop was likely part of an underserved population, and it might have been nice to give him a part of me, whatever the personal risk.

But I didn't.

This morning, I decided to take a stroll through my Marigny neighborhood and see what I could find. Lots of straight couples had moved in after Katrina, but there were still enough gay guys around to warrant a short excursion. Gay ghettoes were limiting, but having no gay concentrations at all would be even more so.

I passed a middle-aged white woman picking up her trash can, a man in scrubs hopping into the mini-Cooper parked in front of his house, and a young black woman with large breasts walking her terrier. A white man about thirty, a tattoo on his neck, passed by on a bicycle without making eye contact.

Finally, I came upon a young Latino sweeping in front of a restaurant on Chartres and Franklin that wouldn't open for another two hours. When he saw me, he smiled and hooked his thumb toward the front door.

The trouble with cruising in your own neighborhood is you see the same people over and over. While I enjoyed playing with a handful of regulars on occasion, I was in the mood for virgins today. At least, virgins as far as my own cock and ass were concerned.

Mormons were supposed to stay married to the same person not only for their entire lives but also throughout all the eternities.

I smiled back and said, "Can I take a rain check?" A fair weather fuck buddy if ever there was one.

"There's a 40% chance this afternoon," Luis told me.

I nodded. "I'll stop by again later."

He held the broom in front of him like an erection and stroked it.

Too public for my taste.

I headed on to a Bed and Breakfast in the Bywater that catered to a gay clientele. The clapboard was painted bright purple, the trim and Victorian porch brackets a bright green, with the front door a bright yellow, gang colors for the Big Easy. Once, a physician in town for a conference invited me to his room here for a blow job, and I'd gone through three other rooms taking care of guests before I headed home.

I waited across the street from the entrance to Bon Sommeil in my usual spot. Fifteen minutes passed with no discernible pedestrian activity. Four cars drove by, three driven by women. The one man I might have given a cum hither look to was staring at his phone rather than cruising his surroundings.

I'd been invited into the Bed and Breakfast another day by a tourist with a two-day beard, deodorant-free for just as long. He looked vaguely familiar, but when you've played with over three hundred men, sometimes you don't recognize second encounters.

Perhaps he'd fucked me from behind at some point and I'd only seen his face briefly. Perhaps I'd fucked him from behind. Perhaps we'd met on the dimly lit third floor of the bathhouse on Toulouse.

But the guy turned out to be Jeremiah, a bully who'd tormented me in seventh grade. He was a Baptist preacher now in Dallas, in New Orleans that weekend for a few days off from both his wife and congregation.

Another time, I'd found a phone number scribbled on a bathroom wall in a male dancer bar on Rampart. A wildly spurting dick had been drawn next to it. I called and a man invited me to his French Quarter hotel room.

When he opened the door, I recognized Brother Parker, my former Institute teacher from back when I was still in the Single Adults program at church. He was embarrassed at first, but then we made a game of quoting verses as we fucked. We even started modifying them.

"I will go and do the things which the dungeon master hath commanded, for I know that the dungeon master giveth no commandments unto his men, save he shall prepare the straps and lube that they may accomplish the thing which he commandeth them."

"Adam bent over that men might cum, and men cum, that they might have joy."

"And if men come unto me, I will show unto them my penis. I give unto men my penis that they may be humble. And if they humble themselves before me, I will make flaccid dicks become hard unto them."

I loved the spontaneity of these encounters. People lost that in long-term relationships, and I wasn't willing to lose it. Just as important, though, was the element of surprise.

Late one Mardi Gras night, I'd ended up in a hotel room on Frenchmen. After an hour of sucking and fucking, this stranger and I lay together for a few minutes, the first opportunity to do much casual chatting. The man told me he was a salesman for Puglia Enterprises. "Pool-ya," he pronounced. "It's spelled—"

"P-U-G-L-I-A," I finished. "I was a door-to-door salesman for a couple of years in Italy."

He nodded. "So you're Mormon, too," he concluded. "I did my mission in Australia."

That's all part of the fun of anonymity. You find out you've just smoked pot with a cop, that you've just barebacked with a microbiologist, that the piss you just swallowed was sweet because the diabetic you picked up at the coffeeshop deliberately cut back on his insulin when he decided to go on the prowl for a hookup.

A curtain moved on the second floor of Bon Sommeil, and a man's face appeared. The guy looked down at me for over a minute. I didn't want to grab my dick or anything obnoxious, but I did scratch my left nipple for a few seconds and then my right nipple. I scratched my thigh, as close to my crotch as I dared.

The curtain closed.

Oh, well.

A black man drove by, looking annoyingly at the road in front of him.

Another woman drove by.

Not a fun way to spend a day off. Might as well be towing disabled cars. At least at work I got to fantasize about the mechanics I met. I'd had sex with several of them at various garages. One liked the blunt end of a wrench up his ass while I sucked him off. Straight, married guy with three kids.

I enjoyed never being in a position to judge.

I'd just made the decision to stop loitering in front of the Bed and Breakfast and head back toward the Marigny when the front door opened. It was hard to tell if it was the man from the window. There'd been too much glare. But the guy waved me over, and after waiting for another car driven by an oblivious man to pass by, I crossed the street, opened a little gate, and walked up to the front steps.

He was a light brown of indeterminate ethnicity.

"Gil," I said, offering my hand.

"Jesús," the man replied with a smile, clasping my hand firmly.

"You don't look Latino." More of those internalized biases. I watched videos and read books to counteract my conservative upbringing, but it was clearly a work in progress.

I followed the man inside and refrained from asking if I could be his Jesus freak for the day. He probably got that all the time. One thing I'd learned over the years was that what was new to one person wasn't necessarily new to the other.

"I get mistaken for just about everything," he said, climbing the stairs ahead of me. His jeans fit perfectly. I wanted to touch his ass. We were safely inside now.

"Is that right?" He had an unidentifiable accent as well, though I supposed it didn't really matter. I'd had a threeway with a Jew and a Hindu once, a threeway with a Japanese man and a fellow from Ghana. I mostly had sex with white guys, but all I really required was a reasonably attractive man with a friendly attitude.

And someone not dangerous.

"Some people think I'm Indian or Polynesian." He glanced back at me. "Folks who don't get out much. I even had a guy at the airport once start talking to me in Farsi."

"I don't suppose there are many Iranians named Jesús."

He laughed.

His room was small, the door bumping into the foot of the bed so that it would only open at a 45-degree angle. I remembered sucking off a dentist in this room. He'd ordered me not to swallow until he could examine my mouth full of cum. He stuck his finger in and rubbed it over all my teeth, taking a couple of pictures with his cell phone and then another after turning out the lamp and plugging in a black light.

Maybe my picture was in a medical journal somewhere.

Jesús closed the door behind us.

"Wow, they've really upgraded the décor," I said, pointing to the bedcovers.

"That's my chasuble," he replied. "I take it wherever I travel. Makes me feel at home."

"Catholic?" I asked.

He laughed again. "You didn't come in to talk religion."

"No, but I'd like to get naked before God, get down on my knees, and worship your cock."

He pondered for a moment and then nodded.

I started to rip off my T-shirt, but Jesús put a hand on my arm. "We'll do this slowly," he said. He took over removing my shirt, pulling it up and over my head gently, brushing a bit of hair from my forehead when he was done.

Following his lead, I reached over and slowly unbuttoned his shirt, moving behind him to carefully pull it off his back. It took more energy to do these things slowly and deliberately than to just jump into bed, but I'd had a solid breakfast, so what the hell? I kissed his bare shoulders before I dropped the shirt onto a nearby chair.

Next came the shoes. I normally just kicked mine off, but Jesús motioned for me to sit on the bed while he kneeled to untie them. He pulled them off slowly, like a shoe store salesman, and then carefully pulled off my socks as well. When he lifted my right foot to his mouth, I thought, "Okay, here comes the kink," but no, he simply kissed the top of each foot gently and put my feet back on the floor.

My father had told me when I returned from my mission that he and my mother knelt together to pray every time before they engaged in "intercourse."

I thought it might be my turn now to remove Jesús's shoes, but he continued working on me, my pants the last major item to address. When I stood again, he slowly unbuckled my belt and then unzipped me, gently pulling my pants to my ankles rather than letting them drop to the floor.

I stepped out of them, and then he returned to my underwear. He leaned forward to kiss the lump behind the fabric softly. Then he pulled those down as well and dropped them on the pile of clothes beside us. He leaned forward and kissed the edge of my pubic hair. He took a couple of slow, deep breaths and then stood.

I wanted to push him over the edge of the bed and fuck him.

Jesús gave me a gentle nod, so I slowly helped him off with the rest of his clothing. I couldn't resist adding a *little* kink, though, kissing each toe one at a time and rubbing my beard against the bottom of each foot.

When his underwear came off, I kissed the shaft of his dick and put my nose into the thickest of his hair right next to it, but rather than take two slow breaths, I kept my face buried in his crotch and began rooting around, under his balls and over to the other side. When I was back up to dick level, I ran my tongue up his shaft and then enveloped his cock, taking in the whole thing and starting to rock back and forth on it.

Jesús put his hands on my head. "Easy," he said. "We've got all morning."

I pulled back. Was going slow some kind of fetish in itself? Some form of prick teasing?

God only knew. Bishop Brooks had told me during one of my worthiness interviews that early in their marriage, his wife had sewn the front slit in his pajamas closed so he couldn't try to have sex with her in the middle of the night.

If Jesús was willing to give himself to me so completely, and only asked for patience in return, I'd make an effort. I spent the next thirty seconds just looking at his dick without reaching for it. "You're uncircumcised," I noted.

"I had the skin restored."

"How long are you?" I asked.

"Seven and a quarter inches."

"Perfect."

He laughed.

I slid his cock into my mouth again and moved up and down on it more slowly. I could feel his hardness getting harder, but I tried to hold back, not terribly easy as I couldn't get enough of his seven and a quarter inches.

I kept the same pace, and after a few moments, something unusual happened. I became completely aware of every centimeter of his cock, every ridge, every vein, the part near the top of his shaft where he widened slightly, the base where his hair started. Normally, I'd have an overall idea of what I was working with, maybe notice a specific anomaly, but now I was enjoying every part of his best part, the difference between a peck on the lips and deep kissing.

Of course, the deliberate pace forced me to make a prolonged effort to get him to cum. Usually, I could get a guy off in a couple of minutes. But I sucked on Jesús's cock for almost ten minutes without the payback I wanted.

Finally, I could feel his skin tightening and adjusted my rhythm, pulling off slowly, hesitating with my mouth around his head, wobbling back and forth a couple of centimeters while I added more saliva, and then going back down faster than before in one fell swoop.

"Ahh."

I repeated my new pattern without any protests, and within twenty seconds, Jesús took over the job, holding my head steady with both hands as he fucked my face. Even then, he didn't go into a wild frenzy like most guys did. But his speed did quicken with each thrust, and I knew I was in for a treat any second.

This was going to be my first time getting a mouthful of Jesus Juice, I realized. Then, considering how Jesús pronounced his name, I amended that to Jesús Hooch. Either way, after nearly fifteen minutes, I was ready.

He shot for probably four seconds. His was probably the biggest load I'd ever taken. Sometimes, a burst of ejaculate could trigger a gag reflex, but despite the volume, the only sensation I felt this morning was pleasure. Better than a mouthful of Reddi-wip.

I buried my face in his pubes again, keeping his cum in my mouth as I breathed in the scent of his crotch, and then I swallowed.

I stood up, and we calmly looked at each other for several moments before he climbed onto the bed and lay face down. I climbed up as well and straddled him, for the first time noticing the can of Crisco on the bedside table. I'd heard tales of guys using it as lube, but I thought that had all stopped years ago, back in the eighties before I was of age.

"How old are you?" I asked, grabbing the can. He looked to be in his mid-thirties, a few years younger than I was, but some guys had great skin. A black guy I'd thought to be in his late twenties had fucked me one day before hurrying off to pick up his grandson.

"Old enough to know what I'm doing."

I dabbed some of the white grease onto Jesús's asshole, rubbed a little over my cock, and pointed the tip into his puckered opening. I eased myself in and rested a moment to give him time to adjust. I'd slipped in so easily with the Crisco, though, that I wasn't sure entering him even hurt.

But I took my time anyway. Part of the fun in meeting new people was learning what they liked and adjusting my performance to make sure I was worth a second encounter, even if we never ended up having one.

I slid in the rest of the way slowly, concentrating to keep from letting myself go and fucking him too quickly. And something odd happened again. By focusing, I seemed to register what was happening along every centimeter of my dick. I seemed able to feel every spot along his rectal lining. I was able to feel what was happening on the head of my cock at the same time as what was happening two inches down, and another inch below that. Rather than one overall sensation, I could detect fifteen individual ones.

Instead of crunching a hard candy, I was slowly letting it melt in my mouth to enjoy the flavor longer.

I felt the skin of my chest against his back. I kissed his neck, smelling the fresh scent of his hair, a hint of almond from his shampoo. I worked my arms under his torso and felt his weight on them, felt my weight added to his. I pressed my cheek against the side of his head. And slowly pulled out and pushed in, the Crisco slick and smooth.

His hair felt soft, his left ear smelled slightly of ear wax, the skin on his shoulders was creamy and unblemished.

His ass was soft and wet and warm and welcoming. I couldn't imagine wanting my dick anywhere else. I couldn't understand how every man didn't want to do this every day.

A burning deep inside my cock soon announced I was getting close. Normally at this point, I would finish like a wild man, but knowing how Jesús had been reacting, I maintained a slow, steady pace instead. It required more self-restraint than I'd exercised since my missionary days when I had to avoid even masturbation.

But with one last, hard, calm thrust, I squeezed Jesús tightly and spurted inside him, my white semen mixing with the white Crisco already there. I stopped and rested against Jesús's back, leaving my cock to marinate in the mixture.

"Thank you," I whispered.

"Thank *you*," he replied. "I'm part of a threesome, but even so, we've been together so long I still need a little variety once in a while."

I imagined Jesús as part of a trinity but kept myself from saying anything out loud. I was sure he'd heard that joke too many times already. I smiled and kissed his neck again.

"You have a towel?" I asked, looking about.

"Not yet. It's my turn now."

"Didn't you already cum?"

"Just the one time."

I pulled out and took his place on the chasuble, but he turned me over to face him, lifting my legs and dabbing some Crisco on my ass. I didn't usually like getting fucked after I'd cum, but Jesús had let me fuck him after he'd cum, so I could hardly say no.

He entered me just as gently as I'd entered him. I held my own legs in the air while he supported himself, but looking into his face as he slowly pulled out and pushed back in was unsettling. His expression was so calm, so gentle, so quiet, his gaze almost too intimate.

Of course, he was already inside my ass. How much more intimate could we be?

"Why so slow?" I asked. I should have kept quiet, but there seemed to be too much time to fill.

Frenzy left no time for thought.

"I like to get to know people." He looked down at me with a relaxed smile, as if he were observing a butterfly on a delicate flower.

I should have felt bored, I thought. "Nice" wasn't very sexy. He wasn't even being playful, just serious, and kind. Normally, my heart beat fast during sex because of the physical activity, but he seemed to be making mine beat a little faster just with his penetrating gaze.

He leaned down to kiss me, and my heart slowed down again, his gentleness utterly calming. Most guys darted their tongues in and out quickly while they fucked, bit my lips, crashed their teeth against mine, but his kiss was so deep and gentle we could have been sitting on a park bench under the moon.

Our tongues were cuddling.

Relaxation was the opposite of excitement, of course. It wasn't what sex was about. Usually, though, by this point, the muscles in my legs would burn just a little, and it would be a race to see if my partner could finish before I was no longer able to keep them pointing heavenward.

Today, I decided to wrap them around Jesús's back. As a rule, I enjoyed the awareness that two foreign bodies were meeting briefly, but this guy made me feel like merging was the only way to overcome relaxation enough to climax.

We stopped kissing and, supporting himself with one arm, while still slowly pumping away, he softly caressed my nipples. There was no tweaking or pinching. He brushed a strand of hair off my forehead again and gently stroked my temple. All pleasure and no pain. I'd never consciously recognized that most guys liked to mix the two. That was usually the only kind of merging we did.

I was used to men with more energy, more creativity. Like the priest who wore a nun's habit and let me crawl under to give him a blow job. Like Casey, the security guard from the bank, who always inserted a butt plug or bullet vibrator before going to the airport, hoping to force a TSA cavity search, and then acting it out later with me. Even my old Institute teacher would have said something to a guy named Jesús like, "I was a stranger and you took me inside you."

"I'm cumming," Jesús whispered. He didn't speed up or change the strength or depth of his thrusts but kept pumping away at the same slow, steady pace.

If only there were a way to make my ass suck him off and get his cum right now.

Jesús took his fingers from my face so he could support himself with both arms again. I hadn't realized his caress had distracted me until it was no longer there, and I was suddenly able to concentrate once more on the dick inside me, making me aware again of his presence filling me up.

Was there anything better than a stranger's cock inside you? It wasn't terribly different from the feeling when your heart was full.

Jesús stopped moving.

I remembered a scene from *Frankie and Johnny* in which Kate Nelligan has sex with Al Pacino. He doesn't climax the way she expects and she asks, "Did you cum?"

I should have felt disappointed, but instead I mostly felt peaceful. We'd never know each other well enough to "make love," but this might be the first time I'd ever made "extreme like." The stillness was a revelation.

This was exactly why I liked anonymous, promiscuous sex. I was always learning a new technique or method, and I could incorporate the best parts of each encounter into future endeavors. I still liked 'fun and exciting,' but there was something to be said for deeply comforting, too.

"Thank you," he whispered.

"Thank *you*," I replied.

He pulled out and we lay on the bed next to each other without even bothering to clean up. He reached for my fingers and held my hand as we looked at the ceiling. A fan twirled softly, sending a gentle breeze down our way.

It was time to go. I could run home and take a shower, grab a snack, and head back to blow Luis at the restaurant.

I wondered if he'd like it slow.

I unclasped my hand and sat up, looking for my clothes.

"There was an ICE raid at my office," Jesús said abruptly, still on his back. I turned to look at him. "I can't go home. I can't access my bank. I only had a couple of thousand dollars stashed where I could get it. Thank God I always keep my chasuble in the trunk of my car." He patted the bedcovers.

There's a scene in *Vertigo* when Jimmy Stewart looks down a stairwell. The camera zooms in at the same time it physically pulls back. I had the same disorienting feeling as I realized Jesús wasn't just some guy to fuck but an actual person.

Not knowing that was the best part of anonymous sex.

"What will you do?" I asked. I'd "loaned" the guy who cleaned the Friendly Bar $50 last week. I could maybe spare a hundred dollars for Jesús. Though I'd never paid for sex before, perhaps this might be an occasion that warranted it. He'd made me…feel things.

This didn't seem like a premeditated con, but then, I supposed that's what made cons effective. "What about your two husbands?"

He shook his head. "It's not safe for them, either." He looked up at me but otherwise didn't move. "I had to abandon the car."

Trouble. Drama.

A chill ran through me. What I used to think was the witness of the Holy Ghost.

"Where will you go?" I asked. I almost offered to smuggle him back into Mexico, but of course, getting to Mexico wasn't the problem. Staying in the U.S. was.

He sat up and took my hand again. "I can pay you in sex and cleaning and doing odd jobs. I got my start hanging out in front of Home Depot and doing construction."

"Oh, my Lord." I reminded myself I knew nothing about this man. Great kisser or not, he could be a safety issue. This wasn't the first time a seemingly routine encounter had turned dangerous. A cute guy I'd picked up at a French Quarter bar late one night had tried to beat me with my bedside lamp. I'd run out of my apartment naked and banged on my neighbor's door for help.

My neighbor hadn't opened up, but thankfully, the guy ran away.

I looked at Jesús again. What if I got arrested for harboring? What if the gentleness that had so impressed me was nothing more than emotional manipulation?

At best, Jesús would put a huge damper on my sex life. Three months of "marriage" was three months I'd never get back.

The hardest part of mission life had been living with a partner I could never escape.

"It's a lot to ask. I know." He kissed me on the cheek. "You're not 'bad' for saying no."

"I don't know you from Adam."

"It's okay. I'll figure something out. I did the first time. I can do it the second."

I stood up and pulled on my underwear and pants, thankful I'd worn the jeans with a zipper and not buttons. I threw my shirt on quickly.

"Can I put your shoes on for you?" he asked.

No.

I sat back on the bed and held out my right foot. Jesús knelt before me and slowly pulled a sock onto it. Then he pulled a sock onto the other foot. He slipped one shoe on and tied the laces, so gently I felt like Cinderella with her glass sneaker. He put my second shoe on and secured it.

We both stood up, Jesús still fully naked. I leaned forward to give him a peck on the lips. But stopped and pushed my tongue inside his mouth instead. I put my arms around him and kissed him for thirty seconds. Forty-five.

"Let me go home and prepare a place for you," I said. "We'll play this by ear. I don't know how long…"

He put a finger to my lips. "It's enough," he said. "Thank you. I'll get my things ready."

I squeezed out his bedroom door and headed down the stairs and back to my apartment, alternately kicking myself and thinking somehow it might end up a worthwhile couple of months. It wouldn't hurt to learn how to like the same person for more than an hour.

Practice in case I ever did decide to settle down ten or fifteen or twenty years from now.

I found myself humming an old hymn about a poor, wayfaring man of grief and wondered which of us was the stranger.

A few blocks later when I turned the corner onto my street, I groaned. My landlord was on my front steps. That could only mean one thing.

"Hi, Gil," he said, nodding as I walked up. "I need to do another plumbing inspection."

I unlocked the door and waved him in, dropping to my knees and unzipping him. I had offered the first time three years ago, but that had somehow turned into an unwritten contract, and I'd ended up blowing him once or twice a month ever since. Thankfully, he was done in less than a minute and was on his way.

I cleared out two drawers in my dresser, squeezing my things into the remaining space. I shoved my clothes to one side of the closet. There hadn't really been much to "prepare." I mostly just wanted one last moment alone in my apartment. I made the bed, checked my hair in the mirror, and headed back to the Bed and Breakfast to offer Jesús some refuge. At least for a while.

But when I knocked, the owner told me two men had come to take him away.

Holy, Holy, Holey

My life of sexual service—not servitude, mind you—began in the Bellevue temple on my eighteenth birthday, right after I'd been ordained to the Melchizedek priesthood.

But the mail carrier didn't need to hear that. He looked to be in his mid-thirties, a mix of Anglo and subcontinent Indian. I lifted my skirt like a can-can girl and spread my legs slightly. Since the postman stood directly in front of my open apartment door, no one else outside could see me. I wasn't going to show up on YouTube. The man's eyes were riveted to my clit. After a moment, he looked up into my eyes, back down again, into my face once more, and down yet again.

I stepped backward slightly, my skirt still raised. The mail carrier glanced around nervously and then stepped into my apartment with no further hesitation. I closed the door behind him and put my back up against it. He dropped his mail and then his pants. I grabbed one arm and his dick and guided him into me. Ever since that fateful day in the temple, I'd been permanently lubricated and instantly ready for penetration.

"Oh my god," the man whispered. "This can't be happening."

These kinds of scenes made up the bulk of my life over the past year since I received my endowments. I'd heard that members going through for the first time used to get naked during the initiatory, but I'd seen nothing sexually inappropriate while I was there.

A little disappointing, really.

My bishop was reluctant to submit my papers to Salt Lake, feeling I didn't have "the right personality" to volunteer as a full-time missionary for two years. What I called progressive he called worldly, but since I hadn't actually committed any disqualifying sins, he had no choice but to grant me a temple recommend.

In the Celestial Room after making my way through the veil, I sat quietly on an overstuffed chair covered in velvet as I tried to persuade Heavenly Father to convince my bishop I was ready to serve.

With a last, prolonged thrust, the mail carrier came, breathing heavily in my face. A mild, pleasant curry enveloped me. The man stood motionlessly inside me another moment until his eyes slowly closed, and then he pulled out. I feigned a demure smile and released my skirt to cover my privates. Glancing down at my skin for the first time since the carrier arrived at my door, I realized I was whiter than usual, with some tiny red freckles across my hands and arms.

These things were impossible to predict. Sometimes, I found tattoos. Other times, I found scarification, henna artwork, and of course every possible skin tone. One guy, I kid you not, wanted a woman with leprosy. Another guy had wanted a man's ass covered with HPV warts.

I know, I know. But sexy is in the eye of the fucker. Since I never suffered any prolonged disability from these aberrations, I just went along with the flow…or discharge.

The postman backed up and stared at his dick as if it belonged to another man. I certainly understood the sensation. "You can come in the rain," I whispered. "You can come in the sun. You can come in the snow."

He was a sub I'd never seen before, so that was always enjoyable. The regular carrier liked to suck my dick for just a few seconds to get himself hard before sliding his own up my ass.

The UPS guy, on the other hand, liked to suck the biggest dick I'd ever had so far, the only man who could take such an enormous thing straight down his throat. His own dick, unbelievably, was even larger, and he liked to slowly insert it inside me, pushing forward at a rate of maybe a centimeter a second, taking almost half a minute to sink the entire thing inside me.

But, of course, I was always ready for anything. Ever since the temple, my body conformed on its own to exactly what the men around me desired. Through the power of the priesthood, I was able to provide an infinite variety of dicks, pussies, and assholes.

Reflecting on my endowments that first day in the Celestial Room, I'd begged Heavenly Father to let me serve him any way I could. I would be a faithful missionary, I promised, and follow every command, no matter how difficult. I would serve everyone I met.

I'd prayed silently for ten minutes, fifteen, until I was shooed away by a matronly temple worker. I'd hoped to detect some sense of Heavenly Father's will before being cast out, but I felt nothing.

I'd walked softly in my Dearfoam slippers to the Men's bathroom and stood at the urinal. I vaguely registered the sound of someone washing his hands a few feet behind me, and then the door opening and closing. I felt utterly alone. When I finished, I stood in silence staring at the drain, watching sullenly as a last drop dangled on the head of my penis. Why, I wondered? Why hadn't the Lord—?

Suddenly, a man moved up to the urinal on my right and unzipped, making me jump. A second after that, a man unzipped to my left. Both began pissing in unison as a voice immediately behind me whispered, "We're the Three Nephites, sent to answer your prayers."

Oh, brother, I moaned inwardly. I knew missionaries always teased newbies, but I hadn't been aware this kind of thing happened in the temple to guys getting their endowments for the first time. "Very funn—" Without another word, the three men in their temple clothing dragged me into a handicapped stall and closed the door.

"Feel free to stop by again any time you're in the neighborhood," I said to the mail carrier. "There are still other holes you haven't tried yet." I kneeled down, licked his penis clean, and pulled up his underwear and then his pants.

"I—I get off at 5:00," he said.

"Excellent. Come back after work and get off again at 5:15."

"Damn," he said. "I hope I don't put the rest of the mail in the wrong boxes." He started for the door.

"Just remember that you can put your male in whichever of my boxes you want."

He paused a second without looking back and then continued on his way.

With a year of experience behind me—and in front of me, and over me, and under me—I'd learned to be coy when necessary, and brazen and trite and clever and stupid, whatever the situation demanded. After all, I'd been initiated by the best.

"When we cum inside you," the tallest of the Three Nephites had told me in the bathroom stall, his hand on my still exposed penis, "your body will change in the twinkling of an eye." He'd been the one standing behind me at the urinal. The smile lines around his eyes crinkled as he lifted his green apron and unzipped. The other two men were already unzipped from their activities at the urinals, their dicks hanging out.

Uncut, I noticed.

"You won't be resurrected just yet," said the guy who'd been on my right, "but you'll remain alive and healthy and young until the Second Coming. At that time, you'll come forth in the First Resurrection, without ever having to die."

He turned me away from him, leaned me over the toilet, and pulled down my white pants and my new sacred underwear. I felt something press against my hole, and for the first time in my life, I had sex with someone other than myself.

I'd inserted a finger up my ass before, but a dick felt decidedly better. Once, I'd unscrewed the top of a bottle of hand lotion and inserted the opening into my anus and squeezed, trying to imagine what a load of cum would feel like. I'd tried a squeeze bottle of mayonnaise. A spurt of toothpaste. I knew instantly that whatever this man in the temple bathroom did to me, it would be better than anything I could do myself. He pulled out and pushed in, pulled out and pushed in.

It felt different when I wasn't in control of the speed. Felt better.

I knew I'd never be going back to lotion bottles.

"What's your name?" I grunted.

"Amalek the Younger," he returned with a deep thrust. "Did you know," he said, panting heavily, "that when the Lord came to the Americas, he blessed the Nephites with copious loads?"

"Unnhh. Moroni must have left that out."

"Well, I'm putting it *in*!"

"Unnhh!" Thrust. "Aahhh!" Thrust. "Unnnhh!" I didn't ever want it to stop.

Watching the mail carrier walk off down the block, I tried to decide what to do next, *who* to do next. That was really the hardest part of this calling, trying to figure out how to find private time with other men. The Three Nephites had encouraged me to have as many repeat customers as possible. It was the quantity of sex that mattered, not the number of new subscribers.

I remembered that three days had passed since someone moved into the house at the end of the block. Welcome wagoning always offered fun options. Today was Saturday, and if I was going to make a move, now was as good a time as any. I grabbed a coffee mug from the kitchen, poured some sugar in it, and walked to the house one lot away from the corner. Curtains were up in the windows. I'd only seen a single man go in but still wasn't sure if a wife or husband was involved. I walked up to the door and knocked.

I could hear rustling inside the house, and a moment later the door opened. "Yes?" The sandy-haired man was in his early thirties, his toned arms suggesting a gym membership, his emerald earring suggesting the gym in question might be popular with gays.

"Welcome to the neighborhood," I said, offering him my sugar.

"Thanks," he said, taking it with a laugh.

"I was wondering if I could borrow a cup of cum."

"Excuse me?"

"I brought my own cup." I turned sideways and patted my ass.

I couldn't determine my new features exactly, but I could certainly feel a Prince Albert in place as my penis began pressing against my jeans. I could feel chest muscles straining against my T-shirt.

It hadn't taken long after my encounter in the temple to realize that my clothes adjusted as quickly as my body. Once, when I'd finally gotten behind closed doors with the District Attorney, I was surprised to discover a chastity belt blocking the entrance to my pussy. But I'd found a key in my pocket and handed it to him with a pleading look. "I'm afraid I can't quite reach the keyhole," I told him. "Can you help me? It needs to be inserted at just the right angle."

The guy was a rising political star. I wondered if our encounter would show up in his memoirs one day.

I supposed some might consider my experience in the temple rape, but while none of the three men specifically asked for my consent, I was totally on board, and I think my smile and the ease with which I complied conveyed my eagerness to participate.

While only God the Father, Jesus Christ, and the Holy Ghost could read minds, the members of the godhood were also capable of passing along the information they gathered. The Three Nephites almost certainly heard it from God himself that I was quite happy not to delay sex another two years while on a mission. Even happier that it was going to be the penetration I fantasized about every day.

One of the biggest cultural crimes was teaching straight men to fear getting fucked. Lots of gay men felt too much shame or worry about it, too. But there was a reason more gay guys were bottoms than tops.

It was *fun* being a bottom.

It was fun even just thinking about it. Like when I looked at the Elders' Quorum president. Or the ward organist. Or the bishop.

I'd worried the bishop had been able to discern I was gay despite my playing on the ward basketball team. Was that why he hadn't wanted to submit my papers?

It wasn't fair. Gay men should be able to serve God, too.

As the first two Nephites from the side urinals fucked me, I kept my thoughts on sharing a missionary apartment with three other elders. There would be so much opportunity to share the work load, the heavy load of missionary stress.

I'd heard Sunday School teachers tell us to "Let Jesus take your load." I'd do my best to take everyone's load, too. After the two men finished, they turned me around to face them again. "Feel any different?" the second guy asked.

My ass burned a little, but I said nothing. I could get used to that. In fact, I already wanted to feel it again.

"Put your hands on your chest," he said.

I did and gasped when I felt rather substantial breasts. I looked down to confirm I wasn't imagining it, and my mouth opened in shock.

"I won't need your mouth today," the third Nephite broke in, the tall guy, "but I do want your vagina." He shrugged. "Sorry. Even after two thousand years, we've never been able to figure out a sexy word for vagina that wasn't somehow a little demeaning at the same time."

I'd never even tried to think of vaginas. But I was soon to learn over the coming weeks that he was right.

As he pumped away, I noted with tingling curiosity the difference between being entered from the front compared to being entered from the back. It wouldn't be many days before I experienced both at the same time, in the bathroom of a private home during a Republican fundraiser. Conservatives needed all the service they could get to divert their energy away from politics.

As the Third Nephite fucked me while the other two braced my body from behind, I searched the man's face, looking for Native American features. The signs were indeterminate, like that of a mixed-race Filipino back in high school who I'd never suspected was part Asian until he told me, and then suddenly I could see it.

Feeling the strong hands of the other two Nephites on my back and ass, I realized I'd always believed that if I ever did run into these guys, they'd help me change a tire or revive an injured deer on the side of the road. I hadn't considered this kind of help.

Maybe that was the real reason there weren't more first-hand accounts of the famed trio circulating throughout the Church. If we weren't even allowed to show bare shoulders or watch an R-rated movie once in a while, no one was going to be at the pulpit during Fast and Testimony meeting talking about their four-way in the temple bathroom.

"Opening yourself to the dicks of unhappy men," the left urinal Nephite whispered as the third Nephite fucked away, "will be your gift to the world."

The right urinal Nephite licked playfully at my ear. "You'll serve mankind faithfully every day until the Millennium begins."

"S-serve?" I managed. Being pounded relentlessly made it a little hard to catch my breath. How did people manage non-stop sex talk, I wondered?

I gained a new respect for pop stars who could follow energetic choreography while they sang. I eventually ended up impersonating a handful of them as well, but the men I met during those encounters weren't interested in hearing me sing.

"Most of the world's misery comes from men acting out when they don't get enough sex. It's mankind's fatal flaw. You'll make sure that the men you come across have no need to lash out financially or politically or physically."

He shook his head. "There are some men, of course, who are simply too damaged and hopeless to work with, for whatever reason. Sex only seems to give them *more* energy to do cruel things. We'll help you avoid those guys by letting you see a dark aura over their heads."

I appreciated that, but I did wonder what kept Heavenly Father from granting that gift of detecting auras to everyone else, too. Most people had the gift of vision and hearing and smell to help them avoid danger. Why not just give everyone's brain this kind of input, too?

The right urinal Nephite who'd already taken a turn leaned over to lick my right nipple. "Sometimes, all this background information takes the tingle away." He reached over and lightly pinched my other nipple. The left urinal Nephite gently licked my earlobe.

"I'm still tingling."

"That means we were right about you."

My new neighbor, still grinning from my surprise visit, set his cup of sugar down. I remembered the day I discovered how good cum could taste when mixed in with a sugary Italian soda. Cum, sugar, and almond flavoring was my favorite, but I tried to keep my mind as open as my various holes.

"We used to call women to this position," the third Nephite had told me as he pumped away. It was true that I could always recall my first time more vividly than any other sexual encounter, and I replayed that glorious time in the temple bathroom almost every day.

Even that long, long afternoon with the talented Chinese businessmen last month couldn't compete. The third Nephite was taking longer than either of the other two to climax. I could taste the salt when sweat from his forehead dripped onto my lips. "But few of them enjoyed a calling they felt they'd already been assigned at birth. If anything, they wanted us to stop them from being forced to serve men all the time."

"So," the right urinal Nephite added, "you're also serving the women who can now get out of having to sexually serve those men."

When I stepped forward and kissed my new neighbor, his tongue found its way instantly into my mouth. My body, of course, instinctively knew how to adjust my kissing to accommodate each partner's preferences. It was rather nice not to have to worry all the time if I was doing things correctly. But in a way, it didn't feel like real service if I didn't have to struggle a bit more. I wondered if worrying I was only a service imposter was what pushed me to seek out more and more men every day. Perhaps it helped push my service to the next level.

I'd had *such* a fun afternoon last week with the guys working on the tenth floor of a new building in the Central District.

"I want more than your tongue in me," I told my new neighbor when we came up for air.

"I haven't unpacked my condoms yet."

"I'm on PrEP," I told him. "We're good."

As if HIV were the only infection to worry about. But whatever the Three Nephites had done to convert my body into that of a living sex doll also took care of disease. I didn't worry about herpes or syphilis or chlamydia or anything else.

Who wouldn't want to enjoy worry-free sex ten times a day? This was a lot more fun than traditional missionary work. Even more fun than doing baptisms for the dead in the temple.

Though subsequent visits to the temple had revealed quite a few workers with baptismal font fantasies. The trick was to satisfy those fantasies strongly enough to displace the accompanying guilt. Religious folks in general were a tough crowd, happy and unhappy at the same time. I didn't want people to end up encouraging their lawmakers to pass even more oppressive legislation. I wanted them to develop a live and let live attitude.

"Many are called but few are chosen," the tall Nephite had said softly into my ear after he finally came that first day. "You'll always be a good lay."

"I hope…I hope I can help make the world a better place," I said, feeling my vagina close up and my breasts disappear after he pulled out. My penis reformed, but it turned out that even my "resting state" now included a bigger, better penis than before, because *I* was one of the people I got to please as well.

"Why do you think there was peace for 200 years after Christ visited the Americas?" The tall Nephite cupped my balls. "You know the scriptures record that the people had all things in common. That included husbands and wives. Sharing everything is the only real way to maintain peace."

The left urinal Nephite patted me on the shoulder. "We used to initiate sex missionaries in the Holy of Holies, but we've found it's easier to do in the presence of plumbing."

We exited the stall together and moved over to the row of sinks.

"You'll find," the right urinal Nephite told me, "that most men need this service daily. At least weekly."

"One person can only do so much," the left urinal Nephite added. "That's why there's still so much aggression—"

"And oppression," the tall Nephite interjected.

"—in the world." The left urinal Nephite sighed. "I'm afraid your mission will last longer than two years." Then all three leaned over to kiss me on my cheeks and forehead.

I looked at the Three Nephites as they dried their dicks and hands with paper towels. I was in the presence of greatness. It was intoxicating.

I wondered if I'd ever be able to convince the programmers over at the BYU cable channel to develop a new show: *Intimately Touched by an Angel*.

Of course, these guys weren't angels.

They were the Three Nephites.

The Book of Mormon was true.

I remembered thinking back in the Celestial Room that if I was finally able to convince my bishop to submit my mission papers, served two years and still came home gay, I might look into surgery. Not to transition to a woman's body but simply to *add* part of a woman's body.

It just struck me as easier to have a hole that wasn't in constant competition with bodily waste, even if I was a happily dicked gay man who wanted to spend my life being fucked by another man.

Much of my time this past year was spent visiting the courthouse, City Hall, and the Federal building on 2nd. A handful of police officers in two different precincts needed a great deal of assistance in reducing urges to take out their frustrations on marginalized people. It was best if I could keep any cathartic shooting confined to my vagina and ass.

Despite my dislike of long road trips, I helped lawmakers in Olympia pass less vindictive legislation, sometimes visiting the capitol two or three times a week when sessions were in full swing.

I was an elderly visitor in nursing homes, a willing doctor or nurse or patient in hospitals, a friendly college student during professorial office hours, and a grateful homeowner in the tax assessor's office.

In a way, the non-stop sex was a little like eating ice cream every day. At a certain point, it's not quite the same treat as when you only get it once or twice a month. But not many people ever turned down ice cream, especially when they could try 30 or 40 or 200 different flavors.

"My lube is packed away somewhere, too," my neighbor told me as I gently stroked his penis.

"I have a bottle of lube right here," I said, putting his hand on my own cock. "You just need to pump it a bit before the lube squirts out."

I let him tug at me a couple of minutes before I deposited a generous amount of lubricant into his palm. I leaned over the sofa and spread my cheeks so he could slap it across my ass.

Our body is a temple, the scriptures tell us. Mine included the most sacred room in any temple around the world. The Holey of Holies.

Unrequited Cum

"Did Jesus ever beat off?" Greg asked, looking directly at me. He was in black jeans and a tight, red T-shirt. I was grateful to have my desk as a shield.

"Of course not!" I said. Why had I pulled my tie so tight? "Jesus was perfect!"

"But Bishop Hammond," Greg countered, "he was also human." He leaned back in his chair, and I could see he'd padded his jeans to flaunt his sexuality. So repulsive.

I stared at his crotch for a moment before forcing myself to look him in the eyes. "A human who never sinned." I looked away from Greg's piercing gaze. A photo of the First Presidency hung on the wall to his left near a photo of the Philadelphia temple. The Family Proclamation was off to the side, and a framed print of Jesus descending from the heavens at the Second Coming just beyond that.

There was a long silence until I turned back toward Greg. He was in his early twenties, recently home from his mission to Scotland and in his second year at Temple University.

No relation to the Philadelphia temple.

"Bishop Hammond," Greg went on, "were you ever annoyed when your kids cried as infants?"

"Yes," I said hesitantly. I could sense I was being set up. I was the one who was supposed to be in control when I was giving someone a worthiness interview. Who did this kid think he was? He wanted to water plants in office buildings, for goodness' sake. I was a leader in Uniform and Refreshment Services at Aramark. We were a Fortune 500 company.

I bit my lip and told myself to be humble. I knew I was supposed to allow myself to learn from anyone.

But did that really include apostates?

"Do you believe Jesus never cried as a child?" Greg asked. "Do you think he never pooped his diaper? Never spit up?"

"Now, Greg," I said, "there's no point in this bizarre speculation. And it has nothing to do with—"

"Do you think even as an adult Jesus never farted? Never got a runny nose? Never had diarrhea?"

I slapped the top of my desk. The framed photo of Sharon and me on our wedding day in front of the Ogden temple fell over. "Greg, one of the Singles accused you of being gay. He's told several people about it already." I used one of my sternest looks. "You haven't acted on it, have you?"

Greg's nose wrinkled as he struggled with an answer. "I suppose it depends on what you mean by 'acting,'" he said. "I wasn't pretending. I knew exactly what I was doing and was fully engaged." He paused a second. "Not like people who pretend they're straight but really aren't."

I looked away again, pleading with the First Presidency for inspiration. I'd heard often about gaydar, though I'd never seemed to have the gift myself. Could Greg tell I was same-sex attracted even though I always used sports analogies in my talks during Sacrament meeting?

I had to get the facts from him quickly, determine if I needed to escalate this to the stake president, and send him out of the office so I could go home to Sharon.

"Bishop Hammond," Greg said slowly, "Jesus had to dig wax out of his ears like everyone else." He paused, and I looked at my fingernails to pretend I wasn't going to listen anymore till he stopped talking.

"Wasn't the whole point that he be human and experience what the rest of us experience?" he went on. "We're the only Christian religion that believes Jesus was married."

He reached up from his seat in front of my desk and put his hands just inches from mine. "When he and his wife had sex, did he never say, 'Oh, baby. Oh, baby'? He had sex in complete silence, efficiency his only goal?"

I pulled my hands away.

"Does that sound like a *perfect* sex partner to you?"

Sharon knew I hated when either of us made any noise during sex. Grunts and groans were so undignified and always made me feel like a sinner.

"So," I said wearily, "you admit you've been sinning." Why did so many of our good-looking young men fall away from the Church? It wasn't fair.

Greg shrugged. "I don't think anything I've done with other men is a sin," he said simply. "Do you need to hear exactly what I've done so you can judge for yourself?"

I was a judge in Zion. I felt the mantle descend upon my shoulders at the thought.

But I knew the danger of listening to verbal porn. When Brother McLellan confessed what he'd done with a female coworker at the restaurant he owned, he'd gone into far more detail than necessary.

Even with a woman as one of the participants, the account had led me to masturbate before leaving the ward meetinghouse that evening, thinking about Ravish, the Indian man I worked with every day at my own gentile job.

Beating off in the bishop's office into a handkerchief thinking of what lay beneath Ravish's nicely tailored slacks. I wondered if it was already too late to save my soul.

But maybe I could save Greg's.

I righted my wedding photo, gritting my teeth. I'd stayed faithful to Sharon for over twenty years. Our twin sons were on missions to Germany. Nothing this man in front of me might say could change any of that. And if he did say something repulsive, I'd kick him out of the office immediately. I might even slap him with my triple combination. That'd show him.

"It started with the hair conditioner," Greg said.

"What did?"

"I was just so curious, so hungry to know."

"Know what?"

"One day when I was in the shower, I pulled a bottle of conditioner from the shelf and took the cap off."

I frowned. Sometimes, I inserted a finger into my rectum when I showered, but since I always used soap as lubricant, it burned too much to do it often.

Greg stood up and acted out the next part of his confession, fully clothed, of course, turning sideways to give me the best view. "I reached behind me and inserted the opening of the bottle into my anus."

"Please, Greg, we don't need—"

"Then I squeezed the bottle as hard as I could." He clenched a fist behind his ass and jumped as if startled.

And hope suddenly rose in my chest again.

I stared at Greg in disbelief, feeling guilty I hadn't had more faith in inspiration. I should have known the Lord worked in mysterious ways. This decadent young man had just given me an answer to my prayers. Perhaps I could stop fantasizing about men and remain mentally faithful to Sharon if I just started buying more hair conditioner.

Well, *return* to being mentally faithful.

Only what *would* I think about with hair conditioner spurting up my rectum?

My eyes fell on Greg's fake bulge again. But…but it looked like it had just twitched. Maybe that lump was real, after all.

Lord help me.

"I went through a lot of conditioner," Greg said. "But after a while, that just wasn't good enough. So I joined a community men's chorus to be around other men."

I'd heard how depraved people in the performance arts could be.

Before I met Sharon, I'd so wanted to participate in the Hill Cumorah Pageant just one time.

"When I confessed to one of the other chorus members about the hair conditioner, he invited me to a party at his house." Greg smiled, his unfocused eyes directed toward the wall behind me. "Eleven of the guys—two of them were even straight—shot into a cup."

"Oh my heck." It was almost as if I could see it happening. Was God giving me a vision?

Why had I pulled this damn tie so tight?

"Then they poured it into an anal douche bulb."

I frowned.

"They had me lie on my stomach in the bedroom, and then they inserted the tip of the douche into my ass and squeezed." He smiled again. "I got eleven loads at one time."

"But that's so…that's so…"

"I know. It was the best night of my life." Greg paused a moment and then sighed. "But of course, after getting real cum, the next thing I wanted was a real cock." He seemed to notice for the first time a plant on the middle shelf of the bookcase off to his right and frowned. Two of the leaves were quite brown. "So I fasted for a cock."

I had to kick this guy out of my office right this second. My hands were too sweaty to pick up my triple combo, but I had more than enough information to give the stake president. "Greg," I said, standing up, "we're going to need to—"

"And I was able to call down blessings from heaven," he said, again with that annoying smile. "The chorus got together for a Christmas party." He chuckled to himself, shaking his head. "The two straight guys were always pretty chill about these things."

I didn't know whether to stay standing or sit back down.

"The Christmas trees for the Christmas village on the coffee table were all butt plugs," he went on.

I sat back down.

"The butt plug Christmas trees were purple. They were black. They were rainbow-colored. There was a real Christmas tree in the corner, but the garlands were whips. The ornaments were nipple clamps and colored cock rings, the tinsel colored condoms. The angel on the top was a stainless-steel butt plug with a red jewel. In the doorway between the kitchen and the living room where the mistletoe might normally hang there was a pair of padded doorway cuffs."

My mouth fell open. The vision was returning. But what in tarnation were doorway cuffs?

Greg wagged a finger in my direction. "That's not the kind of thing you want to do at a party like this." He reached over and lifted my jaw gently with his hand.

There must have been static electricity in the carpet.

"I found myself under the 'mistletoe' without realizing it and got cuffed for ten minutes. I'd tell you what happened, only you might not like it."

"I…I think I can imagine." In fact, I was doing it as we spoke.

Greg's crotch lump was noticeably larger. Did they make inflatable fake crotch lumps? That thing *had* to be real.

I suddenly understood why Catholics said Hail Marys. People needed specific prayers to say during moments of extreme trial. Mormons had nothing. We certainly weren't going to recite the blessing over the bread at a moment like this.

I wondered if Ravish had a special prayer. I could see his lips moving sometimes when he looked at me, when there was no one else around him he could be talking to.

"One of the guys pulled down my pants and started jacking me off," Greg continued, pulling my eyes back to his jeans. "I could hardly protest, could I? Be a party pooper?"

"But you didn't give your consent!" I said. "That's…that's…"

"The guys took turns spitting on my dick while the one guy kept pulling on it till I came." Greg paused again. It was an awfully irritating habit. "But he kept jacking me off even after I was done. It starts hurting eventually, you know."

I'd always felt so mortified that I stopped touching myself the instant I could. It never occurred to me that one could go on. "Did you say something then?"

He smiled. "'Oh, baby. Oh, baby.'"

I shook my head and pointed to the door.

"Do you know what mancream butter is?" Greg asked. I felt like one of the plants he watered on his office route, only he wasn't pouring water on me, he was dripping it like someone performing Chinese water torture. I needed to be strong. I needed to hold onto the iron rod. My eyes darted about the room.

"It's when you keep beating your cum. After a few minutes, it turns opaque and white, like Elmer's glue. A completely different texture and consistency from fresh cum." He stared directly into my eyes. "And taste. The guy made me lick up every last drop off his hand."

I felt dizzy, even though I was seated. Sin was so terribly unhealthy, even vicariously.

Proxy work was supposed to *save* people.

I really needed to keep animal crackers in my office to keep my blood sugar up.

"After that initiation, some of the guys invited me to their exercise class in the director's basement."

Surely, there wasn't more. "I don't need to hear this." I thought about my elderly next-door neighbor who kept turning off his hearing aid every time I stopped by and casually invited him to church.

I remembered that glorious day in the Philadelphia temple when there hadn't been enough women in the prayer circle and I was forced to hold the hands of two other men.

The man on my left had flubbed what must have been an attempt at the Sure Sign of the Nail. It had felt like he was tickling the palm of my hand.

"You have a tiny bit of a paunch," Greg continued, and I put my hand on my stomach. "You know that exercise can get boring. So for the class, the director puts in a porn DVD, and we have to match what we see on screen. By ourselves, of course. Those positions are a lot harder when you're doing them alone. We cue up ten scenes and act them all out, every time the exercise class meets."

I remembered seeing a video on YouTube of Filipino prisoners dancing in sync to Michael Jackson's "Thriller."

Did apostates in Outer Darkness, I wondered, act out sex scenes all alone for eternity as part of their punishment for leaving the Church? To remind them they'd missed out on eternal Celestial sex for their sins?

I shuddered and then thought immediately about never experiencing an orgasmic shudder again. "Think about what you're giving up," I said.

"After we finally get all the moves down perfectly," Greg continued as if I hadn't even spoken, "we pick a partner for the last class where we act out those scenes together. We'll 69 for a few minutes, a guy might fuck my face for a bit, one of us might sit down on the other's cock, a guy might rim me while I'm on all fours, reaching around to jack me off, maybe switching to fuck me doggy style before I cum. Or after.

"Or he might pull out and cum on my back. We almost never get through the entire set of scenes without cumming, so the last class often ends a little early. Then the next time the class meets, we start with a whole new set of scenes we need to match. It's always fun to see the different options available with such a limited number of key body parts."

My brows furrowed. I always fantasized about the same two or three things. I'd always thought that meant I wasn't too depraved and might still be salvageable. Now I realized I was merely boring even in my daydreams.

Ben Stiller wouldn't be starring in a movie about "The Secret Life of Bishop Hammond."

Greg moved over to the desk, pressing against it, the bulge in his pants just barely visible over the ledge. If only I could feel it to make sure it was real.

"Greg." I swallowed. "Thank you for confessing. I'll pass on a summary to the stake president. You'll be hearing from him shortly."

He didn't move.

"Greg, I said—"

"Did you hear about Elizabeth Smart's father?"

"Excuse me?" Was he talking about that poor girl from Salt Lake who'd been kidnapped by Mormon fundamentalists?

"He came out as gay."

"What?"

"Ed Smart came out as gay at the age of sixty-four. Said he wanted to start living an authentic life."

I felt dizzy again. The Smart family were like royalty. Elizabeth had been sent on a mission to Paris because the Church wanted to cultivate her. She spoke at events all the time. There'd been an A&E series about her. The young woman's parents were always so refined and controlled. How could the man throw all of that away?

"Bishop, don't you ever wonder what your life would be like if you lived it the way you want?"

"I *do* live the way I want!" I said, a little too loudly. "I live the gospel!"

"Do you ever wonder why the Apostle John kept describing himself as 'the one Jesus loved'? Jesus loved everybody. So what was so special about the love he felt for John?"

"Nothing! That was all in John's mind! And those scriptures probably weren't translated correctly, anyway!"

Greg looked like he was thinking about what I said. But I knew he was plotting. Sinful people always plotted. I needed to get him out of here.

Why couldn't I get him out of here?

"So an apostle of the Lord was fantasizing about him sexually," Greg said, rubbing his chin in a way that told me he'd planned to say this all along. "And yet Jesus kept him as an apostle. I wonder what that means."

"Greg," I said as calmly as I could, "I need you to leave right now. Do you understand?"

I…I don't *consent* to you staying here, I wanted to add.

But didn't.

"Yes, Bishop," he replied. "I understand completely." He moved over to the door and put his hand on the doorknob. I willed with all my might for whatever spiritual energy I had left to push him out the door. But he turned around. "Sister Hammond told me you talk about a guy from work all the time. Some guy named Ravish?"

I shook my head. "He's not even Mormon. I—" I stood up. "When did you talk to my wife?"

"You know," Greg said, "I'm leaving the Church. I'm already damned. So it's no harm to my soul if you want to take advantage of me one time to get it out of your system."

"I don't want to take advantage of anyone!" I spat. "Ever!"

Greg nodded. "How long have you been married to Sister Hammond?"

I felt dizzy again and fell back into my chair. Surely, I had a roll of Life Savers around here somewhere. "That's different," I muttered. "That's different." I rummaged about in my drawer. Nothing.

Then I found an old Altoids breath mint in the corner of the drawer, the edges worn off, and covered in dust. I looked at it a long moment until I realized the room had gone quiet.

"Bishop Hammond," Greg said from his chair after I made eye contact, "when I studied medieval literature, one of the books we read was Boccaccio's *Decameron*."

I wanted to say, "Bully for you," but kept quiet. If I let him talk, maybe he'd have his say and finally leave.

"The book was translated a dozen times over the centuries, but for a period of a couple of hundred years, English translators kept part of one of the stories in Italian, with a note that it contained so much about witchcraft that the translators found those passages too difficult to translate."

I frowned.

"But the story wasn't about witchcraft at all. It was about a priest who tricked a village girl into having sex with him. He explained that God needed her help putting the Devil in Hell. Every so often, the priest would call on the girl and say God needed her help again."

"Greg…"

"I think even if you didn't take that course, you can figure out what part of his body was the Devil, and what part of her body was Hell."

I felt a bead of sweat rolling down the side of my forehead. I popped the dirty Altoids into my mouth.

"Bishop Hammond, I've brought a condom and some warming gel. And I douched before I came over." He stared at me, and all I tasted was a mouthful of dust. "Why don't we put the Devil in Heaven?"

"Oh my god."

I clapped my hand over my mouth.

"But before you fuck me," Greg went on, "I want you to suck me off." He moved closer to the desk, unzipping. "But don't swallow."

I couldn't quite see through the opening whether he was still wearing his garments or if he'd already become so decadent as to start wearing Hanes. Those boxer briefs online…

"Then I'll lie on the floor naked. You can lean over my ass and dribble that cum into my ass crack." He smiled. "I'll leave the lube next to me on the floor for the next part."

I opened and closed my mouth a couple of times.

"What do you say, Bishop?" Greg reached into his pockets and pulled out a flat, square black wrapper with the word "Skyn" in gold. Then he pulled out a small red bottle of something called "ID," or maybe "ID Sensations." It was hard to tell.

Sharon and I mostly used corn oil. Lamanites had given us maize.

"I am not going to have sex with you," I said, wishing my voice sounded stronger. I felt like a thirteen-year-old whose voice was cracking. Peter Brady singing, "Time to Change."

They didn't make reruns like that anymore.

"But you want to?"

Damn. Those piercing eyes.

"Yes."

Greg pulled out a phone and pushed a button. My heart started beating faster, making me realize it had been beating fast already for several minutes now. Had he recorded this entire conversation? Oh, my Lord. What was going to happen to me? To my wife? To my temple marriage?

I'd say I'd been playing along, trying to get him to confess everything he would.

Maybe I'd have a heart attack.

"Yes, Sister Hammond," I heard Greg say, and his tone told me my life was over. Why didn't I keep a long letter opener in this flippin' desk? At least enough acetaminophen to overdose on? I suspected one of my coworkers at my gentile job took OxyContin. Maybe I could ask her…

Greg handed the phone to me.

"Sharon," I began.

Then I listened. For several minutes. I watched as Greg zipped up, gathering the condom and lube he'd laid out for me. I listened a bit longer, and then I heard Sharon tell me goodbye. I stared at Greg, feeling the way I had my first day as a missionary in Denmark, completely alien and alone, until the other missionaries came to the airport to pick me up.

Greg sat in the chair in front of my desk and shrugged. "She wanted me to lay it on thick," he said. "She wanted you to finally accept who you are."

"She wants a temple divorce."

"She didn't want you to be sixty-four or sixty-five before starting to live your life the way you were meant to."

"We won't have a forever family," I said.

"She also wanted to start living her own life the way *she* wants." Greg leaned forward in his chair. "She loves you, but she loves herself, too."

I put my face in my hands and shook my head. A moment later, I felt a touch on my shoulder and turned to look up at Greg. "Roger," he said, "I made up most of that stuff earlier. Why don't you hang out with me and my friends once in a while? Some of them are your age. Some have kids with their husbands." He squeezed my shoulder. "There's life out here," he said, "sexy and exciting and boring and real."

"And…authentic?" I could barely hear my own voice.

"I can set you up with some nice, easy-to-maintain plants when you find your own place."

Suddenly, I saw another face besides Greg's, besides the one of Sharon in front of the temple, and my heart, which had begun to slow down over the last minute or so, started beating faster again.

I wondered if Ravish would want to have dinner with me sometime. I wondered if he and Sharon would get along, if they'd even want to. I hoped my kids would like Ravish when I finally told them about him.

Assuming he liked me the way I liked him in the first place. "Can you…can you leave the warming gel?" I asked.

Greg smiled and leaned down to kiss my forehead.

Books by Johnny Townsend

Thanks for reading! If you enjoyed this book, could you please take a few minutes to write a review online? Reviews are helpful both to me as an author and to other readers, so we'd all sincerely appreciate your writing one! And if you did enjoy the book, here are some others I've written you might want to look up:

Mormon Underwear

A Gay Mormon Missionary in Pompeii

Out of the Missionary's Closet

Sexual Solidarity

The Golem of Rabbi Loew

Sins of the Saints

Marginal Mormons

Gayrabian Nights

Invasion of the Spirit Snatchers

Mormon Misfits

Escape from Zion

The Mysterious Madness of Mormons

Going-Out-Of-Religion Sale

Gay Gaslighting

Strangers with Benefits

Have Your Cum and Eat It, Too

Please Evacuate

Wake Up and Smell the Missionaries

The Camper Killings

Orgy at the STD Clinic

Breaking the Promise of the Promised Land

Am I My Planet's Keeper?

Racism by Proxy

Recommended Daily Humanity

Constructing Equity

An Eternity of Mirrors: Best Short Stories of Johnny Townsend

I Will, Through the Veil: Gay Mormon Porn

Kinky Quilts: Patchwork Designs for Gay Men

Inferno in the French Quarter: The UpStairs Lounge Fire

Latter-Gay Saints: An Anthology of Gay Mormon Fiction (co-editor)

Available from your favorite online or neighborhood bookstore.

Wondering what some of those other books are about? Read on!

Invasion of the Spirit Snatchers

During the Apocalypse, a group of Mormon survivors in Hurricane, Utah gather in the home of the Relief Society president, telling stories to pass the time as they ration their food storage and await the Second Coming. But this is no ordinary group of Mormons—or perhaps it is. They are the faithful, feminist, gay, apostate, and repentant, all working together to help each other through the darkest days any of them have yet seen.

Gayrabian Nights

Gayrabian Nights is a twist on the well-known classic, *1001 Arabian Nights*, in which Scheherazade, under the threat of death if she ceases to captivate King Shahryar's attention, enchants him through a series of mysterious, adventurous, and romantic tales.

In this variation, a male escort, invited to the hotel room of a closeted, homophobic Mormon senator, learns that the man is poised to vote on a piece of anti-gay legislation the following morning. To prevent him from sleeping, so that the exhausted senator will miss casting his vote on the Senate floor, the escort entertains him with stories of homophobia, celibacy, mixed orientation marriages, reparative therapy, coming out, first love, gay marriage, and long-term successful gay relationships.

The escort crafts the stories to give the senator a crash course in gay culture and sensibilities, hoping to bring the man closer to accepting his own sexual orientation.

Inferno in the French Quarter: The UpStairs Lounge Fire

On Gay Pride Day in 1973, someone set the entrance to a French Quarter gay bar on fire. In the terrible inferno that followed, thirty-two people lost their lives, including a third of the local congregation of the Metropolitan Community Church, their pastor burning to death halfway out a second-story window as he tried to claw his way to freedom.

A mother who'd gone to the bar with her two gay sons died alongside them. A man who'd helped his friend escape first was found dead near the fire escape. Two children waited outside a movie theater across town for a father and "uncle" who would never pick them up. During this era of rampant homophobia, several families refused to claim the bodies, and many churches refused to bury the dead.

Author Johnny Townsend pored through old records and tracked down survivors of the fire as well as relatives and friends of those killed to compile this fascinating account of a forgotten moment in gay history.

This second edition on the 50th anniversary of the fire includes additional research and information not available previously.

A Gay Mormon Missionary in Pompeii

What is a gay Mormon missionary doing in Italy? He is trying to save his own soul as well as the souls of others. In these tales chronicling the two-year mission of Robert Anderson, we see a young man tormented by his inability to be the man the Church says he should be.

In addition to his personal hell, Anderson faces a major earthquake, organized crime, a serious bus accident, and much more. He copes with horrendous mission leaders and his own suicidal tendencies. But one day, he meets another missionary who loves him, and his world changes forever.

Marginal Mormons

What happens when a High Priest becomes addicted to crack cocaine? Should an unemployed bank teller take in a homeless protester from the Occupy movement? Do gay people have positive near-death experiences or unhappy ones? Is there a way to splice the empathy gene into the genome of every human?

Can a schizophrenic woman on anti-delusional drugs still keep her belief in an intangible God? Will a childless biochemist be able to find fulfillment by taking part in a mission to Mars? Should a stay-at-home mom become involved in an international protest against fracking?

Not every Latter-day Saint has a mainstream story to tell, but these soul-searching people are still more than the marginal Mormons headquarters would like us to believe.

Mormon Underwear

Mormon Underwear tells the stories of gay Mormons that mainstream members don't want to hear. Whether it is a young LDS man stripping to his Mormon underwear in public or a virginal 70-year-old finally giving in to temptation, a straight son who discovers his father kissing another man or a group who plots to put gays into positions of power within the Church, these are the stories too shameful or shocking to be told among traditional Saints.

The Golem of Rabbi Loew

Jacob and Esau Cohen are the closest of brothers. In fact, they're lovers. A doctor tries to combine canine genes with those of Jews, to improve their chances of surviving a hostile world. A Talmudic scholar dates an escort. A scientist tries to develop the "God spot" in the brains of his patients in order to create a messiah. The Golem of Prague is really Rabbi Loew's secret lover.

While some of the Jews in Townsend's book are Orthodox, this collection of Jewish stories most certainly is not.

Breaking the Promise of the Promised Land: How Religious Conservatives Failed America

By aligning themselves over the past 60 years with the most conservative wing of the Republican Party, Mormons became leading contributors to the cultural and moral decay of America. Mormon prophets have long declared that God set America apart for the righteous. It was to be a land of freedom, justice, and peace, a place where the Lamanites could blossom as the rose, a country so righteous that the affairs of the entire world would be conducted here during the Millennium.

But when Mormons tired of being "a peculiar people" and chose to side with the most repressive evangelicals, they chose to make America the land of the imprisoned, poor, and oppressed. While declaring their allegiance to the Prince of Peace, they've chosen to support policies that have kept America at war almost non-stop for the last six decades.

Perhaps rather than continue following old men who tell them what an invisible God wants them to do, they should consider doing what they can see with their own eyes the people all around them need.

Wake Up and Smell the Missionaries

Two Mormon missionaries in Italy discover they share the same rare ability—both can emit pheromones on demand. At first, they playfully compete in the hills of Frascati to see who can tempt "investigators" most. But soon they're targeting each other non-stop.

Can two immature young men learn to control their "superpower" to live a normal life…and develop genuine love? Even as their relationship is threatened by the attentions of another man?

They seem just on the verge of success when a massive earthquake leaves them trapped under the rubble of their apartment in Castellammare.

With night falling and temperatures dropping, can they dig themselves out in time to save themselves? And will their injuries destroy the ability that brought them together in the first place?

Orgy at the STD Clinic

Todd Tillotson is struggling to move on after his husband is killed in a hit and run attack a year earlier during a Black Lives Matter protest in Seattle.

In this novel set entirely on public transportation, we watch as Todd, isolated throughout the pandemic, battles desperation in his attempt to safely reconnect with the world.

Will he find love again, even casual friendship, or will he simply end up another crazy old man on the bus?

Things don't look good until a man whose face he can't even see sits down beside him despite the raging variants.

And asks him a question that will change his life.

Please Evacuate

A gay, partygoing New Yorker unconcerned about the future or the unsustainability of capitalism is hit by a truck and thrust into a straight man's body half a continent away. As Hunter tries to figure out what's happening, he's caught up in another disaster, a wildfire sweeping through a Colorado community, the flames overtaking him and several schoolchildren as they flee.

When he awakens, Hunter finds himself in the body of yet another man, this time in northern Italy, a former missionary about to marry a young Mormon woman. Still piecing together this new reality, and beginning to embrace his latest identity, Hunter fights for his life in a devastating flash flood along with his wife *and* his new husband.

He's an aging worker in drought-stricken Texas, a nurse at an assisted living facility in the direct path of a hurricane, an advocate for the unhoused during a freak Seattle blizzard.

We watch as Hunter is plunged into life after life, finally recognizing the futility of only looking out for #1 and understanding the part he must play in addressing the global climate crisis…if he ever gets another chance.

Kinky Quilts

Since patchwork quilts are usually displayed in bedrooms where couples engage in sex, why are there so few quilt designs for folks who want a bit of sexual energy in these intimate spaces?

The original designs in this volume range from simple to intermediate, and with over 250 to choose from, even beginner quilters will find patterns tempting enough to get started.

In *Kinky Quilts*, Johnny Townsend has collected his best designs from *Quilting Beyond the Rainbow*, *Gay Sleeping Arrangements*, and *Queer Quilting*, to offer fun, sexy quilts for men who love men.

Have Your Cum and Eat It, Too

It's 1981, and two Mormon missionaries randomly assigned to work together as "companions" in Napoli find themselves in trouble. They're falling in love, but the Church forbids gay relationships. As missionaries, they can't date anyone at all, much less other men. If they're found out, they'll be excommunicated, sent home in disgrace, and cast out from their families.

In the aftermath of a devastating earthquake, against a backdrop of poverty and repressive mission culture, Elders Grant and Mortensen knock on doors, endure violent assaults, and face the ultimate challenge—will they be crushed by their dedication to their beliefs or will love provide a way for them to escape?

What Readers Have Said

Townsend's stories are "a gay *Portnoy's Complaint* of Mormonism. Salacious, sweet, sad, insightful, insulting, religiously ethnic, quirky-faithful, and funny."

D. Michael Quinn, author of *The Mormon Hierarchy: Origins of Power*

"Told from a believably conversational first-person perspective, [*A Gay Mormon Missionary in Pompeii*'s] novelistic focus on Anderson's journey to thoughtful self-acceptance allows for greater character development than often seen in short stories, which makes this well-paced work rich and satisfying, and one of Townsend's strongest. An extremely important contribution to the field of Mormon fiction." Named to Kirkus Reviews' Best of 2011.

Kirkus Reviews

"The thirteen stories in *Mormon Underwear* capture this struggle [between Mormonism and homosexuality] with humor, sadness, insight, and sometimes shocking details....*Mormon Underwear* provides compelling stories, literally from the inside-out."

Niki D'Andrea, *Phoenix New Times*

"Townsend's lively writing style and engaging characters [in *Zombies for Jesus*] make for stories which force us to wake up, smell the (prohibited) coffee, and review our attitudes with regard to reading dogma so doggedly. These are tales which revel in the individual tics and quirks which make us human, Mormon or not, gay or not…"

A.J. Kirby, *The Short Review*

"The Rift," from *A Gay Mormon Missionary in Pompeii*, is a "fascinating tale of an untenable situation…a *tour de force*."

David Lenson, editor, *The Massachusetts Review*

"Pronouncing the Apostrophe," from *The Golem of Rabbi Loew*, is "quiet and revealing, an intriguing tale…"

Sima Rabinowitz, Literary Magazine Review, *NewPages.com*

The Circumcision of God is "a collection of short stories that consider the imperfect, silenced majority of Mormons, who may in fact be [the Church's] best hope….[The book leaves] readers regretting the church's willingness to marginalize those who best exemplify its ideals: those who love fiercely despite all obstacles, who brave challenges at great personal risk and who always choose the hard, higher road."

Kirkus Reviews

In *Mormon Fairy Tales*, Johnny Townsend displays "both a wicked sense of irony and a deep well of compassion."

Kel Munger, *Sacramento News and Review*

Zombies for Jesus is "eerie, erotic, and magical."

Publishers Weekly

"While [Townsend's] many touching vignettes draw deeply from Mormon mythology, history, spirituality and culture, [*Mormon Fairy Tales*] is neither a gaudy act of proselytism nor angry protest literature from an ex-believer. Like all good fiction, his stories are simply about the joys, the hopes and the sorrows of people."

Kirkus Reviews

"In *Inferno in the French Quarter* author Johnny Townsend restores this tragic event [the UpStairs Lounge fire] to its proper place in LGBT history and reminds us that the victims of the blaze were not just 'statistics,' but real people with real lives, families, and friends."

Jesse Monteagudo, *The Bilerico Project*

In *Inferno in the French Quarter*, "Townsend's heart-rending descriptions of the victims…seem to [make them] come alive once more."

Kit Van Cleave, *OutSmart Magazine*

"While [*Inferno in the French Quarter*] is a non-fiction work, the author is a skilled fiction [writer], so he manages to respect the realism of the story, while at the same time recreating their lives and voices. It's probably thanks to the [author's] skills that this piece of non-fiction goes well beyond a simple recording of events."

Elisa Rolle, *Rainbow Awards*

Marginal Mormons is "an irreverent, honest look at life outside the mainstream Mormon Church….Throughout his musings on sin and forgiveness, Townsend beautifully demonstrates his characters' internal, perhaps irreconcilable struggles….Rather than anger and disdain, he offers an honest portrayal of people searching for meaning and community in their lives, regardless of their life choices or secrets." Named to Kirkus Reviews' Best of 2012.

Kirkus Reviews

The stories in *The Mormon Victorian Society* "register the new openness and confidence of gay life in the age of same-sex marriage….What hasn't changed is Townsend's wry, conversational prose, his subtle evocations of character and social dynamics, and his deadpan humor. His warm empathy still glows in this intimate yet clear-eyed engagement with Mormon theology and folkways. Funny, shrewd and finely wrought dissections of the awkward contradictions—and surprising harmonies—between conscience and desire." Named to Kirkus Reviews' Best of 2013.

Kirkus Reviews

"This collection of short stories [*The Mormon Victorian Society*] featuring gay Mormon characters slammed [me] in the face from the first page, wrestled my heart and mind to the floor, and left me panting and wanting more by the end. Johnny Townsend has created so many memorable characters in such few pages. I went weeks thinking about this book. It truly touched me."

Tom Webb, *A Bear on Books*

Dragons of the Book of Mormon is an "entertaining collection....Townsend's prose is sharp, clear, and easy to read, and his characters are well rendered..."

Publishers Weekly

"The pre-eminent documenter of alternative Mormon lifestyles...Townsend has a deep understanding of his characters, and his limpid prose, dry humor and well-grounded (occasionally magical) realism make their spiritual conundrums both compelling and entertaining. [*Dragons of the Book of Mormon* is] [a]nother of Townsend's critical but affectionate and absorbing tours of Mormon discontent." Named to Kirkus Reviews' Best of 2014.

Kirkus Reviews

In *Gayrabian Nights*, "Townsend's prose is always limpid and evocative, and…he finds real drama and emotional depth in the most ordinary of lives."

Kirkus Reviews

Gayrabian Nights is a "complex revelation of how seriously soul damaging the denial of the true self can be."

Ryan Rhodes, author of *Free Electricity*

Gayrabian Nights "was easily the most original book I've read all year. Funny, touching, topical, and thoroughly enjoyable."

Rainbow Awards

Lying for the Lord is "one of the most gripping books that I've picked up for quite a while. I love the author's writing style, alternately cynical, humorous, biting, scathing, poignant, and touching…. This is the third book of his that I've read, and all are equally engaging. These are stories that need to be told, and the author does it in just the right way."

Heidi Alsop, *Ex-Mormon Foundation Board Member*

In *Lying for the Lord*, Townsend "gets under the skin of his characters to reveal their complexity and conflicts….shrewd, evocative [and] wryly humorous."

Kirkus Reviews

In *Missionaries Make the Best Companions*, "the author treats the clash between religious dogma and liberal humanism with vivid realism, sly humor, and subtle feeling as his characters try to figure out their true missions in life. Another of Townsend's rich dissections of Mormon failures and uncertainties…" Named to Kirkus Reviews' Best of 2015.

Kirkus Reviews

In *Invasion of the Spirit Snatchers*, "Townsend, a confident and practiced storyteller, skewers the hypocrisies and eccentricities of his characters with precision and affection. The outlandish framing narrative is the most consistent source of shock and humor, but the stories do much to ground the reader in the world—or former world—of the characters….A funny, charming tale about a group of Mormons facing the end of the world."

Kirkus Reviews

"Townsend's collection [*The Washing of Brains*] once again displays his limpid, naturalistic prose, skillful narrative chops, and his subtle insights into psychology…Well-crafted dispatches on the clash between religion and self-fulfillment…"

Kirkus Reviews

"While the author is generally at his best when working as a satirist, there are some fine, understated touches in these tales [*The Last Days Linger*] that will likely affect readers in subtle ways….readers should come away impressed by the deep empathy he shows for all his characters—even the homophobic ones."

Kirkus Reviews

"Written in a conversational style that often uses stories and personal anecdotes to reveal larger truths, this immensely approachable book [*Racism by Proxy*] skillfully serves its intended audience of White readers grappling with complex questions regarding race, history, and identity. The author's frequent references to the Church of Jesus Christ of Latter-day Saints may be too niche for readers unfamiliar with its idiosyncrasies, but Townsend generally strikes a perfect balance of humor, introspection, and reasoned arguments that will engage even skeptical readers."

Kirkus Reviews

Orgy at the STD Clinic portrays "an all-too real scenario that Townsend skewers to wincingly accurate proportions…[with] instant classic moments courtesy of his punchy, sassy, sexy lead character…"

Jim Piechota, *Bay Area Reporter*

Orgy at the STD Clinic is "…a triumph of humane sensibility. A richly textured saga that brilliantly captures the fraying social fabric of contemporary life." Named to Kirkus Reviews' Best Indie Books of 2022.

Kirkus Reviews

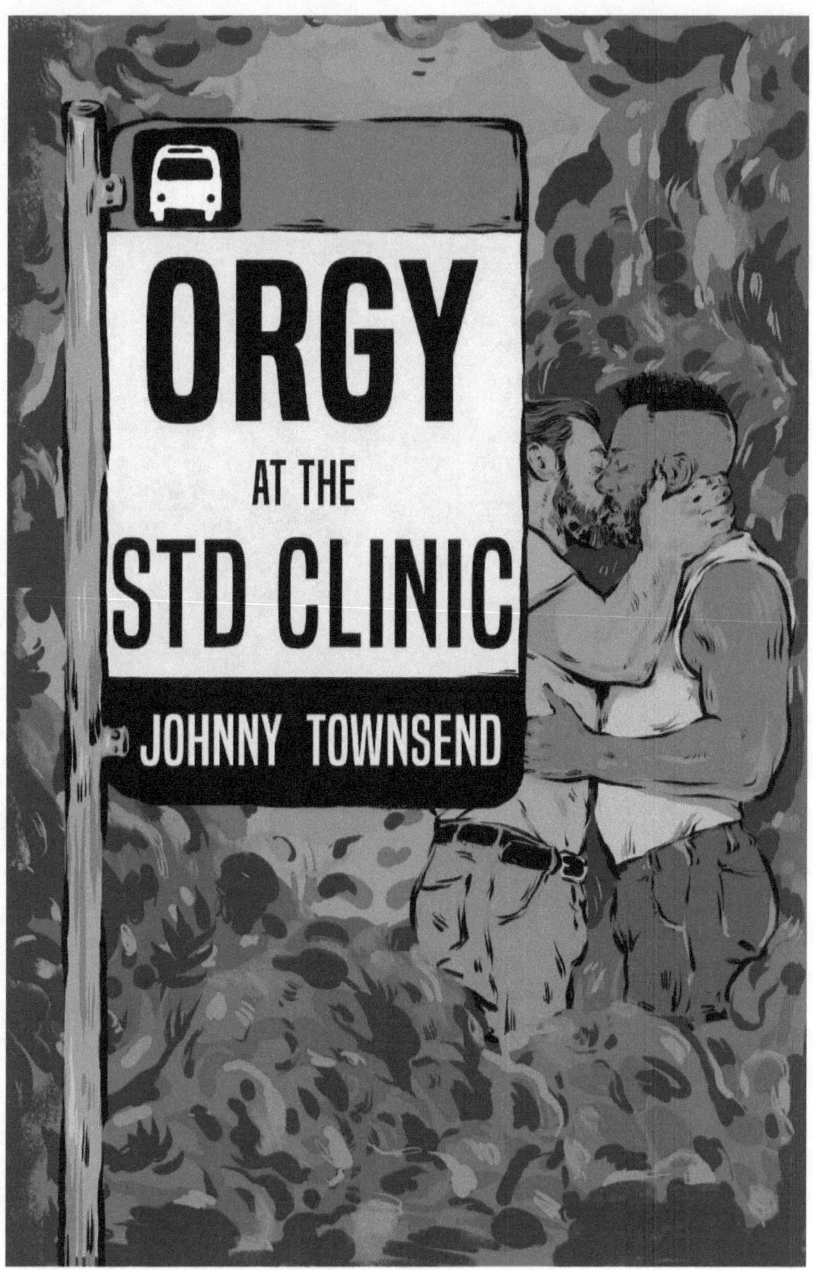
ORGY
AT THE
STD CLINIC
JOHNNY TOWNSEND

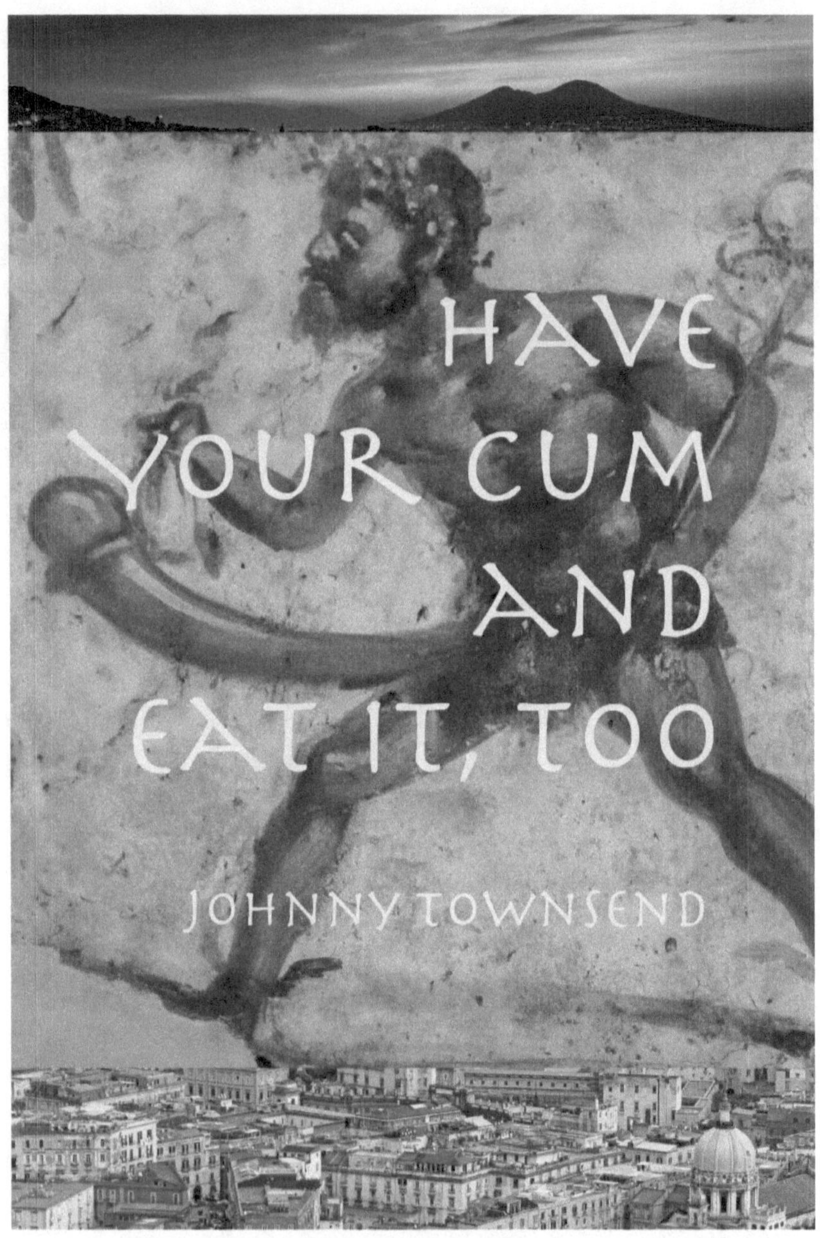
HAVE YOUR CUM AND EAT IT, TOO
JOHNNY TOWNSEND

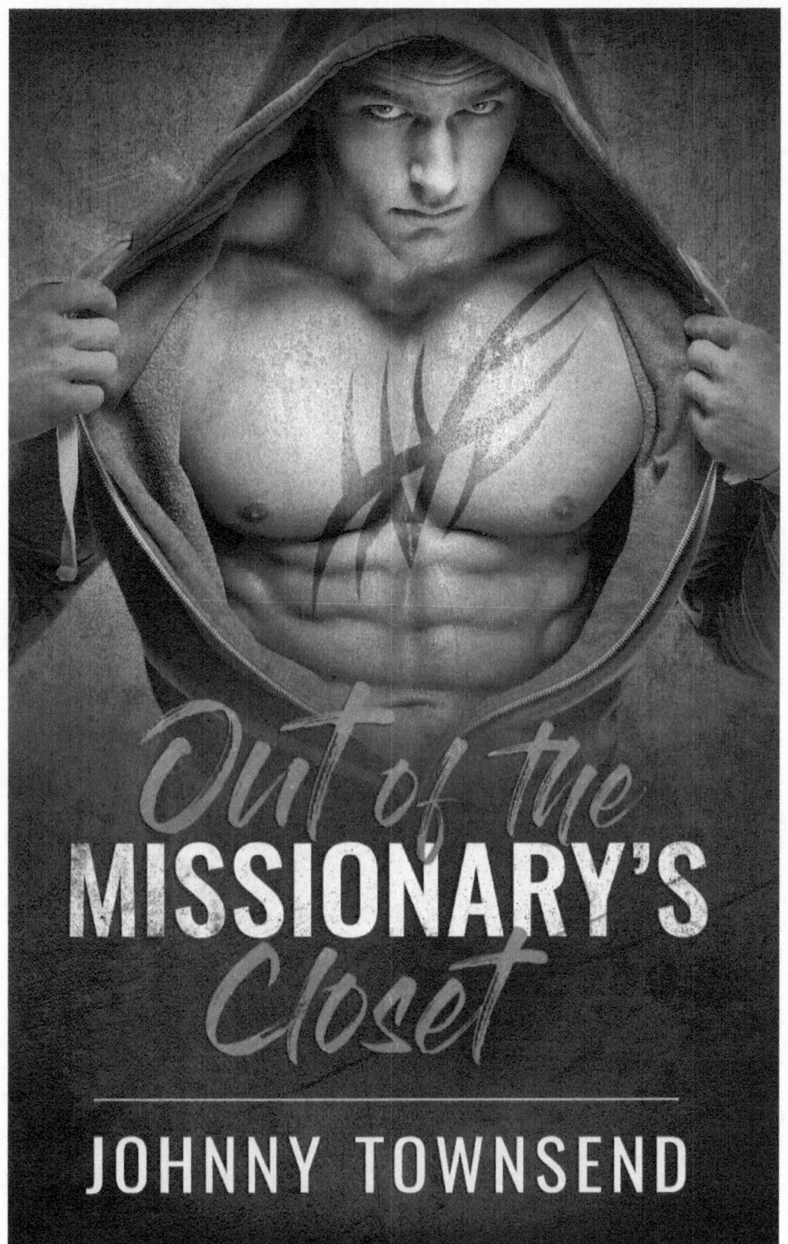
Out of the
MISSIONARY'S
Closet
JOHNNY TOWNSEND